LAST
TRACKS

LAST TRACKS

SUSIE McKENNA

Susie McKenna

ARCHWAY
PUBLISHING

Archway Publishing books may be ordered through booksellers or by contacting:

Archway Publishing
1663 Liberty Drive
Bloomington, IN 47403
www.archwaypublishing.com
1 (888) 242-5904

ISBN: 978-1-4808-3556-6 (sc)
ISBN: 978-1-4808-3557-3 (e)

Library of Congress Control Number: 2016912746

Print information available on the last page.

Archway Publishing rev. date: 08/26/2016

To my husband, Lew, thank you for all your
love, wicked ideas, and support.

CHAPTER 1

The car crawled along a road that was supposed to be a highway. It looked more like a snow-packed country trail than a paved road, the few clear spots evidence that a snow plow had cleared it at one point. Wind had blown snow back onto the road, making it difficult to keep the wheels in tracks left by other vehicles. The passenger, a woman, gripped the armrest with one hand and pressed the other hand into the dashboard, ready to keep herself from going through the windshield if the car slid off the road. The woman didn't move her eyes from the road. Her feet were ready to hit the nonexistent brakes in front of her. But she didn't risk telling the driver, her husband, what to do in the treacherous driving conditions.

Their rental car had front–wheel drive, snow tires, and an indicator on the dashboard that lit up when the tires lost traction. Andy Harris entertained himself by getting the indicator to light up, easy to do on an unplowed, slippery road. His wife, Deana, was mildly amused only the first time the car lost traction and they spun and slid across the road. Andy had laughed and whooped like he was on a thrill ride at a water park. He prided himself on his ability to drive in winter conditions and made fun of the reaction to snow back in their home state of Virginia. At the first sign of even a light snow, there would be a run on milk and bread at the stores. Schools would announce closings and delays.

Driving through Jasper National Park, even Andy was now tense and focused.

"Hang, on, hang on," he muttered as the car started sliding around through the snow. It came to a stop with the front pointed into a snowbank. They were both leaning forward, looking through the windshield over the top of the snowbank into the wild blue yonder. There were no guardrails. Only a pile of snow on the side of the road kept them from continuing to slide over the side of the mountain.

Andy settled down after that and was careful to stay on the tracks in the middle of the road. The newlyweds were on a snowshoeing trip in the Canadian Rockies. Andy had promised Deana an adventure. She hadn't counted on the drive from the airport to be part of the adventure. At the rate they were going, she figured they would be lucky to survive the drive.

They had landed in the sprawling, bustling, big city of Calgary and immediately headed north to the small town of Jasper. The highway to Jasper got more treacherous the further north they drove. They were surrounded by craggy, snow-topped mountains, *real* mountain peaks that reached heights of nine thousand feet—over twice that of the highest mountains in Virginia. The wind had blown off the snow in some areas, exposing sheets of jagged, rocky granite above the tree line. It was beautiful, awe-inspiring, and downright scary.

Deana's breathing was slow and deep, as if she had been sucked into a trance. She tried to think of a word that described what she felt—*ominous,* that was it. They were headed away from civilization into a wild and primal place.

"Andy, look at that massive piece of granite," Deana said, pointing to the highest peak in view.

He glanced at her with one of those how-could-you-be-so-stupid looks, turned his attention back to the road, and said without emotion, "It isn't granite. It's composed of sheets of sedimentary rock."

Deana thought about making a crack about all rocks looking alike but restrained herself. There was enough tension in the car without a smart-ass remark from her. She didn't even look at him. She knew it was his good looks that made her let him off easy when he got sarcastic. She still felt a little twitch in her heart or mind when she looked at him.

They say men let their judgment be clouded by their dicks, but an honest woman will tell you women have the same weakness.

Andy was movie-star good-looking, stood ramrod straight, and seemed to take everything in through dark, intense eyes. He had straight dark hair, sharp features, and a complexion that gave the impression there was Indian blood in him. They say opposites attract, and, if so, they were proof. Deana had curly red hair, freckles, and a careless posture. Just thinking about him, she unconsciously straightened her back.

Love wasn't always easy, she decided, and turned her attention to the scenery and the first part of the day's drive.

The 112-mile stretch of highway between Calgary and Lake Louise was clear. They made good time until they passed the exit for Lake Louise. The famous lake marked the halfway spot on the highway that runs north through Banff National Park. In the winter it was also the last sign of civilization until one reached the town of Jasper. The road conditions worsened as the car crawled along on a snow-packed path. They would be lucky to reach Jasper by nightfall. The eighty-mile stretch of highway between Lake Louise and the northern part of Banff National Park was called the Icefields Parkway for good reason. It passed through glacier fields, which they couldn't appreciate because they were so worried about sliding off the road. Andy picked Jasper for their adventure because winter was the slow season for tourists. He wanted to make sure they would not have to experience nature with a lot of other outdoor adventure seekers.

"This is our chance to make first tracks through snow-covered wilderness. The only sounds will be our snowshoes softly moving through the snow." He mimicked the motion of snowshoeing, gliding around the living room while whispering, "Whoosh, whoosh."

It sounded romantic when they were planning the trip. Now, Deana wasn't so sure. The slow progress and the "Don't Stop/Avalanche Area" signs posted along the road were less than comforting. It was only 140 miles from Lake Louise to Jasper. She calculated it would take four hours to cover the distance, and it would be dark for the last hour of driving. A light snow started falling.

"Honey," Deana said, "maybe we should turn back and spend the night at Lake Louise."

Andy stared at the road, concentrating, and said, "No. If a storm moves in, the road could be closed, and we might not get through for a couple of days. At least we aren't going to get lost." He glanced at her. "This is the only road open. We'll get there. Don't worry. Look around you. Have you ever seen anything more beautiful?"

He was right. The scenery was spectacular. She sighed and started browsing through the tourist brochures about Jasper to try to take her mind off the steep, curvy part of the road ahead. She couldn't help but notice the section on "Things to Do in the Winter" was a fraction of the size of "Things to Do in the Summer." The winter activities were skiing, snowshoeing, and snowmobiling. The photos depicted a rustic, old-fashioned town—nothing like the upscale resorts in popular ski areas. It wasn't easy to get to Jasper in the winter, and most tourists wanted to just look at the scenery. It was easier to do that in the warm months when you could also fish, hike, mountain bike, raft, golf, go horseback riding, and bask in the hot springs. In the summer you could see the green of the forests and the blues and greens of the lakes and rivers. In the winter you saw shades of white. Yes, winter was definitely the time to visit if you wanted to experience the vast wilderness without busloads of tourists.

Suddenly the car lost traction. Andy said, "Shit!" under his breath. He let the car slide while pumping the brakes lightly. "Hold on, hold on," he uttered softly to the car, not Deana. He laughed as he regained control and straightened the car.

Deana shook her head but kept her thoughts to herself. *This is incredibly beautiful, but I'll never again complain about crowd-infested roads and trails in Virginia.* Suddenly the idea of other travelers and an occasional gas station or ugly fast–food restaurant was appealing. They had been warned that there was nothing open between Lake Louise and Jasper, and it had proved to be true. They passed park buildings, campgrounds, signs for trails, and tourist attractions. "Closed" signs were posted on all of them. Entrance roads and parking lots were piled high with snow.

"I don't suppose you can pull up road closings on that damn phone of yours?" Andy asked gruffly. He hated to rely on modern technology and hated to bring it along on a vacation, but even he realized they didn't want to get to the next mountain pass and find the road had been closed.

Deana pulled out her phone and said, "I've got the app to check for weather conditions. It will just take a second."

The car slowed from a crawl to a stop. She looked up to see bighorn sheep in the middle of the road. They turned their heads to glance at the funny–looking intruder approaching them. Large horns curled around the sides of their heads.

"They're males," Andy said. "The females have small horns, like a goat."

Andy turned to the backseat and picked up the binoculars. He scanned the side of the mountain and then handed the binoculars to Deana. "Check out that ridge. Mountain goats." He shook the tenseness out of his hands, stretched, and started to drive again.

"The road is open all the way to Jasper," Deana said. "Andy, do you want me to drive for a while?"

He kept his eyes on the road. "This is not the place to learn how to drive in the snow. I'm fine." He took one hand off the wheel as they passed the bighorn sheep, formed a pistol with his index finger, and pointed it at one as it turned its head to look at them. "Bang," Andy said and laughed. "I'd like to have that head mounted."

Deana thought the sheep's head should stay on the sheep but decided it was not the time to start an argument. Instead, she said, "I understand why the average tourist wouldn't venture out here in the middle of win-ter. We seem to be the only nuts on the road."

Light snow swirled around them. It was a winter wonderland. She was beginning to understand Andy's desire to escape the crowds and upscale tourist towns. The scenery was incredible. She had never seen anything like it. She marveled at the courage and determination of ex-plorers who had broken the original trails through the mountains. They were in a car on a paved road—albeit a dangerous and snow-packed one. Early explorers rode on horseback or mule and had to constantly clear trails. The snow-packed road and slow speed didn't seem like much of a hardship when one thought about early travelers camping out and surviving unpredictable weather.

"Andy," Deana asked, "how would we survive if the car ran off the road, and no one came by all night? Do you know how to build a snow cave?"

He turned his head quickly to look at her for a second and then turned back to the road. "I think we could figure out how to survive one night. It's the second and third nights that get tricky." He glanced at his wife again. "I should guide you to the middle of a wilderness area, confiscate your phone, and force you to use your wits to make it through the night. Our own outdoor adventure survival challenge. You up for that?"

Deana sighed, let out a breath, and said, "No, thank you."

Andy laughed and said, "I didn't think so. We won't be spending the night in the woods. You'll be in a warm hotel room. Stop worrying." He reached over to pat her leg and said, "Wait until we get on fresh snow and make our own trail through the woods. First tracks—and they'll be ours."

They pulled into Jasper safe and sound around 6:00 p.m. The brochures said it had been the site of a trading post in the 1800s. In the dark, it looked like it had managed to hold on to that old-fashioned feeling. There were no high-rise condo buildings or sidewalks full of shopping tourists. They drove past quaint chalets, small hotels, a rustic information center, and a historic railway station. Andy was right. The trouble to get there had been well worth it.

The decor in their hotel room fit the town. A rough-hewn pine bedframe and prints of bears, moose, and antelope made the room look less antiseptic than the usual chain hotel room.

Deana touched Andy's arm and said, "Andy, this is perfect. I feel like we're in a wilderness town. It looks like nothing has changed here in one hundred years. Thank you for planning this trip."

He smiled at her and pulled her close to him. After a tender kiss, he said, "Honey, I'm sorry if I was a little edgy with you today. It was a tough drive."

Andy rubbed his knuckles across Deana's cheek gently and grabbed a handful of her long, curly hair. He opened his hand, and the curls jumped out. He smiled and said, "Curly red hair and freckles—a deadly combination."

Deana felt his warm breath as his lips slowly moved from her neck to her face. She closed her eyes. All the tension from the day melted away. *I'm such a pushover, but this is better than a massage,* she thought to herself as Andy twirled her around and they fell into the bed in each other's arms.

They looked out the hotel window the next morning and saw heavy snow falling. It stopped around 2:00 p.m. They headed out for a short, ten-kilometer warm-up trek on their snowshoes. The trail was close to the hotel and had already been used by other snowshoers. Andy said, "Tomorrow, I bet we'll be the only ones on the trail."

"Andy, if we're making first tracks in deep snow, it will be a lot more difficult than following in someone else's tracks," Deana said.

"Don't worry," he answered. "I'll go first, and you can follow in my tracks."

"All right," Deana said but worried about how she would hold up on the longer hike. It had taken three hours to cover the ten-kilometer trail. Tomorrow's snowshoe hike was a twenty-kilometer hike.

Andy groaned when Deana asked the clerk at the hotel about the risk of bear attacks. The young man laughed and said, "Ma'am, no risk of bear attacks this time of year." She relaxed after that, pleased to be able to enjoy the adventure without carrying bear spray and a noisy can of coins. Their last hiking trip had been in the fall in western Montana. Deana had followed the recommendations of the guide books to scare bears away by filling soda cans with coins and shaking them. She figured it must have worked because they never saw any bears.

The problem was the can shaking didn't seem to have the same effect on moose. She could still see the giant moose crashing through the underbrush. It had hesitated, deciding whether or not to charge, and she remembered trying to decide if she should run or stand her ground. The moose's ears were laid back, and it started swinging its massive head and antlers back and forth. She remembered thinking, *Hell, I've been worried about bears, and now we're going to be mauled by Bullwinkle.* She hadn't moved a muscle and held her breath.

Andy had kept his eyes on the moose and whispered urgently to her, "It's getting ready to charge. Get behind the rock, curl up, and put your backpack over your head." The moose had started stomping its hooves, pawing at the ground like a dog. Andy whispered, "Now!"

Deana moved behind the rock. Andy jumped on top of the boulder, grabbed a branch, and pulled himself up into the tree. He stood on a branch that was just out of the angry moose's reach. He had called down to her in a quiet voice, "Stay absolutely still." They listened to the angry bull stomping around and snorting for a few agonizing moments and then heard the breaking of limbs and underbrush as it retreated into the woods.

Andy had been thrilled by the dangerous encounter. Deana had been upset. He had complimented her on keeping her cool and not panicking, but it was that experience that motivated her to learn more about taking care of herself in the great outdoors.

"*This* is backcountry," Andy said as they drove from the hotel to the trailhead. The fresh snow falling was beautiful, and Deana forgot to worry about the risks masked by the beauty. It continued to fall lightly on the snow-packed mountain road to the trail head. It was the start of their adventure—a twenty-kilometer hike to a mysterious lake that could only be reached on foot or snowshoe. They didn't pass a single car as the road curved along a frozen river and away from the town. The road stopped at the edge of a parking lot that hadn't been plowed. They would have to leave the car on the road.

Andy jumped out of the car, quickly put on his snowshoes, shoved his plastic water bottle in a pocket, and walked over to the trail map next to the trailhead. He brushed the snow away, studied the map for a few minutes, and walked back to the car.

"Okay, let's get moving; if we want to make it back to the hotel before dark, we need to get started," Andy urged.

"Wait, I want to make sure we have everything. Food will help us stay warm, and in case one of us falls or has a problem, we need to take some extra energy bars," Deana countered. She was famous for never missing a meal. Andy seemed to eat half as much as she did. He didn't understand.

She lifted her backpack from the trunk.

Andy said, "Deana, you don't need a backpack. It's just more weight, and it'll slow you down. What do you have in there?" he asked, reaching out to grab the little backpack.

She wrapped both arms around it. "Important things like toilet paper and a little surprise for you. Don't ruin it." She quickly slipped her arms into the straps before Andy could grab it.

He cocked his head to the side and asked, "Toilet paper? You are prepared for just about anything, aren't you?" He paused for a second and said, "Sweetie, we'll only be out for the day, not the weekend. We'll have a nice dinner when we get back. One of those energy bars should last you all day. Don't worry; nothing will happen."

He was being so sweet she didn't want to argue about a few energy bars, so she stopped herself from mentioning the goodies stashed in the great hidden pockets of her jacket. One energy bar might last him all day but not her.

"Okay, ready. No, hold on a minute," Deana said. "Let's check cell reception. The *Parks Canada* paper had a little note about spotty coverage in the parks." She pulled out her cell phone. "The paper was right. No reception here."

"Well, that's a relief," Andy responded sarcastically. "Give me the phone. I don't want you calling your friends. In addition to 'don't feed the animals,' that paper should also say 'twitter-free, email-free zone.'"

Deana insisted they at least take the phone with them. Andy shoved it into his pocket. The drive from the hotel to the trail head took two hours. There was no sign of a gas station or any habitation. Andy was right; it was just like the brochure said: the park is "a place to wander, to wonder … to discover yourself." There was no point in coming this far to get away from it all if they took the hustle-bustle of the world with them. On the other hand, if they got into trouble, email and twitter would be their savior *if* (and it looked doubtful) they could get reception.

Deana had to admit it was exciting to head out into a vast wilderness. The hope and dread of running into an unexpected adventure made all her senses tingle. Until she met Andy, it was a world she didn't know existed. Yeah, she had always liked to hike the trails in Virginia, but Andy was a serious outdoorsman. Hiking with him was like hiking with a naturalist. She had learned a lot from him about the wilderness world on their many hikes. A memory of Andy picking up animal excrement made her smile. She had thought it was a disgusting habit. He would rub it between his fingers and identify the animal and its diet. She changed her mind when she realized it would be helpful to know the difference between bear poop and raccoon poop.

Her natural habitat was a desk and computer, with a cappuccino maker close by. An enormously successful software program for toxicology testing had left her comfortably retired at thirty-five. She continued to do a little consulting work in the field but was happy to have found someone who was from a different world.

She surprised Andy and herself when she enrolled in a hunter education class advertised in one of his magazines. She had learned just enough in the class to be slightly disabused of romantic notions about the lack of serious risks in exploring the rugged western mountains.

The hunter education class was just for women and was taught by a woman. The instructor dedicated a session to survival planning. Sergeant Myers had held up a black nylon fanny pack and pulled out the contents, starting with a small first aid kit and ending up with a smashed, almost empty roll of toilet paper.

The class laughed at the toilet paper, but the instructor said, "It beats leaves. Seriously, ladies, Virginia is not the wilds of Montana—you are not likely to starve to death here—*if* you let someone know about your plans. As important as having a survival kit with you is always letting someone know where you will be in the woods and an approximate time you expect to be home."

"Andy," Deana asked, "you *did* let the hotel know where we were going, right?"

"Yes, Deana," he answered in a tired voice. "They promised to send in Canada's finest on snowmobiles if we aren't back by nightfall." He tilted his head, raised his eyebrows, and asked, "Good enough?"

She smiled, threw him a kiss, and they started out on the trail. They were making first tracks on the path to the lake. Without snowshoes the hike would have been impossible. There was at least three feet of snow on the ground. Deana was thankful it had stopped snowing. At least the snowshoe tracks wouldn't be covered by the time they made the return trip.

There was only blazing white ahead, unmarked except for tracks left by creatures used to easily stepping on top of the snow. The crisp air was made clearer and cleaner by the cold and the altitude. Their steps would be the first tracks left by human trespassers. Andy was finally getting his wish. Deana sighed and looked around, taking in the quiet beauty of a picture-perfect winter wonderland.

"Oh, Andy," she said, "this is incredible."

She thought about the catastrophe a mere two inches of snow would cause at home. Accidents, schools closed, power losses. Here, they were surrounded by thirty-six inches of snow, and life went on without a hiccup. It was cold by Virginia standards, but it didn't feel cold. There was something invigorating rather than chilling about the 20° temperature. It did that funny thing inside one's nose that made the nostrils quiver. A body was on full alert, as if it had received signals from the brain warning it: "Wake up! Danger!" Deana smiled, remembering weather reports in Virginia blaming cold, snow, and wind on Canadian cool fronts. They were at the origin of the cool Canadian high pressure that took the blame for any cold spell that hit the South.

"I love this brisk weather, Andy. It makes me feel alive!"

Andy stopped and turned to look at her. "Enjoy it while you can."

They trekked along quietly until Andy stopped and held his arm out, motioning for her to stop. He turned his head, index finger across his mouth, signaling quiet. They stood still while he listened for life around them.

"We just missed an animal. See the tracks?" He pointed to tracks crossing the path. "Probably a wolf." He looked at Deana's face and laughed. "Don't worry; we would be very lucky to come eye-to-eye with a wolf in the wild." He grinned with a leer and turned to continue down the trail. "Unless they're really hungry."

That was all the motivation Deana needed to pick up her pace and stay close to Andy. She focused on the whooshing sound the snowshoes made when they pushed through the snow. Each step seemed to be syncopated with her labored breathing, followed by puffs of air she could see in the cold. The whoosh, inhale, exhale, puff of air was a hypnotic rhythm. She let herself wonder at the peaceful surroundings and left the navigation to Andy. The snow-covered ground made it tricky to stay on the trail. In spite of her best efforts, she couldn't keep up with him, and she gradually fell further and further behind. Andy turned around to check on her, said nothing, and continued making tracks through the snow. Even he was breathing heavy from the effort of blazing a trail. If there were blaze marks on trees, they weren't always easy to find. They had to assume the trail followed the open spaces but were forced to backtrack a couple times when it became clear they were off the trail. Andy's best guess was that they would reach the lake in an hour.

Each step was like climbing stairs two at a time. The snowshoes sunk several inches into the snow, and it was hard work picking them up and putting them down. As her legs grew tired, she forgot about the beauty she had paused to admire just a few minutes earlier. It required all her concentration to force herself to keep moving. It was easier slogging if she stayed in Andy's tracks, but his longer gait turned Deana's steps into lunges. The distance between them grew.

"Come on, Deana," Andy urged, "try to keep up with me." She picked up her pace and crossed the tips of the snowshoes, tumbling headfirst off the trail into the deep snow.

"Are you okay?" Andy called as he backtracked to help her. He started laughing when she struggled to right herself.

"It's not funny. You could suffocate in this snow. My snowshoe fell off." Deana managed to stand up, brushing snow from her face. She had to reach through the snow to unhook the snowshoe. As soon as she removed the snowshoe, her foot started sinking, at first slowly; then, all at once, it was swallowed and sucked through two feet of snow. It was a struggle to stay upright with the uneven stance. Her forehead wrinkled in exasperation. She hit the snow with the ski poles like a spoiled child.

"Okay, Mr. Outdoors, how am I supposed to get this snowshoe back on my foot?" Deana asked, holding her arms out in the classic "now what?" pose, while struggling to keep from floundering in the snow again. Andy told her to lie on her back and create a bed in the snow. That allowed her to maneuver and get the snowshoe back in place on her boot.

She didn't whine out loud what she was thinking: *My snowshoes are harder to put on than yours!* Andy's snowshoes had an easy-to-use binding that allowed him to cinch them quickly. Deana's had an unwieldy strap that had to be wrapped around the ankle and pulled tight before snapping it shut. She had to remove her gloves, and her fingers were freezing. The snowshoes had been a gift from Andy, and you couldn't complain about a gift.

He didn't rush to his wife's side but just stood there watching, half-amused, while she struggled to use ski poles to right herself. Andy believed in self-reliance and being able to take care of one's self in all situations. He thought they understood each other because they had both lost their parents and had to learn to be strong and independent at an early age. Deana didn't want to disabuse him of that impression by needing his help to recover from a fall in the snow.

Deana sat in the snow and let out a sigh after she finally got the snowshoe back on her boot. Andy was quietly scanning the area around them.

"Honey," Deana said, "maybe we should turn around; it's been almost three hours."

"And whose fault is that?" he answered with a question. "I'm not the one who can't keep her snowshoes on. If we hadn't had stops for you to rest, recover from falls, etcetera, we would have reached the lake by now."

He said all that in a teasing voice with an edge to it. Deana chose to not respond. She had to admit there was some truth in what he said. Yet it was the demeaning, mocking attitude that made her momentarily forget how handsome he was. The sneer was only on his face for a second. It was quickly replaced by a charming smile.

Andy liked to test himself. He wanted the thrill and risk of going out of bounds. He eschewed her attempts at being prepared for emergencies. Andy's claim that the only tools anyone needed were a good knife and matches made Deana squirm at what she now recognized as bravado. They weren't in Virginia's Blue Ridge Mountains, where another hiker would pass by every fifteen minutes. This was a world where the only passersby were carnivores. The bears might be sleeping, but there were still wolves and cougars looking for an easy meal.

Deana had learned not to question his judgment. She got the silent treatment and an icy stare if she did. She resigned herself to accepting the old cliché that the male ego is a fragile thing. No relationship was perfect. At least he seemed to appreciate the parts of her life that were as important to her as much as she appreciated learning more about the outdoors. Andy had never read or seen Shakespeare before they met. She remembered watching him sit on the edge of his seat the first time she dragged him to a play. It had been a compromise—a day of hiking in the Blue Ridge Mountains, followed by Shakespeare and a charming B and B instead of camping. It helped that the play was *Titus Andronicus,* as close as Shakespeare could get to a bloody, action-filled, high-testosterone drama that would please fans who paid to see car chase and blood-and-gore movies. He loved it, and they continued to combine their two passions.

"We should be close—just fifteen minutes more, Deana. Around the bend, trust me."

She glanced at her watch and decided to wait another fifteen minutes before insisting they turn around. Every time she ventured out of Andy's tracks, she sunk far enough that it was turning what should have been easy snowshoeing into schlepping. It also meant she was looking down instead of around and was missing the beautiful scenery. The love affair with winter and snow was beginning to sour.

"We made it; look at this view!" Andy called out ahead of her, arms stretched wide. By the time she reached him, he had the camera out. And it really was an incredible view. They were on the edge of a snow-covered lake, framed by an expanse of jagged, snowcapped mountains. The tree line stopped halfway up, so they were already at about six thousand feet. It was truly spectacular. There was a break in the fast-moving storm clouds, and blue sky peeked out.

Andy leaned against a large boulder and took off his snowshoes. The wind had blown the snow away from a small area at the edge of the lake, and they could walk around in the semicircle in their boots. There were bare patches and snowdrifts on the lakeshore. Andy picked his way over them and around the snow to get a better look at the view. "Okay, this will make a really great shot," he said. "Take your snowshoes off, and walk out a few feet onto the lake. I want that really high peak as a background."

"How do we know it's safe? What if the ice cracks?" Deana worried aloud as she started taking off the snowshoes. She passed the snowshoes into his outstretched hand.

"Trust me; it's safe. We're at six thousand feet, and the lake has been frozen since October."

Trust me were two words Deana hated. In her experience, every time she heard those two words, something bad happened. Muttering the words *trust me,* she ventured out a few feet, avoiding the deep snow, and carefully stepped between the drifts onto the frozen lake. "Hurry up—take the picture before the ice cracks!" she joked.

"You're in the shadows; move out past the tree shadows."

"Okay, okay." Deana grunted and trudged farther out onto the lake, stopping at the edge of the long shadows cast by the afternoon sun. She was still nervous about venturing out onto the ice. It certainly looked frozen, but she didn't know enough about it to know whether it would be as solid in the middle of the lake as around the edges. She did remember headline stories every winter of an ice hut, snowmobile, or car falling through the ice in Maine or off the shore of Lake Erie. Even ice fishermen who supposedly knew something about ice became the object of ridicule when they fell through. She shook off her nerves, reminding herself she wasn't as heavy as a car or snowmobile, and tried to relax and smile for the camera. After the photo was taken, she turned around slowly and looked at the view with wonder. For a moment, time stood still. She felt as tiny as a grain of sand, standing on the frozen lake, staring up at the mountain tops. They had to come back in the summer—in spite of the crowds. She sighed with contentment and marveled they were the only two people there at that moment.

Andy broke into her daydreaming and brought her back to reality. "Come on back, honey. We had better get started. It's almost three."

Deana turned around and took one last look at the view. A spot above the trees caught her attention. She framed her eyes with her hands and squinted. It looked like a ledge, and a ledge might mean a cave. If they did return in the summer, it would be fun to see if there was a cave overlooking the lake.

As Deana slowly made her way back to shore, the sun disappeared behind a winter sky that looked and felt like snow. Andy laid her snowshoes down in front of her. She slipped her feet into them and strapped them on, ready for the hike back to the car. Two steps and her right foot came out of the snowshoe; she landed on her tush. "Andy, wait! There's something wrong with my snowshoe," Deana called out.

Andy picked up the snowshoe. "Damn, I don't believe it. Two rivets popped out, and the decking is split all the way through to the end."

"Well, can you rig something up? If you can't, I'll just walk out without the snowshoes," Deana said, exhaling and trying to stay calm. She remembered how tough the hike in with snowshoes had been. It would be even tougher without them.

Andy rubbed his chin and said, "A couple of cable ties might have worked if it was just the rivet, but the decking is completely split. If we had the traditional snowshoes, it would be an easier fix."

Their snowshoes didn't look anything like the old-fashioned ones hanging on the wall in every bar and restaurant out West. The traditional snowshoes were made of wood and rawhide lacing; their modern (supposedly improved ones) were made of aluminum and a solid rubber sheet instead of laces. The rubber decking was split from the missing rivets to the end of the snowshoe.

"How could it just split?" Deana demanded.

Andy shook his head. "I don't know, but it did. You can blame me. I should have spent more money on your snowshoes."

Deana thought, *Gee, thanks a lot for buying cheap snowshoes,* but she didn't say anything. She could have sworn Andy thought the situation was funny. She turned her attention to trying to figure out how to fix the snowshoes. "What about your belt? Can't you rig something up with your belt?" she asked.

Andy lifted up the edge of his jacket, displaying pants with no belt loops and no belt. "Shoe laces might have worked, but neither one of us has laces on our boots," Andy answered in a calm voice. "Enough talking." He put a hand on each of Deana's shoulders, looked her in the eye, and said, "Deana, here's what's going to happen. I'm going to get out as quickly as I can, fix the snowshoe, and come back to get you."

It took her one nanosecond to figure out she would be sitting out there in the dark. "But ... but it will be dark in a couple of hours."

"That's right. That's why it's so important I start right away. I can move much faster by myself and get to the car before sunset. With the hiking headlamps I'll be able to find my way back to you. You've seen what it's like to try to walk without snowshoes. We would never make it back to the trailhead before sunset, and I don't think you want to be on the trail by yourself. I can move much faster." He spoke quickly and in an even tone. He wasn't upset, just stating the facts, and that made his argument all the more convincing.

While he was talking, Deana was thinking about the animal tracks they had seen crossing the trail just a short while ago. "What am I supposed to do? Just hang out here for three to four hours? I'll freeze to death, and what about the animal tracks we saw?" She added in desperation, "What am I supposed to do if a wolf starts poking around"

"Deana, consider yourself lucky if you ever get eyeball-to-eyeball with a wolf. They are very wary of humans. With an inappropriate wolfish grin(considering the circumstances), he continued, "If you do get *lucky,* stand up and make yourself big." He stretched his arms out above his shoulders.

"Here's something to keep you busy. Collect some rocks or sticks, and keep them handy. *If* you get a courtesy call from Willy the Wolf, stare right into its eyes, and throw the rocks and sticks at it." He paused and said with a little smirk on his face, "Gee, I'm surprised they didn't teach you that in the survival part of hunter education."

"Well, we don't exactly have a wolf problem in Virginia, do we?"

He looked around and knocked snow from the top of the boulder. "Scramble up there and wait. You'll be fine." He fingered her jacket and tapped the logo. "This will be a good test of your yuppie jacket's thermal properties."

"No, no," she said, trying for the same tone of convincing reason instead of hysteria in her voice. "I'm not sitting here. I'll stay in the tracks and move as quickly as I can. You go ahead and come back for me. You'll find me on the trail."

He pursed his lips and blew out a puff of air that formed a long visible stream in the dropping temperature. "I don't think it's a good idea. But if you insist, I can't stop you. Scream at the top of your lungs if you get into trouble. If I hear you; I'll double back. Now, I need to get going." He hugged her quickly, kissed her on the forehead, and turned his back on her to retrace their steps.

Deana was surprised at her self-control and persistence as her mind raced through best- and worst-case scenarios. She wasn't hysterical. She was trying to plan for the worst. "Andy, what if you *can't* fix the snowshoe?"

He turned, fixed his eyes on hers, and said in an even voice, "I *will* fix it. There's rope in the trunk. I'll figure something out. *If* I can't fix it, I'll have to drive into town and get help. If I'm not back within three or four hours, you'll know I drove into town. You can start listening for the sounds of a snowmobile."

"Andy," she said, "don't even try hiking back in. Drive into town and get help. I'd much rather ride out on a snowmobile than hike back out in the dark."

He laughed and bowed. "Your wish is my command. I'll be back with a snowmobile."

She watched him moving through the snow, the only sound the quick whoosh, whoosh sound of each snowshoe pushing a couple of inches through the surface. She was still trying to decide whether or not to try to follow in his tracks or follow his advice and go back to the lake shore. He was only about fifteen yards away when she screamed, "The phone! Try the phone!"

He pulled it out. "Dead, no service."

He turned his back on her again. She yelled, "Andy, the headlamps are in the trunk."

He didn't stop or turn around. She saw the back of his hand raise up in acknowledgment that he heard her. Her mind was racing, dreading the thought of losing sight of Andy when he turned the corner. Each minute that delayed his leaving also delayed his return. Yet she couldn't help calling out again.

"Andy! Let me keep the phone. I'll try it out on the lake." She started to walk toward him. He unzipped a jacket pocket and pulled out the phone, holding it up to her. They were about thirty yards apart.

"Stop right there," he said. "I'm going to throw it to you."

"Shit," Deana whispered, "I better catch it. I don't want to dig it out of the snow." She held her breath and concentrated on the small phone flying through the air. "Got it!" she said with relief. She looked up to see Andy raise his hand to his head in a salute and say, "I'll be back soon. Trust me."

CHAPTER 2

The instant Deana caught the final glimpse of the underside of Andy's snowshoe, she sighed, her shoulders fell, and a shiver ran through her. She rubbed her arms and stamped her feet. It wasn't the temperature that made her feel cold; it was the realization that she was alone. She stood for a minute, thinking, calculating how much time she would have to spend by herself. A funny sinking feeling spread throughout her body. She hated to admit it, but she was scared and nervous about spending even a couple of hours on her own in the wilds of Canada. The beautiful winter wonderland had turned into a spooky snow house.

She grimaced, thinking she had picked the wrong time to remember the article she read yesterday in a park magazine. It warned that hikers and backcountry skiers died every year and in every season. She had read the next sentence aloud to Andy: "Even more risky and more sparsely populated in the winter."

Andy had just laughed and said, "Deana, we aren't hiking into uncharted backcountry on an expedition for National Geographic. We'll be snowshoeing on trails used by cross-country skiers. You worry too much! We'll just be out for the day."

She stared at the bend in the trail, as if staring would bring Andy back, and started to calculate how long it might take him to get back to the car. *At least an hour,* Deana thought, still not moving. He was certain he could fix the snowshoe. She tried to trust in his ability to do that. Worst case, even if his cleverest attempt to fix the snowshoe failed, he would go into town for help. One way or the other, Andy would rescue her. Either he would be back with a working snowshoe or help would come in the form of a snowmobile. She tried to relax as she convinced herself she would not be out there all night by herself.

"You are never more than two miles from a road in Virginia," Sergeant Myers, the hunter education instructor, had told them. Deana repeated the words, pausing after each word. This would have never happened on trails at home. Number one, she would have been able to easily walk into cell phone range. Number two, they would have been lucky to have enough snow for snowshoeing in the first place. She clinched both fists and shook them, forcing herself to stop wasting time wishing she was somewhere else. She needed to use her head. It was almost 3:30 p.m. It would be dark in a couple of hours—by the time Andy got back. That thought made her shiver again, which broke the spell. It was crazy to stand in the middle of the trail for an hour and a half. She took Andy's advice and headed back toward the lake.

As she slowly picked her way, snowflakes floated around her. It was snowing, but it wasn't coming down heavily enough to fill in the tracks before Andy got back to the car. Deana concentrated on staying in the tracks they had just made. She tried not to think about what would happen if it snowed harder and throughout the night. If the tracks were covered, she was sure Andy could still find her. If he had to drive into town for help, he could direct them to the trail they had followed to the lake.

She remembered a tourist photo of the lake without the snow and ice. It showed a boat full of happy tourists gliding across turquoise water. There was no snow and ice in sight. She shrugged her shoulders, thinking if it was summer and there were hikers and picture snappers popping up around every corner, Andy would be complaining about the crowds.

She stopped and listened for a few seconds, hoping to hear sounds signaling an invasion of one or two snowshoers or—even better—the whine of a snowmobile. The idea of summer crowds sounded really good to her. She shuddered to shake off her fears, let out a groan, and crossed her fingers inside her mittens—an irrational but comforting gesture.

Each step held the threat of throwing her off balance if a boot went through the snow. She narrowed the distance between steps to better maintain balance if one leg suddenly dropped a foot or two lower than the other one. Covering the short distance back to the lake was slow. She realized she was holding her breath and said out loud, "Breathe, *breathe*." Every third or fourth step one of her feet slowly pushed through the top snow. Leaning on the ski poles, she carefully pulled the leg up out of the hole on each step and moved forward.

One module of the hunter education class was on survival. Sergeant Myers had skipped over most of it, suggesting the students read through it on their own. She reassured them that, unless they were stranded in the wilderness, they wouldn't need to worry about it. Deana had glanced at it but now wished she had read it very, very carefully as preparation for this trip. Jasper National Park was one of the largest natural areas in North America, a fact she now wished she didn't know. It made the situation seem even more desperate. Deana's stomach clenched when she thought about being in a wilderness that was protected from development and people. It was a refuge for wildlife, not people.

Sergeant Myers had spent a few minutes on preventive survival, which she defined as planning: being in good shape, wearing proper clothing, and carrying basic survival equipment. Deana *had* followed all her advice, but it didn't erase the worry. The recommended expensive-but-ugly moisture-wicking polypropylene underwear and layered clothing she *did* have on were scant comfort. She realized Myers was mostly referring to hiking and hunting in Virginia. Her reassurance that in Virginia one could travel two miles in any direction and find a road was not improving Deana's mood in the Canadian Rockies. Even if she could make it all the way out to the trailhead and the road, the odds of running into another person were not good. There would be no one heading out for a snowshoe hike in the dark. If it continued to snow through the night, no one would venture to the trailhead for at least another twenty-four hours. Andy knew where she was. She had to stop worrying and count on him.

It was the niggling memory of the pages on extractive survival that made her continue to look around nervously. She started to imagine Andy falling and breaking an ankle. He might not make it back to the car for hours. And if he didn't make it back, Deana would likely be out there for the rest of the night by herself. She concentrated, trying to stay in their tracks as she headed back to the lake. She rubbed her forehead, as if a little pressure would help her recall the at-the-time insignificant definition of extractive survival. Something to do with "getting yourself out of a situation in which you should not have been in the first place."

"This certainly fits the bill," Deana said out loud and screamed as her left foot broke through the snow crust, leaving her lopsided and struggling to stay upright. She pulled her leg up out of the hole and forged ahead more slowly, hoping to avoid any more sudden jolts. The end of the trail was tantalizingly close; she could see it twenty yards ahead. The memory of the small clearing at the edge of the lake helped her pick up her tired legs. A loud thump took her by surprise, and she almost lost her balance. Carefully balancing on ski poles, she looked over her shoulder. A melon-sized chunk of snow had fallen from a tree branch and just missed her. Poking it with a pole, she realized it was hard-packed snow. It could have landed on her head. She didn't waste any more time looking around and pushed ahead. The narrow path was surrounded by towering evergreens, their branches sagging under the weight of the snow they held. She glanced up at the dirty white sky and had to bat snowflakes from her eyes.

When she reached the edge of the lake, she could stand around stamping her feet to keep warm and hug herself in the hope of warding off fear, *or* she could use the little knowledge she had to survive. She halted on the word *survive*. The use of the word made the danger real. And it wasn't just her at risk. Andy was out there. The smartest thing to do was plan for the worst. She finally reached the edge of the lake. "Ahh," she said, waving her arms around in circles to shake the tension and walked around the patch free of deep snow.

She thought about the contents of her backpack and remembered the cute little solid fuel stove she had bought. Her idea of a romantic break on the hike was to surprise Andy with a cup of cappuccino on the trail. It was tempting to take a few minutes now and fix a warm cup of coffee, but she didn't want to waste even a few seconds. Instead, she took a small drink of cold water from a bottle as she looked around and considered the options. The wind had not only blown snow from the area but had knocked it from one side of the majestic spruce trees bordering the lake. Deana now eyed the exposed branches for their use as firewood or a bed instead of admiring their beauty. She rubbed her aching shoulders, sore from the strain of leaning on the ski poles all day, and scanned the snow bordering the clearing for animal tracks. There were small indentations in the snow, but she wasn't sure what had made them. The faces of snarling wolves and cougars jumping with oversized claws flashed through her mind. The details of a recent cougar attack reported in the local paper heightened her anxiety.

Another hole in my wilderness knowledge bank, she scolded herself silently. She spent as much time on the material covering animal tracks as she did on the sections on extractive survival that were recommended but not required reading; it had been only a cursory glance. Now, she wished she had memorized the tracks left by predators, as well as harmless creatures. Knowing which one had just passed through the area would have at least told her whether she should be afraid or not.

She started kicking snow off small, fist-sized rocks around the edge of the lake and carried them back to the boulder. It wasn't much, but it was the only defense system she could come up with if something started circling her, working up an appetite. She stopped every few minutes and stood perfectly still while listening and looking all around, hoping to not hear or see any signs of a threat.

She secretly wished Andy was lurking somewhere in the woods, watching, and that this was all part of a perverse survival test he had concocted for his amusement and her misery. She couldn't help herself. She asked softly at first and then louder, "Andy? Andy, are you out there?" There was no answer.

It had taken a half hour to get back to the lakeshore. Now there was maybe an hour of daylight. The darn test in hunter education asked what the three priorities are if you're in an extractive survival situation. She got the answer right: shelter, fire, and signal. The test did not ask how to construct an emergency shelter. At the time, Deana didn't think she would ever have to worry about it. "Shit!" she said, and thought, *Debris huts, snow caves, remember, remember.* She looked around trying to think quickly and decide whether or not to collect branches and build a debris hut, using the boulder and ski poles as the frame or if she should burrow into the snow.

Deana didn't have a handy supply of leaves, and it would be a chore to find loose branches under the snow—not that she would know what to do with either to make a proper debris hut. She might be able to saw through enough smaller limbs to build some kind of shelter. The other option, the snow cave shelter, reminded her of the ledge she had seen from the lake. Scanning the snow-covered rocks above her, she spotted the ledge. There was no point sitting around until hypothermia rendered her loopy and irrational. As long as she kept thinking and moving, she figured she could at least survive until Andy returned. Still staring at the ledge above her, she started to wonder if there might be a real cave behind the ledge. She might waste ten to fifteen minutes scrambling up to check it out, but it was worth it. If it wasn't a good place for shelter, at least she could throw down some of the branches around the ledge and start work on a debris hut.

Her heart leaped as she realized there was a possibility of picking up cell reception from a higher point. Andy had tried the cell phone in the parking lot and on the trail and couldn't get a signal. Deana grabbed the snowshoe, thinking it would be a useful climbing tool. She saw the split decking and screamed, "Ahh shit!" He had taken the good snowshoe and left her with the broken one. Slapping the snowshoe against her hand, she shrugged and wondered why he had even bothered to take one snowshoe with him. *He was in a hurry and meant to take the broken one,* she mused. Well, he would figure it out and bring what he needed for repairs back with him. In the meantime, the snowshoe would make a better weapon and tool than ski poles for knocking snow from the rocks. She turned to work her way up to the cave. Grunting and groaning after going up just a few yards, she stopped and pulled the cell phone out of her pocket. She flipped it open, turned it on, and heard the familiar and suddenly annoying sound the phone played when it was turned on. It was programmed to imitate the sound of waves crashing. She liked it when she bought the phone. She remembered thinking, *Great—waves crashing!* She had smiled, closed her eyes, and pretended to smell salty sea air. Now the sound of waves crashing had her muttering, "Oh great! Waves crashing," with chagrin in her voice. "Just what I need."

"What!" she shouted, so nervous she dropped the phone in the snow. She dug it out and opened it again. The screen read "No SIM card." She shook the phone and hit it with her hand, hoping for an easy fix. The screen stubbornly continued to read "No SIM card." She had used it last night, and the SIM card worked. She keyed in "911," hoping that it might send a signal even if the SIM card wasn't working. "Call Failed" flashed on the screen. It meant she wasn't in a service area. When Andy had tried the cell phone from the parking lot that morning, she remembered hearing the familiar wave crashing sound when he turned it on. She hadn't actually seen the screen to know if it said "No service" or "No SIM card." Now she hoped he hadn't just been pretending to try it to mollify her. It didn't matter. The phone was worthless. Andy had laughed sarcastically and said, "No reception. We're in a dead zone." Deana shivered and shook her head, thinking, *Stop it! Yes, he can be moody, but he is resourceful, and he'll get me out of here.* This wasn't the place or time to worry about Andy's moods. His last words—*Trust me*—she continued muttering softly. She couldn't help thinking it was odd that he had insisted on carrying the cell phone himself. He was normally virulently anti-cell phone, in keeping with the mountain-man, back-to-nature persona he carefully cultivated.

She went over everything in her head again. It had all happened so fast. She knew he was right. They both would have been stuck on the trail in the dark if she tried to hike out without snowshoes. It was impossible. They could have easily missed the trail back to the car and ended up wandering around in the woods all night. There was a cheap compass in her survival kit, but she didn't know how to use it. *Duh!* she thought. The chapter on survival recommended it, and Deana threw it in her backpack. The instructor told the class they could spend a whole day on learning to use a map and compass and suggested finding a knowledgeable person to help if they were interested. Deana thought she was with a knowledgeable person, but Andy dismissed her offer to pull out the compass. "Deana," he said in a tired, bored voice, "forget it. It won't be of any use to us in the dark and without a topo map."

A picture of the young girl who sat next to her in the hunter education class popped into Deana's head. The teenager was wearing a pink T-shirt and a camouflage jacket. Her name was Kimberly, and she appeared to be all of fourteen. Little Kimberly knew how to use a map and compass, Deana remembered. Kimberly made Deana smile when she started a story with "When I was a lot younger ..." Kimberly continued with the confidence of someone much older, "Daddy took us out in an ATV on a fire road. We had to use the compass and a topo map to find our way back on a trail to the parking lot." Kimberly nodded her head, pink-ribboned ponytail bobbing up and down. "Daddy says *everybody* should always carry a compass and a topo map and know how to use them."

There was a pile of topo maps for Virginia's mountains sitting in a bag in the trunk of Andy's car at home. He never took them with him when he went hunting. "I never get lost," he answered when Deana asked why he didn't carry them when he took off by himself. She shook her head to get rid of thoughts that kept her from believing in the perspicacity of her husband. Her life was in his hands. She didn't want to start blaming him as a distraction for her fear.

Deana thought she knew her husband, but she didn't understand his macho creed of solving problems with his brains, a knife, and some matches. It seemed an unreasonable approach to life, but he enjoyed the challenge of dealing with danger. Deana thought it was normal to run away from danger; Andy ran toward it. She ended her psychobabble analysis with the thought, *This will teach him a lesson.* She couldn't decide whether to be mad at Andy or worried about him. Rolling her eyes, she thought, *Now I just have to trust he will handle my investments with better judgment than he seems to apply to our outdoor adventures.*

Her mind was jumping from the broken snowshoe to Kimberley to money and back to wishing Andy would come roaring down the trail on a snowmobile. Deana was hazy about the details of crafting survival huts, but she remembered only too clearly the instructor's advice on hypothermia. The class was warned it was impossible to self-diagnose. To prevent it one needed to avoid getting wet and try to exercise to maintain the body's heat. A trickle of sweat was running down Deana's neck. She rubbed the moisture away with the back of her glove and wished the instructor was here now so she could ask how she was supposed to exercise and not sweat.

She was wasting time daydreaming. She hoped it wasn't a symptom of hypothermia. There was nothing funny about the situation, but she did chuckle softly as she remembered reading it was impossible to self-diagnose. The air temperature seemed to be dropping as the sun moved toward the horizon. It wasn't her imagination; it was real and logical. Nope, she wasn't hallucinating—yet.

Deana knocked snow off the rock outcroppings ahead and above her, so she could see where to put her feet. She pulled and pushed herself in the direction of the ledge and gave a grateful nod to the wind gods for sections of rock where at least some of the snow had blown away. It made it a lot easier to put a foot down on three inches of snow instead of a foot or two of snow. She left a zigzag path behind her as she tried to work her way in the direction of the spots where the snow was not so deep. As soon as she stopped for a few seconds to catch her breath, the bitter cold connected with the thin layer of perspiration between her skin and the sleeves of her shirt. A shiver ran through her. The short climb was hard work. She was dripping wet before she was only halfway up. She stripped off her jacket and tied it around her waist, trying to keep at least one article of clothing dry. She figured that when she finally was able to build a fire, she would take off the wet clothes and wear the jacket. A small fire might be enough to dry out slightly damp, guaranteed-to-wick-away moisture L.L. Bean wear. Deana didn't think the clothing was made to wick away the amount of sweat she was producing on her climb. The possibility of spending the night by herself had become real.

She was instinctively thinking ahead, planning and preparing for a long, cold night. Shelter, fire, and signal—the answer to the hunter education question of how to extract yourself from a dangerous situation. She was working on shelter and fire.

The falling air temperature would be of no use in drying a sweaty body. She would end up covered in a fine layer of ice if she didn't figure out how to build a fire soon.

Looking up, she saw branches from a fallen tree hanging over the ledge. They could be used to help fuel a fire. If she had to climb back down again and get more branches, it would be doable. She had to get up there first to be able to decide whether the ledge or the ground was the best place to build her camp. If the latter seemed the better alternative, she could throw the branches down to the ground. She finally reached the ledge and made herself peek over the edge without stopping to worry about coming eyeball-to-eyeball with a bear. The way things were going, she figured she would meet the only bear in the history of Jasper National Park to wake up from hibernation this time of year.

Her spirits improved when she saw an opening leading to a cave. Instinctively, she called out a "Hello!" and threw a rock into the opening. She listened as it bounced off the wall and echoed. There were no signs of animal tracks in the snow around the ledge, but if a bear was sleeping the winter away in the cave, there wouldn't be any tracks. She called "Hello!" one more time and waited a couple of seconds before climbing the last few steps up to the cave.

"Oh!" she couldn't help saying softly when she stepped onto the ledge. Nature had carved out a section of rock to form a cave behind the ledge. A giant fallen evergreen was being held up by the overhang jutting out a few feet over the ledge. *A nice hidey-hole,* Deana thought. Shelter for the night was taken care of—ancient stone dwelling with view.

She took two steps from the edge of the ledge and eased into the clam-shaped opening. Then she turned and looked out from the cave entrance to the view over the lake. It took her breath away. All the tension and worry slipped from her mind and body. The world slowed down. The view from the cave was even better than the view from the ground. Snow-covered tree tops framed the view out over the frozen lake. Mountain peaks soared above everything, but the color from the setting sun made her realize the mesmerizing view was about to vanish into the blackness of night. She looked at her watch. She had used twenty precious minutes and had only forty more minutes of daylight to figure out how to make it through the night. She sighed and turned to inspect the cave.

The area was about twelve feet wide and eight feet deep. Hidden by the fallen tree, she could now see another hole in the middle of the wall. It was waist high. She knelt down and stuck her head in but couldn't make anything out. She slipped the backpack off onto the cave floor and looked around the space of what would be her shelter for the night. Protection from wind and snow and a spot to build a fire. It was better than nothing.

Rooting around in the backpack, she found the bag with the solid fuel stove and matches. She had hidden it to surprise Andy with a cup of hot coffee at the end of their hike. Big surprise, lover-boy. She laughed as she thought about teasing him, "Add a mini solid fuel stove to your survival list of knife and matches." This was turning out to be exactly the kind of adventure and challenge Andy enjoyed. He loved a risk and had escaped unscathed so many times he took it for granted his luck would continue. She had to hope for both their sakes it would.

She held up the plastic bag protecting a very small box of matches. At least she had kept them dry by putting them in a plastic bag. She took the shiny box advertising a Washington, D.C., restaurant out of the bag. It was about the width of her thumb and the length of her pinkie finger to the knuckle. There were ten matches inside the box. Each one was now more precious than gold. She needed to use the matches sparingly. She put the bag in her pocket and unclipped a penlight hanging from the backpack.

She knelt down, stuck her head inside the opening, and flicked the switch on the penlight. She caught her breath and banged her head on the rock. Someone had been here. There was a small metal box in the middle of the space and a dark, half-full trash bag. Remembering the penlight was as precious as the matches, she turned it off, quickly crawled in, and grabbed the bag and the box, pushing them toward the opening. In the few moments of light, she saw the small cave was about four feet by six feet and only three feet high—just big enough for one or two people to sleep.

She pushed the treasure out into the larger cave and quickly crawled after it, hoping against hope it would be of use. Opening the green plastic trash bag, she couldn't believe her eyes. A ratty old sleeping bag was rolled up inside two trash bags. Someone must actually use this cave from time to time. This meant she could take off the wet clothes and get into the bag. It would help, but she would still need a fire to make it safely through the night. She reached for the small metal box, lifted the lid, and groaned at the sight of watercolor pencils and a small pad of paper. The rest of the contents told her this was someone's idea of an emergency kit: two emergency flares, an unopened package containing a new 9 V battery, and a small plastic bag. A slow smile spread across her face as she held up the last item. The clear plastic sandwich baggie held a fist-sized piece of steel wool. She smiled because she knew what it was for and wouldn't have known *before* the hunter education class.

The class had been advised to carry more than one fire starter in an emergency kit. You were supposed to pack waterproof matches, steel wool, and a 9 V battery. Before Deana could ask how steel wool and a battery could be used to start a fire, Kimberley raised her hand and said, "Coins will work too."

The instructor had arranged the contents of a survival kit on a table. During the break, Deana walked over to the table, removed the steel wool from the baggie, and picked up the battery lying next to it. She barely got the question out, "How does this work?" when sparks started flying, and she screamed. The ladies had a good laugh at Deana's expense, and she learned a lesson in fire starting.

She rolled the pencils in her hand, figuring an artist must use the cave from time to time. She had used up her quota of good luck in stumbling on a cave with a sleeping bag. The good luck would definitely not extend to the artist showing up in a snowstorm to capture the scene and rescue her. She put the pencils down and picked up one flare with one hand and one with the other. She held her hands out and looked at the flares. A crooked grin froze in place as she thought, *I should be happy.* She now had the third requirement for getting out of a bad situation: signal. The only problem was there was no one around to see the signal. She would worry about the flares later. She didn't think anyone would see them; maybe she could use them to scare a hungry cougar or wolf. She picked up the sketch book and opened it. The artist had sketched the view from the cave around the top edge of the page. Under the watercolor rendering was written: "Dear fellow traveler, You've discovered my spot! What a view! If you're in trouble, I've left a small topo map showing the closest ranger station. Please do not leave food in the cave. —A fellow traveler."

Deana's fingertips rested on the last three words for a second. She spotted the topo map on the bottom of the box. Time to look at that tonight. Knowing she had some kind of shelter for the night lifted her spirits and gave her the energy to finish the preparations. She checked out the fallen tree protecting the cave and decided to drop down below the cave, break off branches, and bring them back up to the bare bones room to use for fuel. It might be better to leave the thick branches covering the cave in place for protection. It was hard work, and she was surprised the trusty ole Swiss Army knife was strong enough to cut through some of the branches. Up and down three times, her thighs were burning, her shoulders ached, and her arms hung at her sides like overcooked noodles, but there were enough branches piled up to keep a fire going all night.

CHAPTER 3

The cold, gray, forbidding sky was growing darker; there wasn't going to be a spectacular sunset to cheer her up. Her skin was like a hard shell, barely able to protect the workings inside it. The bitter cold had worked its way into her bones. She forced her arms out and made half-hearted windmills, trying to get the circulation going. Limp with exhaustion, her arms were now stiff, hardened appendages. She stamped her feet and rubbed her arms to try to bring some warmth back, not taking her eyes from the view as she watched the last light fade from the sky. The gorgeous view depicted in the sketch book showed shades of green, blue-green water and sky, and a rocky glacial peak in the background. She was now looking at the same view in black and white. The artist could draw the winter version with just charcoal and pencil. No matter how talented though, he or she could never capture the piercing cold. Deana felt alone and scared in the Alberta wilderness. It was beautiful and awe-inspiring but not comforting like the friendly Blue Ridge Mountains she was used to. The mountains at home had a gentle beauty. She decided the Rockies offered breathtaking vistas, but their ruggedness and immensity was a constant reminder of the dangers people faced when they tried to exist in them.

As the last light faded from the sky, she made a circle out of loose rocks on one side of the opening to the cave; in the center she laid a bunch of pine cones. Even if they wouldn't burn, they would make a good base around which to pile the branches in a teepee shape. Remembering 4-H camp tips on building campfires years ago, Deana tried to build a pyramid with the logs and branches. She didn't remember much from the week-long camp, but the camp counselors must have made quite an impression when they showed the campers how to build a fire. They were ten years old, and each child marched up and propped a log or branch on the fire to form a pyramid. The counselors said a pyramid fire would burn slower and last longer than just throwing logs one at a time on the fire. Deana smiled, remembering chubby Johnny Binkley's grin when he walked up and knocked the almost finished pyramid over. Johnny's punishment was to sit while the rest of the kids rebuilt it. He grinned through his punishment.

If ever she needed a slow-burning fire, it was now. Lighting the match, she used a piece of paper from the sketch book and managed to get a little fire going. Some of the pine cones flared up; others spewed a trail of smoke, but they created enough heat to catch the branches on fire. Deana knelt down and listened for a few seconds to the comforting hiss and crackle coming from the circle. There was no hurry to go anywhere and plenty of time to think. That was the trouble—plenty of time to think and worry.

She looked at the fire and then out into the night, straining to hear sounds of someone calling her name or crashing through the woods. She clasped her hands together to stop her fingers drumming on her legs. She was stuck here until Andy got back. The priority was to stay safe and alive, and that meant eating and sleeping. If the fire went out, she had enough supplies to get it going again. Andy would see the tracks going up and down to the cave. He would find her. She shook her head, knowing she wasn't expecting to fall into a deep sleep under the circumstances. She would be wide-awake, listening for the sounds of a snowmobile or Andy calling her name.

She began to fix a cup of cappuccino with the little stove. If she used the water bottle now, she could go ahead and melt some snow in the container and keep filling it up. She cherished each sip of the cappuccino and every bite of the energy bar, chewing slowly and deliberately, wiggling her toes in her boots. The boots advertised they would keep feet warm and dry down to minus 25F°, and so far, they were working.

She could still feel her toes. She pulled out the topo map and held it close to the fire to read it. There was an *X*—you are here—marking the cave next to the lake. The trail winding out to the parking lot was a thin line from the cave. Deana caught her breath when she saw the ranger station marked directly across the lake from the cave. She scrambled up and stared out through the darkness across the lake. There really was a chance. It would be much easier to hike across the lake than to try to get out to the parking lot.

She found the compass, still in its packaging, and knelt down next to the fire to take a look at it. It was the size of a silver dollar, plastic, with "Made in China" stamped on the back. The red and white arrows, which she assumed were meant to indicate the direction, were bouncing all around because her hand was shaking from excitement and the cold. She laid the compass on the floor of the cave and put the topo map next to it, trying to place it where she thought the marked trailhead was located. The arrows stopped moving and landed on *E* and *W*. She sat back on her heels, puzzled but not defeated. In the light of day she could figure it out. She palmed the compass, kissed it, and stored it in a zippered pocket. It was like a newfound treasure—another tool that might help her get to safety.

She turned her thoughts again to making it across the lake. At least the snow on the lake had been blown into drifts by the wind, and she could pick her way around the heavy snow fairly easily. She snorted on the words *fairly easily*. Picking her way around drifts was easy compared to slogging through the deep snow in the woods. If she could see the ranger station, she would have a landmark that would help in figuring out how to use the compass.

She thought about the problems she would face if she tried to retrace their steps through the woods. There was no trail to follow. Even if she could figure out how to use the compass, she wasn't sure she could trust the little two-dollar piece of plastic. She couldn't move through the snow any faster than a snail. If she did make it to the parking lot, the likelihood of anyone being around was slim, and that meant being stuck in a snow-packed parking lot at the end of a remote snow-packed road with no shelter. It was too dark to see, but she turned again to face the direction of the lake. Heading out to a goal she could see made a lot more sense than guessing about which way to go in the woods. The ranger station was the goal. She would strike out as soon as the sun was up. If it was locked, she could break in and have better shelter than the cave. It had to be stocked with a supply of canned goods or something to eat. She couldn't see the station and couldn't see lights, but she had a plan, and that gave her hope. Remembering the flares, she realized they would be more noticeable at night. She jumped up and grabbed one of them. If she set one off close to shore, someone in the ranger station might see it.

Buoyed by the cappuccino and a survival plan, Deana worked her way down the rocks to the lake. It had stopped snowing, and there were a few stars twinkling in a break in the cloud cover on the other side of the lake. Lights shining from shore would have been better, but even a little starlight was surprisingly helpful to a scared, lonely soul. She stuck the flare in the snow, lit it, and watched it burn. Then she shut her eyes and willed the rumble of an approaching snowmobile to drown out the low, hissing sounds coming from the burning flare. Nothing—just the fizzing of the flare. She opened her eyes and looked in the direction of the trail, hoping to see the light from headlamps bobbing along the trail. Nothing—just darkness. After a deep breath and a sigh, she forced herself back up to her "cozy" home or grave.

She climbed into the sleeping bag, boots on, and curled around the fire. At least dropping down to light the flare had given her a chance to empty her bladder before she froze to death. Mom would have been happy; she'd freeze to death with clean underpants. It was cold, but she wasn't shaking yet. If the shuddering started, she would fix another cappuccino. What a way to go ...

She checked her watch again. It was now a little after 7:00 p.m. She remembered sitting in the restaurant eating breakfast before they headed out. As soon as the sun came up, they were staring at an elk that had bedded down for the night outside the hotel. Andy hadn't shared her excitement. He'd glanced up from his paper at the huge creature and said, "It will be dark by 5:00 p.m. Only nine hours of daylight."

Daylight wouldn't come until just before 8:00 a.m. That meant thirteen hours of waiting for another chance to look for help. It would be a long, cold night. The only sound was the sporadic crackling of the fire. She stared into the fire and conjured up Andy's face. She wanted to see a smiling image, but the flames licked around a stern face with eyes reddened by the fire. A shiver ran down her spine. She blinked to erase the picture.

She started thinking about Andy and how they had met. It was a blind date arranged by a friend who had met Andy through an Internet dating service and thought they would hit it off. So how much did she really know about him? She remembered thinking, *Wow, what a hunk,* when Cindy guided him across the room to introduce them. It wasn't just the jet-black hair and the angular, masculine features that turned heads. It was the rigid, straight posture, the measured steps of someone in complete control of himself. He caught her eye and maintained contact until they stopped in front of her and held it through the introductions and handshake. Deana felt like he saw straight through to her soul when he put both hands around hers, held them for a minute, and said, "Deana, I'm really glad to meet you. Cindy has told me so much about you. She says you're the best."

He had torn at her heartstrings when he explained he was alone in the world, widowed, parents deceased. He didn't have any close friends in the area and said he wanted to start a new life after his wife passed away. He grew up in a small town in Indiana and played the accordion. Deana learned he was sensitive when she couldn't stifle a laugh after he announced he played the accordion. "What?" she had said. "You mean polkas?"

He wasn't amused. She learned he actually could play the accordion really well. He entertained her with everything from classical to popular music. The memory of Andy playing "Lady of Spain" outside her bedroom window was fighting in her brain and heart with the memory of today's Andy—at times impatient and sarcastic and then confident and decisive. There had been little sign of the retro-accordion-playing romantic.

The day had started out so well. It was exciting to be alone in a vast wilderness, making first tracks through new snow. She imagined bonding with early explorers and trappers who had to live in such harsh conditions. She shook her head. Any romantic notions of reliving the good ole days had disappeared. Now, she wanted to be in a nice, modern, warm hotel room and in a town with cell phone coverage. She pulled out the worthless cell phone. Andy's words, *We're in a dead zone,* replayed in her head, sending an unconscious shiver down her spine. She also recalled her own words before climbing into bed yesterday: *I'm charging the phone in case we need it tomorrow.* She opened the back of the phone and saw the battery in place. Everything was as it should be. The battery worked, she already knew that. The SIM card was defective. She didn't want to turn it on again and waste any of the precious charge left on the phone. There was always the chance the 911 feature would work without the SIM card.

Andy should have been back by now. If he wasn't here by daybreak, she would stick to her plan and try to cross the lake to the ranger station in hopes of finding help. The hike out on the trailhead would have been so much easier on snowshoes. She thought about the traditional snowshoes she had seen and looked at the straps on her backpack. She shook her head in disgust. Why hadn't Andy thought of that? They could have cut the straps and made a kind of web around the frame like the old interlaced rawhide. It might have worked. Holding the cell phone, she sat up and looked at the broken snowshoe. *We're in a dead zone* kept running through her brain as a theme song. It was almost too improbable a coincidence for both the cell phone and the snowshoe to fail on the same afternoon and under the worst circumstances. Andy's unpredictable moods, swinging between romantic and sarcastic, added to her uneasiness about the serendipity in their day.

She had given up hoping he was hiding nearby, watching her, putting her through some perverse survival test. She looked at the watch: 7:22 p.m. Where was he? Questions to which she needed but didn't have the answers popped into her mind, one after the other: Did Andy make it to the car? Did he have an accident? Was he on his way back now with help? What was wrong with the SIM card?

Disappointment and disgust were beginning to replace the trust and respect she had for Andy's independence and knowledge of the outdoors. Too late she was beginning to realize knowledge of the outdoors was only valuable if you paired it with common sense, which Sergeant Myers had defined as "planning and preparation." Andy's lack of willingness to be prepared in favor of adventure and a challenge had landed them in this predicament. Deana had insisted he tell the front desk they were heading out so that someone would know where they were. He'd just laughed and said there was nothing to worry about. She had refused to get in the car until he followed her advice. He finally walked back into the hotel lobby and gave the front desk their hiking itinerary. She shrugged, realizing that's what he said he did. If he had, why hadn't someone been out here looking for her—us, she corrected. It was a young kid working behind the desk. His shift probably changed, and he was now sitting in a warm bar with friends. He wouldn't give a couple of strangers a second thought. The hotel wouldn't miss them until they passed their checkout date.

She sat up and reached for the damaged snowshoe. Holding it close to the fire, she looked at the split in the webbing and ran her fingers along the edges. A clean cut, no frayed edges. Andy would have blamed it on cheap imported rubber. She hadn't stepped on anything that would have sliced it. The snow was so deep she couldn't have sheared the rubber webbing on a rock. She couldn't and didn't want to find the words to ask if it was possible Andy had sliced it with his knife. What was more depressing—the danger she was in or the fact that she was starting to suspect her husband of deliberately leaving her to survive—or not survive—a night in the wilderness with a damaged snowshoe and a malfunctioning SIM card?

She stood up straight and looked around. If this was all part of a sick idea of Andy's to test her in some way, he would live to regret it.

"Andy, are you out there?" Deana yelled and listened for any sound. "This isn't funny!" There was no answer.

It had started to snow again, harder than earlier. Andy told her he checked the weather forecast for the day of the hike, and there was nothing worse than light flurries predicted. Had that been a lie? Had he really checked, or did he check and know the prediction was for several inches of snow? She didn't know what to think. She had to give Andy the benefit of the doubt. He could be out there on the trail or trying to survive the night in the car.

She was scared, and paranoia was filling her with doubts. The uncertainty was as chilling as the cold. A shiver ran through her. She heated up another cup of cappuccino and tried to sit up next to the fire to keep more of her body off the cold stone. By the time she took the last sip of the warm drink, the shivering had stopped. She lay back down, relieved that the fire kept burning. She dozed off, but her dreams were full of worries and plans for the next day. Half in and out of sleep, the sound of her voice calling "Hello! Anyone there?" woke her up. She sat up quickly and rubbed her eyes. In her dream she had crossed the lake and found the ranger station. She looked around, confused and surprised to realize she was still in a cave and not standing next to a snowmobile parked in front of the park ranger station.

"Oh man. Let's hope dreams come true," she said out loud, remembering her plan to hike across the lake. She decided to eat half the remaining food before she started out across the lake and save the other half.

Aching with cold and the extra firm "bed," she checked her watch: 4:12 a.m. Only four more hours until daylight. The best way to pass the time would be to sleep. She was afraid of the dreams that might come with sleep and afraid of rolling away from the fire and freezing. The distant howl of a local coyote or bobcat shot through the otherwise quiet night. Winter nights in the northern wilderness were quiet, as if all sound were tamped down by the cold. There were no birds talking, insects working, or small mammals moving around; there was just the sound of wind and the music of predators announcing a kill or calling a mate. The sounds of cars or trucks roaring down a highway, jet engines overhead, or the ground shaking from an approaching train would all have been welcome intrusions. The lack of noise and sounds announcing civilization, knowing there was no safe retreat, made her feel at odds with the primal world. It was not a friend; it was an adversary.

Her mind started wandering ahead to making it through another night. The big question was how long she could survive if she didn't make it across the lake and find shelter. There was plenty of fuel to keep a fire going, but her body needed fuel too. She was ready to eat worms but knew she wouldn't find any wriggling in the cold. If she could break through the ice on the shore, maybe there was something— snails, burrowing fish, roots—in the frozen mud. She would worry about that if she didn't make it across the lake.

She slept for a few minutes, forced herself out of her cocoon, and stood to do pathetic jumping-jacks. One more cup of cappuccino and a buffalo jerky stick. Chewing each bite slowly, she thought about supplies for the walk across the lake. Matches and the remaining food would go with her. The sleeping bag would stay in the cave, but she would take the damaged snowshoe. It might come in handy to test the ice or break a window when—not if—she got to the other side. Anger at Andy and his risk-taking, thrill-seeking bent rose in her as she looked at the snowshoe. She was only slightly ashamed of her anger when she remembered he could be lying injured along the trail or the road. His absence might also mean he was dead. *If he weren't dead, and they both lived through this, she would be the one to kill him,* she thought to herself wryly.

Climbing back into the sleeping bag, she hoped the sun would come out for the walk across the lake. Sun and images of warm sandy beaches occupied her dreams for the next hour of waiting. She jumped up, startled out of her dreams. It was daylight, 8:00 a.m. She had actually gotten a couple hours of sleep and hadn't frozen to death. Stiff with cold, she climbed out of the sleeping bag, rolled it up, put it back in the plastic bag, and shoved it into its hiding place. She left the fire smoldering instead of dousing it with snow. It wasn't as if the cave would burn down.

The cell phone was tucked inside her bra. It was a crazy idea, but she thought if she kept it warm, it might work. She stood at the edge of the ledge and pulled it out. She looked at it and prayed aloud, "Please work for me, little phone." She turned it on; the greeting played. Her shoulders fell when she read the screen: "No SIM card." Exhaustion, cold, and lack of food might contribute to fuzzy thinking, but a clear memory of the conversation with the cell phone salesman popped through the fuzziness. She remembered his words as he fiddled with the new phone. He had snapped a little card into the phone, put the battery in, and casually mentioned, "The SIM card is the guts of the phone."

She opened the back of the phone again and this time removed the battery. She rubbed a finger around the empty indentation under the battery. The SIM card was missing. No wonder that the phone wasn't working. The SIM card didn't malfunction; it was missing. SIM cards don't simply fall out of phones. They have to be removed. She had not done it. That meant Andy had taken it out. He was the one who had carried the phone all day. She tossed the worthless phone from one hand to the other while she thought. Logic overcame any desire to excuse Andy from responsibility. The phone had been working at the beginning of the day. Her hands curled into fists. "Damn him," she said. He must have removed the SIM card during the hike and forgotten to put it back in when she asked him to throw the phone to her.

If this was a fictional mystery, money would be at the heart of the crime. She certainly had enough money. The hand holding the phone fell back to her side as she remembered adding Andy's name to her stock account after they returned from the trip to Montana. A couple of weeks before they left, she asked Andy to take a look at her investment portfolio. He did a thorough, professional job, presenting charts and graphs that illustrated how much faster her investments would grow under his management. They worked out the details, added Andy's name to the account, and put her name on his. She was happy Andy would continue to use her broker's company to execute the trades in what was now their joint account.

He had saved her from the marauding moose on the Montana trip. But that was *before* his name was on the account. She married him without a prenuptial agreement because it felt right. A prenup seemed like an escape clause. Her girlfriends had tried to talk her into asking Andy to sign one. She asked him what he thought of the contracts, and he took her hands in his and said, "That's for people who don't trust each other. If we don't trust each other, we shouldn't get married. I know you have more money than I do, but I'm well-off and perfectly willing to share everything I have with you." He kissed his fingers, touched her forehead, and said softly, "Make up your mind if this is what *you* really want."

She felt like a creep, apologized, and they were married, "sharing all our worldly goods." Deana shook her head, trying to force the doubts away. What was happening? Did he hope to find her dead, frozen to death, and inherit the entire estate? He could get his hands on the large stock account, but he wouldn't get everything. She had talked to her lawyer before she and Andy got married. He recommended not changing the terms of her will for a few years. Charities and a school would be the beneficiaries of everything outside of the account that now had Andy's name on it.

She remembered the lawyer's advice: "Young lady, I know you're in love, and I respect your wish to not have a prenuptial agreement. However, let me give you one piece of advice." He went on to explain that as long as she kept accounts in her name only, they would not be considered joint assets in the event of a divorce.

The account that now had both of their names on it was worth $2.5 million. Crimes were certainly committed for a lot less than $2.5 million. She shook her head and tried to tell herself it made no sense. She replayed the conversation the afternoon Andy had finished looking at the equity account.

"Honey," he said, "I know Scott is an old friend, and he works for a very reputable firm. It isn't that he's done a bad job for you. He's put together a portfolio of blue chip stocks and bonds that would be a great fit for a ninety-year-old lady with blue hair."

"Andy," Deana protested, "I told Scott I didn't want anything risky."

"Just listen," Andy continued. "I'm not suggesting you liquidate everything and start buying new stocks. I just want authority to move on a company when I think it's a good fit for you. It might mean reducing your holdings in one area and giving you an opportunity to take advantage of some growth areas. I just need to be able to move quickly when there *is* a good opportunity."

"Okay," she agreed. "What do you want me to do?"

"Just put my name on the equity account. I can buy and sell in that account, and the proceeds will stay there. Scott will still get credit for the trades." He hesitated and smiled. "Deana, I'm not accusing Scott of taking advantage of you, but it is fairly standard for brokers to discount their commission on large trades. Scott hasn't given you a discount on any of the stock purchases in your account. I'll negotiate a discount on all future trades. How does that sound?"

It sounded logical and reasonable. Andy finished by suggesting he put her name on his stock account. He had put his hand over hers and said, "We need to start thinking in terms of *our* portfolio and not *yours* and *mine*." She remembered signing something, but now she had to wonder if her name ever made it to his account.

"Stop it!" she ordered. This was a waste of time. This isn't fiction; it's real life. She had to focus all her energy on making it through the rest of the day and night. Andy might have had to drive out on the snow-packed road in the dark for help; he may have run off the road or gotten stuck in the car, waiting for daylight, just like her.

Deana was furious with Andy if he was guilty of no more than carelessness and enraged if he was a scheming killer after her money. The anger energized her. Now she couldn't wait to get back and confront him. If Andy had gotten into trouble on the hike back to the car and was holed up somewhere in a snow cave, the fastest way to find him was for her to get to a phone and get help. The first question she wanted to ask him was why he had removed the SIM card from the phone.

She stuffed the fire starters in her pockets and the rest of the dwindling supplies in the backpack, including the flare and water bottle. She looked at the little solid fuel stove and put it back on the floor of the cave. This was not the time to be sentimental or impractical. She threw the ski poles over the ledge to the ground.

Hoping she was leaving the cave for the last time, she made her way down the rock face. The snow that had fallen during the night had filled in all her tracks. There was no sign of the path she and Andy had made through the woods. It made the decision to strike out across the lake easier. Without a trail to follow, she would end up disoriented and lost, possibly in even more dire straits than she was now. The sun was shining. When she paused at the base of the cave for one last sentimental look up at her refuge, she felt relieved and optimistic. She took a deep breath and turned to face the lake, pausing at the edge to scan the other side for signs of the ranger station. Nothing but trees.

She pulled out the compass and the topo map. Turning the map to line up with the lake and the cave, she was able to figure out the ranger station was *NE*. The other revelation was that the red arrow pointed north. "Yes!" she said and pumped a fist. She didn't need to worry about seeing the ranger station. The compass would guide her to it. After tucking the snowshoe into the backpack, she muttered, "Here goes nothing," and she took her first step onto the lake. Worried about weak ice, she used the ski poles to poke through the snow ahead of her. The lake was solid ice. Testing and poking the ice would make the crossing take even longer. She gave up testing the ice and used the ski poles as crutches. The snow was crusty, and each step was uneven. At this rate, it would take three hours to cross. She hesitated for a minute, hoping her logic in choosing the route to the ranger station instead of back down the trail made sense.

She started unconsciously humming "a marching we will go." Pick up one leg; put it down; pick up the other. She should have been exhausted, but fear and adrenalin kept her going. She reminded herself to not get too confident—yet. Anything could happen. If her frozen body was found, the obituary would say, "She was headed *NE*." She could make it if she just kept pushing.

Halfway out, she rewarded herself with water and a jerky stick. She picked the compass out of her pocket and laid it in the palm of her gloved hand. Great—she was staying on course. Her heart did a flip when she squinted and thought she could see a chimney peeking out of the trees on the shore. Relief flooded through her. Yes, she would make it across. The sun felt great, and the physical effort made her feel something close to warm. The relief was shattered by a vibration that shot through the air and the ice. Deana felt and heard it at the same time. Sheer terror ran through her. The sound echoed around her. She knew it was the sound of ice breaking.

She stood stock-still, shaking, eyes closed, afraid to breathe, as close to praying as she had come in a long time. She finally got the courage to open her eyes and look around. There was a crack in front of her, but she didn't know if it was the only crack. She had to get off the ice and back to shore before there were more of the deadly vibrations. She remembered Andy's words: *Trust me … don't worry. The lake has been frozen since October.* He definitely didn't know what he was talking about. The scowl on her face, triggered by disgust at Andy's confident assurance the ice was frozen, was replaced with a grimace. In just the few moments of standing there, she had become chilled. She was trembling. Her face was frozen. She started hitting it with her hand. Then she pulled her fingers into fists inside her mittens. She had to start moving to get warm. Shivering, tears turning to icicles on her cheeks, she slowly, carefully turned around and tried to retrace her steps, placing each foot down gingerly to lessen the impact of her weight. She paused after each step, holding her breath, and listened for sounds of cracking ice. She slowly inched herself away from the cracked ice and back to the wrong side of the shore. If only someone were in the ranger station and would see her. Her back was turned to any chance of being saved as she retraced her steps back to the cave.

At least she would be back at the cave with enough daylight to collect firewood and melt more water. She chastised herself for heading straight across the lake. It would have been smarter to have hugged the shore. It would have taken longer, but it would have been less risky. She wanted to run as fast as she could, but running was impossible through the uneven snow and ice. The adrenalin rush of anger that had propelled her earlier and the terror of the cracking ice now left her feeling exhausted and drained of energy. If she sat down to rest for even a few moments, she was afraid she'd close her eyes and fall asleep.

Deana felt a little woozy. She had been staring intently at the snow, walking carefully, looking for signs of ice or open water. She kept blinking to clear the spots from her eyes, but it wasn't helping. She stopped and dropped to her knees to let the dizziness pass. She lifted her head to look around and rubbed the crick in her neck. She realized she wasn't depressed, feeling sorry for herself, or too scared to move or think. She was determined to survive. She waited a few minutes to make sure her vision was okay and thought about how every living creature instinctively fought to live and hide from predators. The desire to keep fighting might be instinctive, but she had to use cunning and brains to come up with a plan: get back to shore, check on the fire, collect more fire fuel, and think about food. Catching an animal with her bare hands was a little far-fetched. All she could think about was food, but she knew the most important thing was to keep warm. There was one jerky stick left. That would probably be enough food for some people for two days. She just had to get back to the cave and get warm.

Head down and eyes just one step ahead of her body, she stared at indentations in the snow left by her boots as she retraced her steps. Her eyes rested on each footprint for signs of a break in the ice. She didn't want to look up to check how much further she had to go. The shore and safety would seem too far away, and the disappointment would slow her down.

"Yes!" she said softly when the shore was just a step away. She jumped quickly onto land, hugged herself, and then bent down to kiss the snow. She was so relieved to be on solid ground that she forgot for a few seconds she was still in serious danger.

It was just after 3:00 p.m. by the time she had a big warm fire going. She hovered over it, rotating her body to let all parts soak in the warmth. She tried to imagine the smell of a steak sizzling on the fire. Instead, the hissing sound around her ears gave off the smell of musty mittens drying out. The memory of Sergeant Myers telling the class about her squeamishness on her first squirrel hunt made Deana smile. She had tried to hide her "Oh yuk!" look when two of the women talked about the quickest way to skin a squirrel. Right now, she was hungry enough to eat a squirrel raw. The memory of Kimberly's culinary recommendation on how to cook a squirrel made her smile. "Daddy brought a lemon and a bag of herbs with him." She had proceeded to explain how her dad prepared and fried the squirrel at their campsite.

There were no herbs and lemons around, but Deana was hungry enough to just put it on the stick she was using to poke the fire and roast it. Kimberly had concluded her enthusiastic description of a squirrel dinner with, "Tastes just like chicken." At this point, Deana decided squirrel, whatever it tasted like, would be fine eating.

Tomorrow, she could try to get to the cabin again by skirting around the edge of the lake. Stepping onto the lake again was not an option. She would never forget the terrifying sound and the echo that followed when the ice cracked around her. A feeling of sadness swept through her. Her shoulders dropped with the harsh realization that she might not wake up in the morning. She wouldn't die from starvation. Hypothermia was the biggest threat. Deana shook off the sadness and negative thinking. She *would* wake up in the morning.

Eating very slowly, she started nibbling on the jerky, reminding herself again that shelter, fire, and signal were the top three priorities for survival in a serious situation. She left a few bites of the jerky stick for later. Food was not one of the big three.

When Deana had asked Sergeant Myers why food wasn't on the list, she laughed and said, "It takes a very long time to starve to death. You'll die from hypothermia days before you'll starve to death. Water is more important than food." Myers held up a book on edible plants and reminded the class again that they would be found before they had to eat native plants. She left unsaid the words *in Virginia*.

Deana hadn't really been any more than mildly curious about the brief segment on survival. She paid enough attention to pass the test. Sergeant Myers passed out a flyer announcing a three-day class devoted to wilderness survival. Deana didn't even glance at it. Her own idea of survival had been how to deal with gas station coffee and the fried-everything food offered in every restaurant in the South. Now, her mouth watered at the thought of biting into an artery-clogging hamburger, washed down with day-old coffee.

She decided to drink a little water and go down one more time before settling in for the night. She would wait until sunset, climb down, and set off the second and last flare. She curled up in the sleeping bag to rest for the thirty minutes before sunset and stared at the sparks in the fire. Dozing off, she dreamed of a warm Virginia night alive with fireflies.

Armies of miniature lanterns descending through the night sky and landing in the tall grass. Once they landed, the little lights kept moving. She woke up suddenly, shivering. Her hat had fallen off in her fitful sleep. Three hours had passed.

Her hand flew to cover her mouth as a wave of nausea hit. She took a couple of deep breaths and reached for the last flare. "Push. Come on, you can do it," she whispered. Eyes shut tight, she forced herself up off her knees. She was conscious of moving slowly as she stuffed the fire starter tools in her pockets—matches in one, steel wool and battery in the other. She stopped and moved the steel wool into the pocket with the matches. The way her luck was running, there would be a miniscule hole in the plastic bag holding the steel wool, and it would ignite the battery, setting her pants on fire.

It was overcast but not snowing now. If there was any chance for the flare to be seen, she had to take it. She had been up and down the rocks to the cave so many times she could do it with her eyes closed. Still, instinct and the fear of taking a wrong step in the dark made her pull out the little penlight and scan the edge before taking the first step down. She stepped and fell anyway, sliding down a few feet on her rear end before bracing a foot against a rock. She let out a breath, rubbed her forehead and then her bottom to make sure she was still in one piece. She was so sore and cold it was impossible to tell if she had an injury. The cold had numbed everything—nature's painkiller. She slowly picked her way down without falling again.

Deana walked to the edge of the lake. It was unreasonable to hope a crazy hiker would want to make first tracks and take the same trail she and Andy had followed. *Highly unlikely,* she thought. *Real backcountry skiers and hikers would not take unnecessary risks. They would not deliberately head out into bad weather. No one would find her by chance and no one would be looking for her. Andy had left two days ago. If he'd made it out, he would have been back with help by now. That meant Andy had* not *made it to safety and was in trouble or dead. Their car was in the parking lot. If Andy had not been able to get back to the car, someone would find it and know to look for them.* She tried to push all the "what ifs" out of her head.

The ranger station represented civilization. Rangers probably did some work in the winter as well as the summer. If no one was looking for her, the best chance of rescue rested on someone seeing the flare. Deana stuck the flare in the snow at the edge of the lake and lit it. The "psst" sound of the flare fizzling instead of lighting took all the air out of her. She had taken for granted it would light like the first one did. Humph, she had taken a lot for granted in the last few months. She angrily kicked it and then quickly stepped to grab it out of the snow. There might be something left in the flare if she put it in a fire. If no one saw the fire at night, someone might see the smoke from the fire during the day.

She closed her eyes and pressed her fingers against her aching forehead. Hunger or cold or stress or all three were giving her a pounding headache. She got as close to the edge of the lake as possible without stepping on it and was amazed at her own strength as she dragged broken branches across the snow, cut them, and shook the snow off them. By the time she was ready to light the fire, she had stripped down to her shirt and was thoroughly exhausted. The sweat turned icy cold as she stood and tried to catch her breath. Her hands were shaking when she pulled out the matches and the steel wool and battery. Sparks flew from the battery, and a branch caught fire. She lit a match quickly to help it along, but the smoke generated from the still-damp branches forced her back.

Deana fanned the fire with her jacket. She was so tired that even waving the jacket was a huge effort. A couple of small flames flicked. She bent down to place the flare in the flame. She jumped as a loud boom filled the air. The flare exploded and then fizzled. *Great, going out with a bang,* she thought. The vibrations echoed around the lake, and that was it. There was a lot of smoke but no fire. She left the smoldering, smoky fire until morning.

Deana turned to make her way back up to the cave. It started to snow again—beautiful small flakes all around. The job of finding dry branches had just become more difficult. Everything would be covered with another layer of snow by morning. She leaned on the snowshoe, not able to even turn around and look at the snow swirling around her. If she looked, she might give up. Even worse, she might start crying. She closed her eyes for a second, took a deep breath, and willed her body back up to the ledge.

She settled back in the cave, her stomach rumbling, and her own body odor so foul she could no longer smell the dank cave. She was shivering and feverish. Curling around the fire, not knowing whether this would be her last night or not, she had finally reached the point of misery where people don't care if they live or die. Staring into the fire, she thought again of hot, humid summer nights at home. She remembered a film of sweat on her upper lip when she tossed and turned, trying to fall asleep in the heat. Even those memories couldn't stop the shivering.

She closed her eyes and smiled as she pictured foamy cappuccinos, hot chocolates—anything and everything hot. She caught herself rubbing her stomach and remembering wonderful meals, planning her first meal back in civilization. She couldn't smell the fire. She smelled the aroma of an apple pie and felt saliva dribbling down the side of her mouth. She didn't care any longer if she was dreaming, hallucinating, or lying to herself. She hugged herself and listened for sounds or anything to tell her she wasn't alone in the world.

A moment later, she sat up straight; she had heard something new. The sound grew closer and louder. It was the roar of a snowmobile. She kicked her way out of the sleeping bag as quickly as she could and stood on the ledge, looking for signs of a light and listening for the sounds of an engine. *Andy did make it,* she thought with relief. *He's brought help. It must be him coming back on a snowmobile.* Stomping her feet and clapping her hands, she listened with excitement as the snowmobile drew closer, shattering the still night. As soon as she made out a light bouncing off the trees, tears of relief started rolling down her cheeks.

The snowmobile roared to a stop at the end of the trail. She called out from the mouth of the cave "Andy, up here!" The snowmobile driver took off his helmet. It wasn't Andy.

"Hey, are you okay? Can you climb down?" the man yelled.

CHAPTER 4

Her eyes were trying with difficulty to open; why were they so heavy and hard to open, even a little? Coming out of a dream, the lines from a poem ran over and over in her head: "All I could see from where I stood was three long mountains and a wood." Then Deana remembered that she had frozen to death. No, wait a minute. She started to realize that she was alive and slowly waking up from the heavy, dream-laden sleep of the bone tired. This time she opened her eyes wide and tried to sit up. Her arms and shoulders ached. Memories of dragging branches up into the cave explained the aches. Flash: the memory of the snowmobile savior roaring through the woods made her sit up straight and look around. She remembered hearing the sound of what she had always referred to as *damned snowmobiles* moving closer and closer. She had been happy to hear the buzzing engine instead of cursing it for disturbing the peace. She slowly rubbed her temples and conjured up a hazy memory of someone calling out. But after that, she couldn't recall anything.

Now she was lying on a small bed, bundled up in wool blankets. The smell hit her. "Whew! That's me," she realized, holding her nose as she breathed through her mouth and looked around. She was confused and surprised about how she ended up in this small, plain room. Her fingers slipped from her nose, and she gasped. The nasty smell of her dirty clothes and unwashed body were like a heavy dose of smelling salts. She pinched her nose shut again. Wallboard had been painted a dingy white. There was just enough room for the door to open and not touch the edge of the single bed. A wildlife calendar, open to the month of July and dated last year, hung on the wall. Her eyes stopped on the only window. It was two by two feet, but iron bars ran vertically from one end of the frame to the other. Had she been saved or captured? She smelled so bad she figured no one would want to get close enough to hurt her. It was time to find out. She gingerly got out of bed and stood up to check her aches and pains. She still felt chilled and wrapped one of the blankets around her shoulders. The rough-hewn wooden door was slightly ajar. *Maybe she had been rescued,* she thought with relief.

Deana stood in the doorway, one hand holding on to the door-jamb, and looked around the room. She could feel the heat from the wood-burning stove coming from the opposite corner of the room. It was a log cabin, and the stucco between the logs was bright white, as if newly applied. There was one small window on the wall next to the door. It had bars on it, just like the window in the bedroom. A long table with an assortment of electronic equipment, a jug of water, cans of food, and a lantern was shoved up against one wall. A rocking chair with a blanket spread across it sat under the barred window. She realized she must have slept in the bed of the hunched-over man working at the paper-strewn table in the middle of the room.

Still standing in the doorway, not sure if she should step into the room, she cleared her throat and said, "Hello, uh, what happened?"

"Well, well, you're finally awake. Hi, I'm Jim Jessup." He pointed to his shirt with the park insignia and said, "Park Ranger. I went out to bring in some more wood, heard an explosion, and saw light I figured was coming from a fire. You're awfully lucky I decided to investigate."

Deana stared at him for a second and said, "It was a flare. Uh, the explosion, I mean. I had one flare left, and I threw it into the fire."

He looked at her and nodded, "That was smart. I wouldn't have noticed a fire if I hadn't heard the explosion."

She nodded back at him and tried to force a smile. "Good," she said. Her arms were hugging her body tightly.

Jim spoke softly, as if to reassure her, "I assumed the park was empty. The parking area at the trailhead was empty."

Deana's head snapped up. "What? There weren't any cars in the parking lot?"

He answered calmly, "That's right. And the snowplows don't come back in here until after they've cleared the main roads. I didn't see any signs of snowmobile tracks going into the parking lot."

He leaned forward and rested an arm on his knee. "Do you feel up to telling me how you ended up out here all by yourself?"

That was an invitation to cross the threshold and join this seemingly nice man who had saved her life. Deana hesitated. Her eyes darted from Jim to the stove and the pile of wood next to it. The promise of warmth overcame any reluctance to move, and she stepped into the room. It was nice and toasty, but she kept the blanket wrapped tightly around her body. Jim motioned for her to join him at the table. "Take the hot seat," he said, smiling. "Sorry, bad pun." He moved a chair close to the stove and looked at her expectantly.

She sat down and shut her eyes, trying to push the news that there were no cars in the parking lot from her mind. "First, tell me where we are and how I got from the cave to this cabin. I remember hearing a snowmobile coming through the woods but can't remember anything else."

"You fainted! Good-looking guy like me—that happens a lot," Jim joked.

He *was* a good-looking guy—maybe early fifties, hair starting to gray, rugged features, but there was a nasty scar on his left cheek, and half of his left ear was missing. *Not the time to ask how that happened,* she thought to herself.

Jim said, "This cabin is the ranger station. It's directly across the lake from the cave where you were holed up. I had to use the snowmobile to get to you. I couldn't go across the lake. It's too dangerous."

"Yeah, I know," Deana interrupted in a barely audible voice.

"I pulled up in the snowmobile, looked up, and saw you. You called out the name *Andy* and then collapsed. I put my snowmobile suit on you and got you back to the cabin. You kept mumbling the name. Who is Andy?"

"Andy is my husband. We were snowshoeing and ..." she hesitated and looked away from Jim's kind eyes, "my snowshoe split." She looked at him again and finished the explanation quickly. "Andy went for help. He should have been back two days ago. Do you know anything? If he's okay?" Before he could answer, she asked, "How long have I been here? I'm sorry; thank you, thank you for saving me!"

"I've already called the RCMP, the Royal Canadian Mounted Police. No one's been reported missing in Jasper." Jim scratched his head and looked away, as if thinking out loud, and said, "No one's been up and down that road since Wednesday. I drove in late Wednesday evening and didn't see any cars when I drove by and no sign of anyone last night when I rode by on the snowmobile and found you." He turned his head back to look at her. "Your husband, Andy, is he an experienced outdoorsman?"

Deana couldn't look Jim in the eye. Keeping her head down, she sighed and answered slowly, "Y-e-s. Yes, he is. But I'm not sure how much he knows about surviving out here." She jumped up and said, "We've got to look for him. He might have run off the road!"

Jim stood up and held out his hands, palms facing her. "Hold on. Hold on. I'll contact the RCMP and tell them to start looking for your husband. You didn't appear to be injured, but I thought the safest thing was to get you back to the cabin and drive out today in my truck. I was waiting for the road to be plowed this morning so that we can get back into town. The police can get them to up the priority on the plowing and look for any signs of a car on the side of the road."

Deana stared at the cell phone in Jim's hand. "You're going to use a cell phone? I thought there wasn't coverage out here."

"It's spotty, but I can usually get through. Sometimes I have to go outside." Jim pointed to the table with electronic equipment. "Battery-operated two-way radio is my backup."

Jim put a sweatshirt and sweatpants on the table. "I thought you'd like to get out of those dirty clothes." His face reddened when he pointed to a small container of hand wipes sitting on top of the clothes. "Sorry, no running water here.

"I'll make the phone call, we'll get some hot food in you, and you can tell me the rest of your story."

If the phone had been working, she might have been able to get cell reception from the edge of the lake. She couldn't get the malfunctioning cell phone out of her head. She barely heard Jim say into the phone as he moved toward the door, "Let me get outside. You're breaking up."

She snatched the clothing from the table, frustrated and angry, as she struggled to make sense of everything that had happened. Alone, tired, and hungry in the cave, she wanted to blame Andy for the broken snowshoe. Now she struggled to convince herself that the most logical explanation for the missing SIM card was Andy's determination to make sure they enjoyed the day without interruptions from the modern world. But even he wouldn't have stuck to eschewing the connected world if it meant leaving her in the frozen wilderness. He would have fessed up and pulled the SIM card out of his pocket and tried the phone on the lake or back on the road.

Deana stood perfectly still and slowly exhaled. It felt great to get out of the grungy clothes, but she now had an urgent personal problem to address. She had to pee badly. There didn't appear to be any other doors. That meant there was no indoor plumbing.

Jim came back in. A rush of cold air came in with him. "They'll check the road to the trail as soon as they can get through. There is no record of him being picked up by an emergency vehicle."

Deana nodded. Worrying about Andy was temporarily pushed aside by an urgent need. She started to ask, "Excuse me, but where's the ..." Jim smiled and answered before she could finish.

"Sorry, no indoor plumbing. The port-a-potty is around back."

Deana nodded and swallowed. She didn't want Jim to see that she was afraid to leave the warm cabin. It was silly. She had survived two nights in the worst conditions. Now that she was safe and warm, she didn't want to budge. Her bladder didn't give her a choice. The smell of bacon and coffee was filling the air, and hunger proved to be a strong motivator. She held her breath, grabbed her jacket, quietly opened the front door, and went in search of the port-a-potty.

When she was done, she hurried back into the cabin and shut the door behind her. "What's that noise?" she asked.

"A generator."

"What's with the bars on the windows?"

"Keeps the wild animals out. A large cat could climb up and break the window, but it won't get through the bars. Eggs sound good?"

"Yes!" Deana answered. "That would be great." She was starving. The promise of real food seemed to mark the end of her nightmare, but she still felt uneasy. She looked down and saw she was slowly rubbing her hands and pressing them together while she worried about Andy. She continued to think about Jim's information that there had been no sign of him in Jasper.

If Andy did make it out of the woods and drove the car to safety, he hadn't gone to the police, and he hadn't come back for her. She shook her head and pulled her hands apart, wrapping them around her arms. He could have reached the car and then driven off the road. Here she was salivating over the prospect of eggs and bacon, and Andy could be unconscious in a ditch. Andy could be shaking from cold. Here she was standing close enough to a stove to turn any exposed skin bright red. It couldn't be warm enough for her. Never, ever would anyone hear her complain about Virginia's hot, humid summer days. Deana closed her eyes and enjoyed the luxury of being able to stand still without shivering and not having to flagellate herself to keep her circulation going.

"Jim, it's Friday morning, right?" she asked. Her watch read 8:30 a.m., but she wanted to be sure she hadn't lost a day.

He turned from a pan of sizzling bacon to another pan, flipped an egg, and said, "Yes, Friday morning. You've been here since last night."

While he fixed breakfast, Deana recounted her tale of snowshoeing gone wrong. When she got to the part about the ice cracking on the lake, she stopped after the words *I heard this vibration, and the ice started cracking.*

She put her hand over her mouth. Jim asked, "Are you all right?"

"Yes, I'm okay. I mean, I'm alive, right?" She laughed with more than a touch of sarcasm. "What was that sound I heard? It was terrifying."

"It's the temperature swings we get here. During the course of a day, we might have a twenty-degree swing. The sound you heard is one of the scariest sounds in the world. Sometimes you can hear it echoing across the lakes at night. That's why I took the long way around the lake to you. I've known too many people who have gone through supposedly frozen ice to even consider crossing a frozen lake."

Deana processed what he said and thought, *Yes, he's right. It is a terrifying sound.* But even more terrifying was the uneasiness she had about Andy. Deana pulled her phone out of her pocket. "The SIM card is missing. The only explanation is Andy removed it so that I wouldn't ruin his nature experience with technology." Deana looked at Jim with a question in her eyes.

"Let me take a look at it." Jim opened the phone, nodded, and handed it back to Deana. He said succinctly, "Interesting."

Jim pointed to her plate. "Finish that. I'll call the police and find out if they've checked your hotel yet. It will be a while before the road gets plowed and they're able to look for a car. They can at least check your hotel. He could have made it back and passed out."

He walked outside. Deana quietly ate the rest of the breakfast. She didn't have to wait long. The look on Jim's face told her she wasn't going to like the news. Jim slipped his phone in his pocket and sat down across from her at the table. Deana put her fork down and pushed the half-eaten breakfast away, her appetite suddenly gone.

"Deana," Jim said, looking her in the eyes. "There was no sign of Andy in your hotel room. Clothes are hanging in the closet, personal items in the bathroom." Jim frowned. "I'm sorry. I didn't see anything off the road Wednesday evening. Unless he made it out the entry road and then got into trouble."

Deana said, "He'll be okay. There's water in the car." She hesitated and then said quickly, "Flares. There are flares in the trunk."

Jim was quiet. He was probably thinking what was in the back of Deana's mind. Andy could have been knocked unconscious in the car and was already dead. Jim reached over and patted her hand. "I know you're sick with worry. You survived. You said your husband knows a lot about the outdoors. If you figured it out, you have to trust he will."

His voice lowered. "We'll find him." Dead or alive was left unsaid.

Deana jumped up. "I can't just sit here. There must be something we can do. Will you take me out on the snowmobile to look for him?"

"Deana, there isn't enough extra gas to do that. We're stuck here until the road is cleared. I don't want to leave you alone. And you are in no shape to be riding around on a snowmobile. I'm going to load the snowmobile on my truck while we're waiting."

Deana sighed. Jim was right. Every bone in her body ached. She wanted to crawl right back in bed.

Jim went outside to call for a status report on the plowing. He came back in after a few minutes. "Beautiful day out there!" he said. "Friggin' cold, but sunny and clear. Listen, I called my wife. It looks like you're going to be in town for more than a few days. We'd like to invite you to stay with us. You'll be more comfortable than in a hotel." He smiled, "and I have a feeling you and my wife, Linda, will get along great."

The idea was appealing, but Deana turned him down. "No, I'll be fine. I should stay in the room, so Andy will know where to find me. I appreciate the offer."

"You'll at least join us for dinner." Jim responded.

"I'd like that."

While they waited for word that the road had been cleared, Jim sat down to work on his report on porcupines being tracked with radio collars.

Deana stared at the back of his neck as he worked at the table. She mumbled, "Saved by the porcupines."

At the sound of her voice, Jim turned around. "Did you say something?"

She tilted her head and put a smile in her voice. "Were you out here to check on the porcupines?"

Jim rubbed the scar on his face and looked at her over the top of his reading glasses. "Yes, that's right."

"Then I was saved by the porcupines, right?"

Jim chuckled. "Hold on to that sense of humor, young lady." He returned to his report.

Deana was quiet on the long drive back to Jasper. In spite of the bizarre situation she could still appreciate the beauty around them. Jim slowed the Jeep to a stop and pointed to the right side of the road. A huge gray dog stopped at the edge of the roadway and turned its head thick with winter fur to glance their way. In that brief glance she felt, *He belongs here; we don't.* His jaws held lunch or brunch—a limp bundle of fur.

Jim said, "The wolf. Beautiful, isn't he? Consider yourself lucky; accidental sightings are rare."

Lucky, yeah, right, she thought but said, "Yes, he is beautiful—majestic."

They rode the rest of the way without talking and pulled up in front of the hotel. Jim got out of the truck. "I'd like to go up to the room with you. Make sure everything is as you left it. Then I'll drop you off at the clinic. After all you've been through, a check-up is a good idea."

Deana stared at the young man leaving the hotel as they were going in. "Excuse me," she called out to him, "you were working the day my husband and I left the hotel three days ago."

The intensity in her voice made him take a step back.

He looked from Deana to Jim and then answered her question. "Yes, I remember. Your husband came into the lobby and asked who won the hockey game in Calgary the previous night. I asked him what your plans were for the day. He said you were heading south to watch ice climbers."

"Did he say anything about a snowshoe hike?" Deana demanded.

"No. I would have remembered that."

Deana looked at Jim. She didn't care if the young man heard her. "I asked him to go into the hotel lobby and tell this young man where we were going."

"Uh, I'm sorry," the young man started to talk.

Deana held up a hand signaling him to stop. "Thanks. It's okay." She exchanged a glance with Jim. He followed her into the hotel.

Deana opened the door of the room. The air was stale, the drapes drawn shut. Jim said, "Take a look around. Did you leave any money or credit cards in the room? Make sure nothing's missing."

Deana opened the closet. Her hand reached out to touch Andy's windbreaker hanging next to her clothes. She mumbled, "Passports." Her favorite hiding place for anything valuable was inside a folded sweater. She rushed to open the dresser drawer. Her hand came out with one passport. She grabbed the sweaters in the drawer and shook them. Nothing. Hands on hips, Deana said, "Jim, Andy's passport isn't here. I'm positive I put both passports here before we left."

Jim didn't say anything for a minute. "Maybe he took it before you left on the hike. Go ahead and get changed. I'll wait for you downstairs."

The door closed, and Deana unconsciously felt a shiver go down her spine. The room gave her the creeps. The pine smell of Andy's aftershave lingered in the air. Deana couldn't wait to get out of the room. She ran down the stairs to the hotel entry.

"Ma'am," the clerk behind the desk called. "You are scheduled to check out tomorrow. The room is reserved, and the hotel is full."

Deana looked at Jim. "Go pack. You're staying with us. I'll call Linda." He shooed her away.

Deana came back to the lobby, pulling a large black duffel bag. She waved to Jim and stopped in front of an ATM machine.

"Oh shit!" she yelled. The balance in the joint checking account was $20. Deana punched buttons until she saw the last $400 withdrawal had taken place two days ago.

She motioned for Jim to join her at the ATM machine. "There was a $400 withdrawal on our account. Look at the date."

Jim said quietly, "Anyone else have access to that account?"

Deana shook her head.

"We can track the location from the ATM withdrawal. Print that statement," Jim ordered.

"Jim, if he emptied out that account, he might have taken more from an equity account." Deana's voice was angry and getting louder.

"Whoa. Slow down. Not here."

Jim took the duffle in one hand and Deana's elbow in the other. They headed out the door to his truck. Deana slammed the truck door harder than she should have. "Sorry," she told Jim.

Jim drove from the hotel to town while Deana talked to her broker. He heard Deana ask questions: Where are the proceeds? Are they in the money market account? She was quiet for a minute. Then he heard her say, "Scott, I don't know anything about an account in the Caymans."

She sat without moving a muscle, shocked. She was more angry and hurt by the betrayal itself than the missing money.

The truck stopped in front of a picture-perfect log chalet. The juxtaposition of the peaceful dwelling with the ugly conclusion she had just reached was otherworldly.

"Son of a bitch," she said, dragging out each word. "I preferred to worry something had happened to him rather than believe he left me out there to die. I've been played for a fool. My husband concocted this plan to let me freeze to death—all for money."

Deana cocked her head. "Jim, you suspected something, didn't you? That's why you insisted on going into the hotel room with me."

Jim leaned forward, resting his arms on the steering wheel. "Yes, I did think there was something fishy about the situation. I take it from your conversation with your broker there is money missing."

"Yes. $2.5 million," Deana whispered.

"That's a lot of money. But his plan didn't work." He patted her on the back. "You're alive. What doesn't kill us makes us stronger. Let's get you inside."

A tall, slim woman dressed in jeans and a sweater waved at them from the front door. It wasn't until they got closer that Deana saw the long hair was streaked with gray. Her face was lined with the wrinkles that told Deana she was probably in her early fifties. The warm smile and kindness in her eyes told Deana she was in good hands. Deana was shocked out of her stupor by the beautiful and ferocious animal standing next to the woman.

"Good lord!" Deana cried, "is that a bear?"

Jim laughed, "No, that's our alarm system. Bear is part German shepherd and part Samoyed. He scares everyone, but he's really a very gentle dog." Jim said something to Linda in a quiet voice.

Linda put her arm around Deana and said, "Young lady, I'm here to help. If that means being your chauffeur in Jasper, then just tell me what you need to do first. Let me look at you." She kept her hands on Deana's shoulders as she looked her over. "Sleep, food, and a hot shower, and you'll be fine. I'm dying to hear how you survived in that cave. I got trapped by a surprise snowstorm once in the fall and had to wait for help. Very, very scary." She gently led Deana down the hall to a bedroom. "Go ahead and grab a quick shower. Jim is going to call the RCMP. He wants them to come to the house to talk to you."

Deana started to thank her, but she interrupted, "I'm a retired teacher, and I've reinvented myself as an artist. That and curling keep me busy, but I'm in between projects, and things were getting a little boring around here. This is also the most exciting thing to happen in our little town in a long time. Rescuing you was a big thrill for Jim. He used to be a detective in Vancouver. It was a dangerous job. I'm sure you noticed the scar and the ear. It happened on the job and led to an epiphany that the wilds of Alberta were safer than the wild streets of Vancouver. We love it here, but ..." She paused, looked Deana in the eye, and added, "Rescuing you gives new meaning to his role as a park ranger. A lot more fulfilling than those porcupine reports he has to do."

Linda turned to leave the room. "I see Bear likes you," she added as the monster dog pushed against Deana's leg for attention.

CHAPTER 5

Deana reached out and touched the door frame. Her hand lingered on the wood, fingers tracing the dark patterns of the grain showing through the golden wood. She stepped through the door into a room decorated to cheer up even the most miserable guest. It was an oasis of yellow and white. The log walls glowed from polish lovingly and regularly applied. A quilt made of yellow and white squares hung on the wall above the antique iron bed. Wispy white curtains, covered with a yellow daisy pattern, were pulled back from the windows, and the snow-white bedspread was trimmed in yellow.

Linda and Jim's home was a rustic, cozy log chalet, but the showerhead was a modern, powerful one. Deana adjusted it to let the warm water pummel her body. She wasn't in the mood for a gentle spray. A strong stream of water would wash away the days of grime and sweat; more importantly, it would wash away the memory of the tears that rolled down her cheeks when she thought about her husband leaving her to die. She scrubbed hard with the soap and mumbled into the water running over her face, "I will find you; I *will* find you."

Deana walked into the kitchen at the same time as Jim. She watched Linda put a plate of sandwiches on the table and had to remind herself she was back in civilization. Stifling the urge to grab one of the neatly cut sandwiches and scarf it down, she forced herself to sit and politely put one of the delicious-looking baguettes stuffed with lettuce, ham, and cheese on a plate and proceed to methodically chew and savor each bite while Jim filled them in.

"I just got off the phone with Lowell Hopkins," he said. "He's the most experienced officer at the Jasper RCMP station. He'll be right over."

Before Deana could reply, there was a knock at the door. It turned out to be Officer Hopkins of the RCMP.

"I heard you were back—small town," he smiled. "I thought it might be easier for you to talk here than at the station."

The uniform would have been impressive on anyone else. It hung loosely on Lowell's wiry frame, as if he had recently lost weight or liked his clothes comfortable and baggy. Deana relaxed just looking at him. He shared her hair color and had more freckles than she did. On Lowell the red hair and freckles contributed to an innocent little boy look, but the worry lines around his eyes made her think he was at least forty years old. Pushing an unruly shock of hair away from his forehead, he sank into a chair at the kitchen table. He nodded yes to the offer of coffee and bumbleberry pie, pulled out a small notebook, and got right to the point.

"Jim told me about your ordeal. I'd like to hear it from you. Please start with what brought you to Jasper. I know this is difficult, but the more we know about you and your husband the better our chances of helping you."

His easygoing, businesslike approach made it easier to talk. Deana was surprised she was able to retell the story without shedding a single tear. She stuck to the facts when she described the plans for the trip. It was impossible to keep the sarcasm out of her voice when she referred to what Andy called a romantic second honeymoon trip. Her voice started to quiver when she described the cracking ice and falling asleep in the cave for what she thought would be her last night on earth. She resumed her matter-of-fact demeanor, looked directly at Lowell and summarized her thoughts.

"Please don't tell me to wait until we find my husband to condemn him. He planned this for a long time. One, he insisted on keeping my cell phone and told me we were out of range when we got to the parking area. Two, I discovered the SIM card was missing, meaning Andy must have removed it. Three, snowshoes are supposed to be indestructible. Except mine broke after I left them with my dear husband for a few minutes. Four, which actually should be number one, my husband's name was added to my very large stock account a few months before this trip. He gets all of it—$2.5 million—if anything happens to me. He has been selling positions in the account. The proceeds were transferred to an offshore account in the Cayman Islands a couple of days ago."

She paused, folding one hand over the other. "Five, his last words to me when he left me on the trail were *Trust me.* Any idiot knows they're about to be screwed when someone says 'Trust me.'"

Lowell let her talk uninterrupted and showed no emotion through the end of the tale.

When she finished, he stopped taking notes. Deana waited for him to look at her, not wanting to see pity in his eyes. Lowell didn't disappoint her. When he slowly raised his head and looked directly at her, she saw respect in his eyes.

"You are one lucky lady." Drawing the words out, he asked, "Where do you think your husband could be?"

Deana didn't have any answers. She half-listened while Jim and Lowell discussed the case. Her thoughts turned to the absurdity of the situation. She was sitting in a stranger's kitchen, telling another stranger why and how she thought her husband had planned her death. She was still alive, but what would happen when she returned to their—make that *her* home—in Virginia? Andy liked to finish what he started. Her demise was unfinished business to him.

She tuned back in to hear Lowell explain they had already checked on flights and rental cars. The rental car had not been turned in.

"That doesn't mean he didn't leave it in a lot," Lowell said. "It'll take us a little longer to check the rental car lots at the airports. No one has flown out of Calgary or Edmonton using your husband's name in the last few days. We'll keep working on tracking the car down. It would help if we could get a picture of Mr. Harris as soon as possible. I would like to ask around and see if anyone remembers seeing him." He cleared his throat, looked at Deana, and hesitated before saying, "Uh, to the best of your knowledge, would your husband have access to a passport under another name?"

Deana smirked and said, "Lowell, it wouldn't surprise me one bit. The answer is no, not to my knowledge." She couldn't help muttering, "If he did, Dick Head would be appropriate." She caught Jim and Lowell exchanging a glance. Jim tried to hold back a smile. Lowell laughed. Jim winked at her and motioned for Lowell to continue.

"Deana," he said, "the truth is he could be anywhere. We are doing everything we can to trace his movements from the time he left you on the trail."

"Lowell," Jim interrupted, "she isn't safe until we find him. We have to consider he might hang around for a few days to make sure Deana doesn't survive. It will be hard to keep the story quiet." He raised an eyebrow and leaned toward Deana.

"This is a big deal. You survived for three days in a very dangerous situation. You kept your head and used common sense. The story will hit the news, and your husband will disappear." He cleared his throat. "We can hope he won't worry about being seen as long as he thinks you're an icicle. If we can keep it quiet, the police will have a valuable head start in looking for him."

"Ohh," Deana said, "I see."

"I hate to bring up the question of money right now, but do you have access to any other funds, or did he wipe you out?" Jim asked.

"Yes, I still have some investments, bonds, and SEP/IRAs that are just in my name." She looked at Jim. "I won't starve to death. She looked away and said, thinking out loud, "And the house and other real estate are in my name." She let out a breath. "Gee, guess I'm lucky Andy didn't want to hang in there for all the property. My lawyer advised me to keep accounts in my name only." Deana said with a sneer, "He was worried about a divorce, not murder."

"Okay, in the meantime, do not generate any activity that would alert Andy to the fact that you are still alive. Do not use your credit card."

"I'll have to call my broker and sell something. Normally we get a written notice a few days after a transaction." Deana slapped her forehead. "Ugh. The last sales orders Andy put through will be waiting at the post office for me." She shook her head. "Now I understand why he was always so quick to pick up the mail."

"Can you trust your broker?" Jim asked.

"Apparently more than I can trust my husband."

"Call him, and change the routing for any sales orders. You could use a friend or relative's address. The proceeds could be wired to a bank in Jasper. If you open an account here, you can use our address. We'll receive and forward statements to you until you're established and safe."

Deana nodded. It made sense. "I'll use cash for everything." She swirled toward Lowell. "I just thought of something. Andy might return to the house in Virginia. There's a little cash, coins, and jewelry in a home safe."

"You'll need to be careful." Lowell said. "Andy left all his clothing in the hotel room, trying to create the impression no one had returned. He has all the money he can get from you." He paused. "Alive or dead. I'm sorry to say we can't provide round-the-clock protection. I doubt you'll be able to get that in Virginia either. If you can afford it, hire someone to at least cover your back. Jim has a lot of contacts. He can probably hook you up with a private investigator/bodyguard. It will be hard to keep this story quiet. Once word gets out you survived, he knows you'll push to track him down."

Deana looked at Jim. Jim said, "Deana, Lowell is right. If you're dead, he knows the pressure to find him will gradually fade away."

Lowell said, "You're in danger here, as well as when you return to Virginia. Mr. Harris may be waiting around here for a few days to see if your body, uh, excuse me, I mean to say, he might try something else. We haven't released any details about your ordeal to the media yet. When we do and if he is still in the area and hears about it, it will increase the danger. You'll need to be on your guard at all times. On the other hand, posting his photo with the story may help generate leads in tracking Mr. Harris."

Deana looked at Jim. He nodded, and she asked Lowell to go ahead and contact the media.

"Deana," Lowell continued, "I'm very serious about the danger you could be in. Your husband has access to significant amounts of money, money that could be used to hire the services of someone who would hurt you for him."

"Here, in Jasper?" Deana responded, not shocked that Andy might consider finishing her off but shocked that he could find someone in Jasper to take care of his dirty work. "He could find, what, a hit man, here in Jasper?" she asked, laughing.

Lowell's answer was sobering. "Yes, here in Jasper. We have poachers and drug dealers, as well as drunks and petty criminals that pass through on their way to bigger towns or are on the run from trouble somewhere else. You won't read about it in the Canada Parks brochure. I repeat, please be careful."

Deana couldn't help thinking one probably wouldn't read about husbands abandoning their wives in the Canada Parks brochure either. Disposing of unwanted spouses on cruise ships or islands seemed to be more popular methods. She started to think about the chances of surviving in the ocean with sharks versus freezing to death in the mountains. When she shook herself back to reality, Lowell and Jim were talking. She heard them but didn't hear the words. Something was bothering her.

"Wait, stop," Deana said. "There's something I don't understand. Would someone tell me why, if Andy wanted me to die, why didn't he just knock me out on the trail and leave me? I would have frozen to death and died. Why go to all this trouble?"

There was a moment of silence before Lowell and Jim started talking at the same time. Lowell stopped and said, "Jim, you explain. You took some profiling courses, I seem to remember."

Jim said, "It's too early to tell. We don't have enough information about the circumstances and your husband; however, there *are* killers who don't like to get their hands dirty. They get off on planning and organizing their victim's demise." He paused, sat down, and put his hands on his knees, looking right at her.

"Deana, there are a lot of sick bastards out there that you and I can never begin to understand. There's a whole group of people who kill for profit and not to satisfy violent urges." He cleared his throat and, with a sly smile, said, "Count yourself lucky that he might be one of that ilk and not one of the monsters driven by a desire to kill with their own hands. He stole your money—he's a thief—but he could have done that without killing you. His elaborate plan to leave you to freeze to death didn't work, but he probably thought it was foolproof. He took the money and ran. At least that's what it looks like now. We don't know yet what we're dealing with here. Okay?"

"Okay," Deana said. "Lucky, huh?" she asked, finding it hard not to let a smile replace her grimace. "One more question. Why didn't I see it?" She was remembering the last night in the hotel, when they made love. She didn't need to share that with Jim and Lowell.

"Deana, that is exactly why some people get away with murder. They are very, very good at presenting themselves to the world as normal, charming, functioning members of society. They don't look crazed, and they are expert liars."

She thanked Jim for the explanation. It didn't really help, but it did give her something to think about. She had been taken in by blue eyes and a rugged profile. A memory of a character in Melville came to mind. It was something she had read in college. At the time Melville's description of an evil man seemed too far-fetched to be realistic. Her book review of Billy Budd received a *B-*. The teacher's response to Deana's criticism of the character that plans evil deeds yet appears friendly was: "Take a psychology class." A little late for that.

Deana excused herself and went into the bedroom. She didn't want an audience when she called Cindy. She knew Cindy had a picture of Andy. The fastest way to get a photo to Lowell was to ask Cindy to email it. The picture was from their wedding. Andy in the middle, Cindy and Deana on either side. Cindy was very proud of the fact that she was the one who helped two people find love.

Now Deana stared at the phone while she considered what and how to tell her best friend what had happened. She sighed and punched in Cindy's number.

Cindy picked up after two rings. "Hey, you're supposed to be on vacation. Is everything okay?"

"Cindy, stick to your day job. You're a lousy matchmaker," Deana said.

"What? You two lovebirds have a fight? Wishing you had a prenup?" Deana heard her chuckle at her little joke.

The silence on Deana's end of the phone instead of a smart retort had an effect. Cindy said, "Deana, what's wrong? Are you all right?"

"Yes and no," Deana answered and took a deep breath. "Just listen, okay?" She then proceeded to tell Cindy in as few words as possible what had happened.

Cindy couldn't believe it. Once she got over the shock, she was mad. She said, "Sure, I'll email the photo ASAP. Then I'm going to make a copy of it and burn it!"

Deana asked her to keep everything to herself for now. She promised to call and let Cindy know when she'd be back in Virginia.

Linda offered to drive Deana to town. She handed her a thick woolen cap to pull over her head. "It will keep you warm and hide that red hair," she said. Deana picked up a new SIM card for her phone and took care of business in the bank. Armed with cash, they scoured the small shops in Jasper for a winter wardrobe. Luckily, Jasper was not Aspen, and she didn't need anything fancier than slacks and sweaters; at least she had a warm jacket and boots. Linda had thrown Deana's jacket in the washing machine. It was not as good as new but was now like an old friend. She had no intention of replacing it.

Deana stood at the window of the bank, looking out at the train station across the road while she waited for Linda to finish her business. Jasper was an interesting western mountain town. It seemed to have spread out from the historic train station, a busy point of arrival and departure for tourists in the summer months. In the winter the railroad yards were busy with long freight trains carrying goods across the rough northern country. An image of Andy sitting in the dining car of a train rumbling along the tracks away from Jasper flashed through Deana's mind. It would be too good to be true to hope he had jumped on a train and was now on the other side of the country. If he had, she preferred to think of him shivering in the corner of a grubby freight car.

There was the usual proliferation of tacky gift shops but none of the chichi high-end shops you would find in the Colorado resorts. The amazing mountains soared up all around the town. "Beware of Bear" signs posted at the city limits were a reminder the little town existed in the middle of a huge, protected natural area.

She remembered Andy's words when they drove through the gate at Banff National Park: *Say good-bye to strip malls and chain stores, Deana.* She was impressed at the time that he had done a lot of reading and research for the trip. Now, she understood why. He had searched out the perfect spot for his plan and regaled her with promises of beauty and solitude. She looked up at the sky and then closed her eyes and grimaced as she remembered something else. It was one of those unscientific, impossible-to-prove, tingling sensations people sometimes get when they sense danger. She remembered now—too late, much too *late*—a shiver of fear that went through her when they passed through the gate. At the time, she shook it off and ignored it, thinking it was just fear of leaving civilization behind. From now on, she would listen to her gut instincts.

The women finished their shopping and walked back to the car. Jasper had a comfortable, been-here-and-will-always-be-here feel. They passed a few art galleries that looked interesting; a lot of stores had signs in the window that said "Closed 'til spring." Linda explained that spring and summer were the high season. The tourists took over starting in June. Adventurers looking for unspoiled wilderness might have discovered Jasper in the winter months, fallen in love with the beauty, and decided to make it their home. Putting up with the few busy months was worth the slow, quiet pace the rest of the year.

Deana stopped suddenly at the sound of an accordion playing. Linda turned and saw the look on her face. "What's wrong? Are you all right?"

The music was coming out of a bar sandwiched between an art gallery and a tourist shop. Weathered strips of lumber covered the exterior wall. There was a small window covered with a curtain. This was a drinker's bar; you didn't go in there to watch the world go by. You went in to drink. A dingy sign on the sidewalk advertised "Live Music after 9:00 p.m."

Deana held her breath and pushed open the door without answering Linda. She looked at the young, long-haired guy on the dark stage and let out her breath.

He stopped playing and asked, "Can I help you ladies?"

She stammered, "I know someone—I mean, I used to know someone who plays the accordion. I heard it and thought … you're good."

"Thanks. Come on back tonight. We've got a tour group coming in from Quebec. The place will be packed. If you like the accordion, you'll hear a lot of it tonight." They turned to leave. Deana caught her breath and spun around to look at him again. The haunting sounds of "Lily Marlene" echoed through the empty bar. She was in trouble if a corny accordion could make her blood run cold. *Get a grip,* she thought.

As soon as the door of the bar closed behind them, Linda put her hand on Deana's arm and asked, "Okay, now, what was that about?"

"Sorry, I'm a little paranoid. Andy plays the accordion," she explained, adding that "Lily Marlene" was a standard in his repertoire. "It was always the last tune he played." She shook it off and hoped she could get the damn melody out of her head.

"Deana, I know Lowell and Jim want you to be careful, and so do I. Even if Andy is still around, he's smart enough to not stroll into a bar and start jamming with a band.

"I think Lowell and Jim are scaring you to death, talking about Andy hiring someone to put a hit on you. You're staying with us. You're not alone. That should be enough to deter him if he is still hanging around Jasper." She stopped and put her arm around Deana's shoulder for a quick hug.

Deana sighed and tried to relax. She didn't tell Linda what she was thinking: *It would be easy for Andy to disguise his appearance.* She knew Linda was trying to help, but her support was less than reassuring. "Linda, this isn't fair to you and Jim. I need to move into a hotel. I could be putting both of you at risk."

Linda pooh-poohed her fears and insisted that Deana remain with them.

Deana had offered to treat Jim and Linda to dinner that evening, but Linda suggested Jim do the cooking at home. "You must be exhausted," she said. "Let's save going out to dinner for later this week." Then Linda hesitated and asked softly, "Deana, do you know how to shoot a gun?"

"Andy tried to teach me. I didn't like it. It was too noisy, and I was afraid of shooting myself in the foot instead of the bottles and cans lined up as targets."

"Aren't you an American? I thought all Americans knew how to shoot!" She laughed. "I'll talk to Jim when we get back. He's a certified shooting instructor for the youth program. He taught all the women in my Gentle Ladies Garden and Shooting Club."

Deana looked at her with a raised eyebrow and said, "Garden and Shooting Club?"

"Deana, in the West, everyone needs to know how to handle a gun, especially a shotgun. You never know when you might have to face a bear or wolf or cougar. It would be a good idea for you to learn to handle one. When you get back to Virginia, you might even want to pick up a hand gun." She paused and winked. "You might want to form an Eastern Gentle Ladies Garden and Shooting Club!"

"Linda, my girlfriends all have fancy security systems installed in their homes and carry cans of pepper spray in their purses—no guns— but I'm going to take you up on the offer of shooting lessons. If Jim has time. If not, that's on my list as soon as I get home."

Deana told her about the women from the hunter education class and her plans to take shooting lessons from a man named Snooky. Linda rolled her eyes and asked, "Snooky? You've got to be kidding!"

Linda glanced at her watch and said, "I've got to be at the curling rink in an hour."

"Curling?" Deana asked, with the same look of disbelief Linda used when she made fun of the good southern name of Snooky. "You've got to be kidding!"

Linda gave Deana a raised eyebrow look and explained she was the coach for the junior curling team and had to meet the kids at the rink in an hour. "Big bonspiel's coming up, and we plan to win!" she said. She invited Deana to come along, but Deana was exhausted. She asked for a rain check.

Linda dropped Deana off at their log cabin with her purchases, parked the car, and walked to the curling rink. "Tell Jim I'll be home for dinner," she called out, "and lock the door!" Bear greeted Deana and followed her into the bedroom. Deana lay down for a quick nap. Her eyes closed, and she smiled at the sound of the huge dog's body plopping on the floor at the foot of the bed.

Bear was restless. She thought he was trying to tell her he needed to get outside. She got up and absentmindedly shoved the pepper spray in her back pocket. As they walked out the back door, she spotted the handgun Linda had threatened to teach her to use and grabbed it as well. A short way down the path to town, she and Bear turned at a sound behind them. The shaggy-haired accordion player from town was striding toward them on snowshoes, laughing and pointing a shotgun at her. Bear lunged as he pulled the trigger. She screamed as Bear fell to the ground, pulled the handgun out, and unloaded it in the direction of the man sprawled on the ground.

The door flew open. Jim and Linda were standing next to the bed when Deana bolted up, confused and upset. "You were having a bad dream," Linda explained as she gently shook Deana's shoulders.

"It seemed so real. The guy from the bar tried to kill me. Bear knocked him down." Bear jumped on the bed and started licking Deana's face at the mention of his name.

"You're all right. Bear's all right. I'm sorry. We're probably scaring you to death. Let's forget about all of it for a few hours."

Deana rubbed her eyes and sat on the edge of the bed. "Linda, no one is scaring me. I've been thinking that you're right; I should learn how to protect myself, and the best way to do that is to learn how to handle something more powerful than pepper spray. As soon as I get home, I'm calling Snooky."

"Snooky?" Jim asked. Linda shushed him and told him she would explain later.

"Dinner will be ready in an hour," Jim said. The two of them left her to get herself together. Deana had to laugh when she heard Jim ask Linda in a tone not meant to be heard by her. "She really knows someone named Snooky?"

She sat a few more minutes on the edge of the bed, absentmindedly petting Bear. A picture of Andy leaving the house to head to a shooting range was frozen in her mind's eye. "See ya' later. I'm off to practice," he'd say and then turn and smile, pointing a cocked finger at her. "Bang," he would sometimes whisper and smile. Deana shivered at the memory and reached down to give Bear a big hug.

Bang, bang right back at you, she thought, making a pistol with her hand. She winced as she remembered sending a contribution to a gun control group. Annie Oakley was replacing Patty the Pacifist.

Linda was right about Jim's cooking. He whipped up a mean venison chili and cornbread. Dinner conversation covered their life in Jasper, the weather, Canadian politics—anything and everything except Deana's life in Virginia with Andy. Deana carried the plates to the sink and sat back down at the table for coffee.

"Look, Deana," Jim said, the expression on his face telegraphing the topic would not be pleasant, "we don't know what Andy will do if he finds out you're alive. I'm assuming you're going to want to get your money back, and that means tracking your husband." He paused and smiled when she nodded. "You're going to need help and protection. I'm not suggesting you work outside the legal system, but I will tell you the system can sometimes move slowly. If you have the money, you would be smart to hire a professional. I know a guy in Seattle. He's a retired FBI agent and now takes on a few jobs as a private investigator. He isn't cheap, but he *is* good."

She didn't need to think about it. Immediately she said, "Okay. I don't care how much it costs. I *will* find Andy. How do I get in touch with your friend?"

"Whoa … slow down. I'll call him tonight; his name's Ed Robbins. You can get in touch with him tomorrow."

Deana pushed Jim and Linda out of the kitchen and cleaned up. Bear was on the floor, watching her every move, hoping for a scrap.

Linda had called over her shoulder when she left the kitchen, "No scraps for Bear!"

Deana couldn't resist the big brown eyes. She broke off a small piece of the tasty cornbread for Bear. He took it daintily from her hand and looked up, hoping for another piece. "That's it," she whispered, and they headed to bed.

The next morning, Deana called Ed Robbins. She didn't know what Ed looked like, but he had a voice that inspired confidence. He said, "You're one lucky lady from what Jim tells me. And you're in good hands with Jim and Linda. We met on a case when I was with the FBI and have stayed in touch."

He explained that his contacts within the FBI and law enforcement helped him get things done. He would work as a bodyguard and investigator for her. "You are one of many cases for the police. They do not have the resources to offer you 24/7 protection. It's a little complicated as far as the police are concerned. Right now, it's just your word. You could be the bad guy, and your husband's body could be somewhere along the trail."

Deana protested. He said, "No, no. Calm down. Jim believes you and the Canadian police believe you, but right now, there's no evidence of a crime. I know money has been moved out of accounts. But as your husband, he had a right to execute those transactions."

Deana groaned. "I need your help, Ed."

He laid out the rules and costs. Number one, she had to agree to follow his orders. His first order was to change her appearance and keep a low profile until he got there. "No blond or red hair; people seem to remember blonds and redheads. Dye your hair, change the style, and get a pair of glasses." He spoke calmly, but there was no doubt he expected her to do what he said. His final words, *keep a low profile,* were said in a voice that combined an order and a warning.

Deana didn't tell him she was born with not only red hair but curly and hard-to-control red hair that people did in fact remember. Growing up, the kids called her "Red."

He would be in Jasper tomorrow. His rates were high—$300 a

day—but that was the cost of staying alive. She was happy to pay. Ed gave her a list of things to have ready for him: a photo of Andy, his social security number, friends and family names, addresses, and phone numbers. As she worked on the list, she realized that all their friends were really her friends. Supposedly he had no family.

Jim was at work. Deana argued with Linda again about moving to a hotel. Linda insisted they welcomed the company and agreed to let Deana treat them to dinner that night. She laughed when Deana told her Ed wanted her to change her appearance and not to go blond or red. Linda said, "I've got just the thing. Hold on."

She left the room and came back in a few minutes with a couple of hatboxes. She sat them on the table and lifted the lids, spread her hands like a magician, and said, "Voilà! Two nondescript, boring brunettes. Take your pick."

There were two wigs. Deana tried on one and then the other. "This one's perfect," she said. Perfectly straight brown hair, styled in a bob that moved easily and covered half of her face. She patted the long straight bangs and looked at herself in the mirror Linda held.

"I don't recognize myself. This is great! Where did you get the wigs?" Deana asked.

"Cancer. I beat it, but I lost all my hair during the treatment." She smiled, "It seems I have a pointy head, and it didn't look good bald. The wig looks great on you."

Deana still needed a pair of glasses without magnification to complete her disguise and wanted to walk into town. Linda would only agree if Bear went with her as a bodyguard. Armed with a pepper spray canister and her cell phone, she whistled for Bear.

"You'll see," Linda said, "people will cross to the other side of the street when they see you two coming. Bear has good instincts. If his hair stands up and he growls, pay attention."

Linda saw the worried expression on Deana's face and laughed. "Don't worry. He won't attack anyone unless they make an aggressive move. Just don't get excited with the pepper spray and hit yourself or Bear by mistake. It will take four strong men to carry that dog home."

CHAPTER 6

Deana started walking into town, pausing to glance in store windows. At the first glimpse of her reflection, her head whipped around. The layers of clothing made her look like a chubby little kid sent outside to play in the snow. Perched on top of the snowwoman body was a head with silky brown hair. She was certainly in disguise. Her eyes scanned the window without seeing the handmade local pottery on display. She looked instead for reflections in the glass, worried Andy might suddenly show up behind her. It would be easy for him to pull her into a car and drive away. Hearing the sound of a car pulling into a space behind her, Deana quickly turned around. False alarm. It was a handicapped space. The driver, a gray-haired woman, was walking to the sidewalk with a cane.

Deana looked down at Bear. She patted his head and gently grabbed a handful of fur. Bear would put up a fight if someone tried to grab her. He seemed to sense her unease and stayed close, bumping her knees as they walked along. Deana almost toppled over him when a painting displayed in the window of an art gallery caught her eye. She stopped abruptly and stared at the painting. The fears and bitter cold that had worked its way into her bones the night she stood at the edge of the cave watching the last light fade from the sky took over her mind and body again. She was back there, feeling alone and scared. She remembered thinking the artist who left a sketchbook with colorful drawings of summer views would never be able to capture the piercing cold of the winter view. She was wrong.

Bear barked and Deana patted his head. She shook off the memory and stamped her feet, just as she had done on the night outside the cave, trying again to bring some warmth back into her body. "Bear, that's it," she whispered, "that's my view from the cave."

She looked around and spied a parking meter right in front of the store. An image of Bear running down the street and dragging the parking meter flashed through her mind, but she was too excited to worry about the wisdom of tying him to it. She had to find out about the painting and the artist.

"Bear, be good," Deana said to the dog, looking him in the eye and holding his massive head in her hands.

She turned to the gallery, took a deep breath, walked through the door, and headed straight to the saleswoman sitting behind a desk. "Please tell me about that painting. Where was it painted?" she demanded.

The woman was in her thirties, stylishly dressed in an expensive-looking sweater and slacks. Expertly applied makeup and lots of gold jewelry. She looked the part of a saleswoman in an expensive art gallery. Deana certainly didn't look the part of a typical paying customer.

The woman looked at her nervously and slowly pushed herself out of her chair, keeping the desk between them. "It was painted by a local artist. I'm sorry, I don't know the exact location of that picture." She reached for the phone. "I, uh, I'll call the gallery owner. He'll know."

"No, not the gallery owner. The artist!" Deana demanded again.

Deana knew she needed to calm down and be reasonable and charming if she expected any help from the saleswoman. "Look, I'm sorry," she said. She sunk her bulky-looking body into the chair next to the woman's desk. Deana had worked herself into such a state that she actually felt warm—a condition she never thought she would feel again—and unzipped her jacket.

"Let's start over," Deana said, trying to keep the excitement and urgency out of her voice. "You said the artist is local. What's his name?"

"Jack. Jack Hanson." The woman must have decided Deana was no longer a threat because she slowly removed her hand from the phone. "He lives here in Jasper."

"Okay, thank you. Could you tell me how to get in touch with him?"

"Oh no, I'm sorry. We're not allowed to give out personal information."

Deana nodded and forced a friendly smile. "How much *is* that painting?" she asked, pointing to the picture.

The woman had her hands on the edge of the desk, ready to push herself up and out of there if Deana became too scary. The desire for a sale finally overcame the woman's reticence. She tried a start of a smile and said, "Actually, *that* painting isn't for sale. We'll be offering numbered prints for sale. The unframed print will be $400. Would you like to put your name on the list for a print?"

Deana thought about what she said and asked, "*If* the painting were for sale, what do you think the price would be?"

The saleswoman relaxed a little and smiled a real smile. "Well, Mr. Hanson's paintings usually sell in the $5,000 to 10,000 range. I think that one would be at the top of the range."

Deana nodded her head and said, "I *would* like to put my name on the list for a print." Deana gave her Cindy's name and address and promised to call later with the credit card information. Cindy would be willing to make the call for her best friend. Deana wanted to make a graceful exit but knew the saleswoman would be telling her friends about the woman wearing too many clothes who looked like she was wearing a wig and had the nerve to inquire about a painting she could never afford. Deana could only hope she was wrong about the wig being obvious. She knew she wasn't wrong about being part of a good story. Ed warned her to keep a low profile, and the first thing she did was create a scene.

At least she had kept quiet about why she wanted to get in touch with the artist. There was no need to write his name down—Jack Hanson; she would never forget the name. Jim and Linda would help her find him.

Bear and the parking meter were just where she left them. She bent down and nuzzled Bear's head. She was eager to get back to Jim and Linda's to ask them if they knew Jack Hanson. And she wanted to check with Lowell to see if Cindy's email with the photos had come in. She glanced beyond the Jasper train station and was fascinated by all the tracks coming and going. It appeared to be freight traffic and looked like the type of busy train junction one would find in a large city, not a small town.

The snowwoman and the huge dog crossed the street to walk in an area that bordered the train tracks. The rhythmic sounds from the rails were interrupted by Bear's abrupt, low growl. There was a man walking toward them through the snow. Deana tensed, and Bear started howling and pulling on the lead. The frightened man turned and walked quickly back toward town. "Thanks, Bear. Good dog." She didn't call out to apologize to the retreating figure, even though she knew it wasn't Andy. The man was too small. She didn't call out because she remembered Lowell's warning that it wasn't just Andy himself she had to fear. They hurried home, Bear leading the way. *If I had a gun,* she couldn't help thinking, *I wouldn't be afraid. I might not love shooting, but I will learn and become good at it.*

Linda was working in her studio. Deana paced outside the door, waiting for her to take a break. "Jack Hanson?" she exclaimed when Deana told her about the painting. "Oh, he's a great guy and a very successful landscape painter. You think he was the artist from the cave? Wow—that would make sense. He does a lot of hiking, and it would be just like him to climb up to a cave for a special scene. He hangs out at Fritz's sometimes. That's where we're going for dinner. His wife passed away last year—cancer—and he pretty much keeps to himself. He stops in at Fritz's a lot and eats at the bar. Let's see if we run into him there tonight."

They bundled up and headed out to walk to Fritz's Bistro for dinner, but not before Jim and Linda discussed both Lowell's and Ed's recommendations that Deana should be careful. Jim wanted to stay at home, but Linda said, "Honey, Lowell might be able to keep Deana's rescue out of the national papers and news for a few days, but the Jasper locals will know about it. Right now, all anyone knows is that you brought in a woman who survived a night or two in the park. They won't know that's who's joining us for dinner. It will be good for Deana to get out, and she'll be with us. She'll be safe. She'll wear the wig and glasses."

Linda and Deana waited outside for a minute while Jim looked around to make sure there were no strangers in the restaurant. He waved them in, but Deana hesitated inside the door. The fear of stumbling upon Andy kept her alert. She quickly scanned the room before following her friends.

Fritz should have called his restaurant Fritz's Weinstube. He was from Switzerland and had recreated a charming Swiss atmosphere in his Jasper restaurant. Jim and Linda seemed to know everyone and spoke and waved to friends as they were led to a booth. Deana settled into the banquette and turned her attention to the men at the bar. One of them might be her savior. She asked Jim and Linda if they saw Jack.

"Yep, that's him—second from the left." Linda answered.

She looked at the man and thought about the beautiful painting of the view from the cave. He had straight brown hair with traces of gray. He sensed her stare and turned his head to look around. Deana saw a long face, strands of hair in need of a trim dropping over a wide forehead. His nose was maybe a little too long to be perfect. It was obvious, even from twenty feet away, he needed a shave. Wrinkles and creases on his face looked like they came from exposure to the weather and not age. He glanced around the room. His face looked relaxed but curious. He shrugged his shoulders, and one hand reached up and ruffled his hair. He didn't seem to care about his looks.

That not-quite-handsome, unassuming, weather-beaten man saved my life, she thought. And then she wondered how someone who looked so casual and ordinary could have painted the incredibly beautiful and powerful piece of art she had seen hanging in the gallery. Deana had met a lot of Cindy's artist friends in D.C., and he wasn't dressed like any of them. They favored the chic, all-black city garb and stylishly long hair-dos. Jack was wearing jeans and a woolen sweater with a loose turtleneck falling around his neck. Deana's gaze took in battered hiking boots and a knapsack resting under his bar stool

She stood up, and Jim and Linda followed her gaze. Jim put a hand on her arm and gently held her back. "Low profile, remember?" He looked at Linda and asked, "Do you want to ask him to join us, or should I do it?"

Linda hesitated and said, "I know him better, and I wanted to ask him about talking to the local arts group. You know, Jack used to curl with us. He was a good third."

Deana looked at Jim with raised eyebrows and mouthed, "A third?"

He laughed and said, "Curling talk. Deana doesn't know what a good third is."

"Oh," she laughed, "sorry. It means he was a very good shot maker. We'll get you out on the ice." Linda made a pistol with her hand and pointed it at her. "That's two things you need to learn: how to shoot and how to curl."

Deana cringed inwardly but kept the expression on her face unchanged. It brought back the memory of Andy making the same gesture. It certainly was an unfriendly expression for one so popular.

Linda stood up and said, "Now, let's see if I can talk Jack into showing up at the curling rink and the next meeting of the arts group."

Deana watched intently as Linda walked to the bar, oblivious to Jim shaking his head in disapproval. Linda sat down on the bar stool next to Jack Hanson. They talked for a few minutes, and Linda came back to the table smiling. "He'll finish his dinner and join us for coffee and dessert."

Deana didn't waste any time. As soon as he sat down, she stuck out her hand and said, "Hello. My name is Deana North, and you saved my life."

His head jerked back in surprise. Then she saw a smile in his eyes. "Please! Tell me how I saved your life. I've been accused of a lot of things, but saving someone's life is not on the list."

Jim jumped in before Deana could explain. He said, "Jack, please keep everything Deana is going to tell you to yourself—at least until you read about it in the paper. You'll understand when she tells her story." Jim nodded at her, but he didn't smile. He folded his arms across his chest.

As Deana summarized her plight in the cave, Jack's demeanor

changed from relaxed and congenial to alert and intent. He looked at her and said, "Deana, the sleeping bag and metal box have been in the cave for over four years. I slept up there when I was working on sketches for the painting. I wanted to see it from daybreak through sunset." He stopped talking, placed both hands over hers, and continued, "I'm so glad you found that cave."

Deana had stared at the table through most of the story, but now, with Jack's warm, strong hands on top of hers, she looked directly at him. It was difficult not to notice that he was good-looking, but not in the traditional way. His features weren't perfect, but he was at ease in his own skin, and that made him attractive. One could almost feel the kindness in his eyes. The simple gesture of placing his hands over hers indicated this was a man not afraid to show his emotions. He reached out in the same way a woman might.

Or, she thought, *maybe it is true that men don't make passes at girls who wear glasses and who look like they've been living in a cave for three days.* She wondered if he would look at her the same way without the wig and glasses. And then she reminded herself she was not in the market for flirtations or sexual interest. Chocolate and vigorous walks had more appeal than even a kiss.

Just as naturally, he removed his hands and asked, "What about your husband? Where is he?"

Right on cue, a slim, fit-looking man in his thirties walked over to the table and greeted them. "Hey, guys. There's a rumor floating around that Jim brought in a young woman who spent a few nights in the park. I had to ask. Is that you?"

His question was met by a rolling of the eyes from Jim and a smile from Linda.

Jim introduced Deana to Patrick Dupree as an old friend of Linda, visiting from Florida. Jack's head turned from Jim to Deana. She smiled at Patrick and didn't say a word. She was officially in hiding, but her cover was going to have to be better conceived. The poor guy was staring at her, probably wondering why she didn't have a tan.

Jim said, "Patrick, the woman we brought in from the park is very weak and recuperating. We'll have you over for a beer next week and give you all the details. It's nice to see you."

Patrick took the hint and returned to his bar stool. Jim said, "He's a good guy—good outdoorsman and hunter. He would be genuinely interested in hearing your story."

Deana dropped her head. The borrowed hair fell forward, covering half of her face. She removed the decorative glasses and rubbed her eyes. Jack also took the hint. He cleared his throat and said, "A good time to change the subject, I think."

She looked at him, this time seeing concern in his eyes and furrowed brow. She whispered, "Yes, please change the subject." She did not want to relive the experience by telling the story again tonight. She wanted to have a decent meal and something resembling a boring, normal, "weather and what did you do today" conversation.

Jack looked from Deana to Jim, met Jim's eye, and said, "I'm working on a new painting; it's a winter scene from the cave. I wanted to hike up there this week. You won't be up there in the ranger cabin, will you?"

Jim said, "If you're wondering whether you could sleep at the cabin, we can work it out. You tell me when you want to go up, and I can schedule my trip at the same time."

Jim and Jack chatted about weather and dates and a plan to allow Jack to sleep in the ranger cabin for a few nights. Jack said, "Look, I've got an idea. Why don't you all come out to my place for dinner?" He looked down at the table and continued. "I've been living like a hermit for the last year. It'll give Linda and me a chance to talk about my session with her arts group, and I have a feeling Deana would like to see some of the sketches from the cave. Tomorrow evening all right?"

"You know, it's a little spooky. I was planning to hike up there again this week."

He hesitated and looked at Deana, the smile gone from his face. "I might have found you there." The word *dead* was left unsaid.

He shook his head and said, "Thank goodness I left those supplies there. Your story is amazing." He stood up and said, "Seven o'clock okay?"

After Jack left, Linda said it was an honor to be invited. She was dying to see his studio and home gallery. He didn't sell all his work. He kept some of the paintings and loaned them out to museums for special shows. Deana didn't know anything about contemporary artists; according to Linda, Jack was famous and successful. Jasper was a surprising little town—famous artists, quaint restaurants, nice people, beautiful scenery. It was easy to understand why travelers would find it hard to leave.

There was a message from Lowell when they returned to the house. He wanted to meet with Deana at the RCMP office at 10:00 a.m. the next day. Ed Robbins was arriving early. Deana planned to fill him in and invite him to the meeting with Lowell.

She sat in bed thinking about the artist who had saved her life simply by leaving a ratty old sleeping bag and a few flares in a cave. She wanted to have a print or painting of his series from the cave: winter, spring, summer, fall. The winter scene would definitely not be on a wall where she saw it every day. She did want to have it to look at now and then as a reminder that she was a survivor. Spring and summer would hang in the living room. One day, she wanted to go back to the cave and see those views for herself. Deana reached for the phone to call Cindy back in Virginia and ask her to call the gallery in Jasper and order a print.

The next morning, Deana woke up to a quiet house. Jim was at work, and Linda was in her studio. She poured a cup of coffee, winked at the moose staring at her from the side of the coffee mug, and strolled to the window overlooking the snow-covered front yard. A car pulled up in front. She held her breath for a second. She let it out and put the mug down.

She recognized Ed from Jim's ex-cop's description: five feet ten, gray hair, receding hairline, square jaw, muscular. She watched him walk up the sidewalk from the living room window. Stocky, fighter's build, mid-to late-fifties, and confident. She liked the look of him. He walked like a man on a mission. She needed someone with that kind of drive.

She opened the door and said, "Ed, hi! I'm Deana."

Before she could say another word, he dropped his bag on the floor, put one hand on a hip, pointed at her hair, and said, "What's this? I said no red hair."

Deana laughed and said, "Hold on." She returned to the room with the wig and glasses in place. "I don't leave the house without the wig and glasses."

He relaxed and said, "Okay. Sorry to jump at you. Good work. You look completely different in that getup.

"Jim filled me in, but I would like to hear the whole story from you. I have to warn you, expenses multiply quickly, and tracking someone like your husband could become very expensive. Think about that before you decide to hire me."

She assured Ed that money was not a problem. After listening to her version of events, starting with how she had met Andy, Ed asked the question everyone else was too polite to ask. "How did you get your money? Inherit it or did you earn it yourself?" She told him about the college toxicology research project that had given her the idea for a software program that analyzed test data on drugs. She developed it right after graduation and got lucky, selling it to the major company involved in pharmaceutical testing. She still got calls to help companies set up their testing programs and could be picky about the jobs she accepted.

He continued to pepper her with questions, and she realized how easy it was to deceive someone who was of a trusting nature. She had to admit she had never seen Andy's birth certificate, social security, passport, or voter's registration card. He asked about Andy's computer.

Deana said, "He left it at home. My best friend, Cindy, has a key. She could go into the house and see if it's still there."

"The problem is we still don't know where Andy is. He could still be here in Jasper or he could be spending your hard-earned money on the other side of the world. It looks like he's been planning this for a while and has probably laid the groundwork for his disappearance. If he does find out you're still alive, which we have to assume he will, the logical place to finish the job would be back in Virginia. It will be much easier for him to be invisible in an urban setting than it will be here in Jasper.

"I don't want your friend going in alone. Let me get in touch with the police and find someone to accompany her to the house. If the computer is there, I want it removed before Andy gets there. I know the area well from my time with the FBI. I have a lot of contacts with the FBI and the police in the area. We don't need a court order or search warrant. The computer is as much your property as his. I just don't want to endanger your friend by asking her to go into the house alone," Ed explained.

Deana pulled out her cell phone. Ed pointed at it and asked, "Is that your old cell phone or your new one?"

"It's the old one. I had to get a new SIM card, but it's my old phone."

"Have you used it yet?" Ed asked quickly.

"Just to make one call. Why?" she answered.

"Shit!" he said. "Give it to me. A tracking device is tied to the serial number of the phone. Even with a new SIM card, someone could still trace the phone. You'll have to get a new phone." He tapped his fingers on the table, glanced away, and then looked at her. "I'll hold on to the old phone. We could call your service provider and ask if the tracking device is on, but we aren't going to take that chance. If you're dead, you wouldn't be calling, right?"

"Uh, right," she said. She handed the phone to Ed.

"I have an idea," Ed said, tossing the phone from one hand to the other. "We might be able to use this to our advantage. We have no way of knowing if he is tracing calls from that phone. We need to be on guard in case he is."

They parked in front of a modest house that was built of rough-cut pine siding. The corners were framed with pine logs. A small sign attached to the front porch identified it as Jasper's RCMP station. Lowell explained his office would do what they could to help. He apologized, saying their resources were limited, and he was glad Ed would be working on the case. At least there wouldn't be any energy wasted on territorial disputes and egos. Lowell recited what he had found out about Andy's mysterious exit from Jasper. The rental car still had not been found. A railroad worker returned from a three-day shift to find his car missing. Lowell didn't know if Mr. Harris was the culprit or not. They assumed that he was smart enough to not continue driving the rental car. The storm on the day Andy left Deana in the park kept all private and commercial planes grounded in Jasper from the afternoon through the evening. Either Andy stayed in Jasper or took his chances in the storm and drove away as far as he could get.

Deana was impressed by how much trouble Lowell had taken and thanked him. "Ma'am, once we establish he has left Jasper, I can't really do a lot for you. Ed explained to you that since both of your names are on the stock account, he was within his rights to execute transactions. We're looking at a missing person's case. You yourself will have to report that in your home state. At your request, I can tell Mounties in other jurisdictions to work with Mr. Robbins."

Lowell had already sent an officer with a copy of Andy's photo to canvas the stores, hotels, and gas stations in town. No one recognized him. Deana promised to deliver the original photos to Lowell as soon as they arrived. Ed and Lowell exchanged contact information. They agreed it would have been difficult for Andy to have left town without anyone seeing him unless he had help. Deana tried to not react and replaced a scream with a swallowed gulp. That meant there was another threat, someone she wouldn't recognize.

There was a phone store across the street from the RCMP station. Ed looked around and told her to go ahead to the phone store. His rental car was parked in front of the station. He could watch her and the store from the car.

A mud-caked pick-up truck honked at her as she crossed the street. She turned to see Jack, the famous artist, waving at her from the truck. Her head snapped around at the sound of a car door slamming. Ed was running across the road toward her.

Deana looked from Ed to Jack and said, "It's okay, Ed. This is Jack Hanson, the artist. You know, the artist who left the sleeping bag in the cave."

She looked at Jack and said with a grimace, "Meet Ed Robbins, my bodyguard."

Jack pulled his truck into an empty spot and got out to shake hands with Ed. "Bodyguard? I didn't know you were in danger. I was just going to invite you for a cup of coffee."

Deana felt Jack was owed some form of explanation. Now was as good a time as any to answer the question left unanswered last night: what happened to your husband?

"Ed," she said, "let me grab a cup of coffee with Jack. If he gives me a lift back to Linda and Jim's, will that be safe enough for you?"

Ed agreed. Jack waited outside while Deana bought a new phone, and they walked around the corner to a coffee shop. She was nervous, not sure where or how to begin.

Jack broached the subject of her adventure. "Listen, Deana, it's none of my business, and you don't have to answer the question I asked last night." She started to interrupt. He held up a hand, motioning her to stop. He smiled, exposing a gap between his front teeth—another imperfection that gave his face character.

He continued, "You've probably told the story several times, and I can get the details from Jim at some point. The important thing is that you're safe." He paused and gave a wry look. "Well, maybe not completely safe if you have a bodyguard."

In as few words as possible Deana gave Jack what she considered the sordid details of her life in the last few days: her loving husband tried to kill her; Jim's friend Ed was now protecting and helping her. He was right; she had a bodyguard.

She watched him for a reaction, expecting pity or shock or even fear for his own safety. Instead, there was admiration in his eyes.

"Deana," he said, "you're one tough lady. Most people would be too afraid to go outside after all you've been through. I'm impressed. Are you still up for dinner at my place tonight? No problem with canceling if you would rather just …"

She stopped him, "Don't worry, I'll be a different person by this evening. I'm dying to see your paintings." There would be no need for the wig and glasses this evening. She caught herself wondering again what he would think of the real Deana. Right now, she needed friends, and it looked like she had made another friend in Jack. She was as comfortable around him as she was with Linda and Jim.

There was an awkward pause. Desperate to change the course of the conversation, Deana blurted out, "Linda says you're a famous artist. She's a bit in awe of you. You seem too nice to be a temperamental artist."

"I'm only temperamental when I'm painting. Don't interrupt me in the middle of work. Outside of that, I'm pretty relaxed," he laughed.

"Linda says you're also a good curler. Was she able to talk you into curling with the club?" she asked.

Jack said, "As a matter of fact, I came into town to buy a new pair of curling pants. My old ones have a hole in the right knee."

Deana asked why the pants would wear out in the knee, and Jack proceeded to give her a passionate tutorial on curling. She grinned and said, "You sound like a diehard football fan in the States. It sounds like you love curling."

Jack offered to give her a curling lesson. She agreed to take him up on it, forgetting for a minute that she was supposed to keep a low profile.

Before they said good-bye, Deana said, "Jack, I want you to know that the sleeping bag, flares, and topo map saved my life. They gave me not just tangible help but hope, knowing that there was a possibility of survival. Thank you, thank you, thank you! I couldn't believe it when I saw the view from the cave in the art gallery." She hesitated, looked down at the table, and glanced back at Jack. "I *had* to find you and say ..." She couldn't finish.

He seemed embarrassed and said, "Aw shucks, ma'am, it was nothin'," in an exaggerated cowboy drawl.

Linda was certainly right. Jack was a great guy. A very nice man who could afford a Range Rover and drove a beat-up old truck. She nodded her head; people were often not what they seemed.

The biggest problem, if Jim and Lowell were correct, was staying safe until they could track down Andy. At the end of the meeting earlier, Lowell's warm and reassuring interviewer's voice disappeared and was replaced with a stern and tense warning: "You're a witness. You survived, and that makes you a threat to him. Be careful. You're now the hunter, and he's the prey."

CHAPTER 7

Deana found Ed hunched over the computer when she got back to the house. "Hey, get in here; I think I've got something. Cindy called. She went into your house with an undercover officer and only found your computer, not his. That's good news and bad news. The good news is either Andy or an accomplice got into the house. It wasn't a random break-in or random crime. The house had not been burglarized except for the money and jewelry you thought were in the safe. That's gone. It didn't appear to your friend that anything was out of place. The bad news is we still don't know where he is. He might have headed straight to Virginia from Jasper, or someone else might have gone into the house for him.

"There was a short article in the Jasper paper and the Calgary paper about your ordeal. We have to assume he knows you're alive. I think," Ed continued, tapping the desk with a pencil, "he'll want to eliminate you."

Deana cocked her head to one side and stared at Ed when he said the word *eliminate*.

"Sorry," Ed said and smiled, "I thought *eliminate* was a better choice of words than *kill*."

"Ed, dead is dead. You don't have to worry about me bursting into tears at this point. Save the euphemisms for someone else!" She motioned with a hand for him to continue.

He went on to explain that, alive, she could continue to press for Andy's capture. Dead, there would be no one to keep the pressure on the police to make finding him a priority. Newer crimes would take precedence, and her case would slip farther and farther down the pile of unsolved cases.

"I'd like to go ahead and get the story out to the news media and get Andy's photo out in the U.S. and Canada. I've got another idea, but it will need Lowell's cooperation." He hesitated and looked at her. "And your permission. I'd like to release an article saying Mrs. Harris was readmitted to the Jasper Hospital for complications as a result of hypothermia. It might lure Andy back to Jasper if he has left, and it could also make your life safer. If he thinks you're in the hospital, he won't be on the lookout for you here or in Virginia.

"If Lowell agrees to work out the details at the hospital, you'll have to stay out of sight. It will mean not staying in touch with your friends for a period of time and not returning to your town house until we're sure he isn't going to take the bait."

"You're going to use *me* as bait to lure him to Jasper? Will I actually have to stay in the hospital?" she asked.

Ed answered, "Yes, to the first question and no, to the second. It won't be you in the hospital room. A policeman or woman would be on duty, waiting in the hospital room. You'll be with me, and we'll probably be back in Virginia in a couple of days. What do you think?"

"It's a great idea. What about Cindy? She already knows I'm all right."

Ed made a face. He looked uncomfortable. "This Cindy. She's your friend and the person who introduced you to Andy." He held up a hand. "I'm going to ask you a difficult question." He paused. "Are you 100 percent sure you can trust Cindy?"

Deana responded with force. "Absolutely. She's like a sister. You can't think Cindy would be involved?"

"I had to ask. She introduced the two of you. Is there anyone else in her life?"

Deana hesitated before answering. She was thinking about trust and how she had been fooled by Andy. "No, there is no special man in her life. Look, Ed, Cindy is the one who tried to convince me to get Andy to sign a prenup before we got married. Why would she do that if she was in cahoots with him to get my money?"

Ed considered this. He leaned forward. "Tell me why you trusted Andy."

Deana looked away for a few seconds and thought. "He saved me from a marauding moose. That was on a hiking trip in Montana." She glanced away from Ed. "Of course that was *before* his name was on the stock account. After the moose rescue, he convinced me he could do a better job managing my investment portfolio than my previous broker. Speaking of trust, when I broached the subject of a prenup with Andy before we married, he said it was for people who didn't trust each other." She rolled her eyes. "I bought it hook, line, and sinker. We were married, 'sharing all our world goods.'"

"It's looking more like he isn't working alone. I don't know Cindy—you do. If you are confident you can trust her, that's good enough for me. That's also good because we can use her help. If we tell Cindy the truth, she can help spread the lie you're still in Canada and in bad shape. She's a close friend, and it makes sense for her to go in and out of your home. I know you're anti-Facebook," Ed said, "but how about Cindy?"

"She's definitely not anti-Facebook," Deana answered. "She chronicles everything in her life on Facebook—except her bowel movements," she added with a half-smile.

Ed gave her a thumbs-up and said, "Great. We'll ask her to post something on Facebook about your condition. Something like 'Keep Deana in your prayers.'"

Deana sputtered and said, "Ed, you better change the wording. Everyone would know it's pure fiction if you use 'Keep Deana in your prayers.' Cindy is not the praying type. She'd write, 'If anyone out there prays, please, please, include my friend Deana in your prayers. Send cards to me, and I'll forward to her. Keep you posted.'"

Ed nodded and put the paper and pencil down carefully on the table. He squirmed in his chair, rubbed the stubble on his chin, and said, "There's something else I need to tell you. Deana, Andy isn't Andy

Harris. I traced the social security number he used for your shared brokerage account. It belongs to a man who would be about Andy's age,
except that Andy Harris is dead."

"What? You're kidding!" she said and jumped up out of the chair.

She should have been past shock and surprise, but this bit of news was
like the proverbial nail in the coffin. As quickly as she had jumped out
of the chair, she collapsed back into it and said, "Well, I'll be damned!"

Ed sat quietly, watching Deana as she stood up and started pacing
in front of him.

"The man you know as Andy Harris has not generated any income
that would trigger an income tax or social security record. The real Mr.
Harris died twenty years ago." He paused for a few seconds, watching
her reaction. "We need to find out who Andy really is. That could be
the key to tracking him."

Deana stopped pacing and sat down, dumbfounded. "I can't believe
this. Was everything he told me a lie?"

Ed said, "Probably. Welcome to my world. A world full of accom-
plished liars and cheats. We have to assume Andy has changed his appearance and is traveling under another name. As carefully as he seems
to have planned your demise, he probably had another identity ready
for this disappearance. Even if he has changed his hair color and style,
someone might recognize him from his current photo and call it in. We
need to get his photo out."

Ed laughed. "Hah, I'm showing my age! They'll tweet it in before
they'll call it in. It's a lot harder to disappear today than it was even
ten years ago. Andy thinks he's smart. That's what trips these guys up."
Ed paused and raised an eyebrow. "The bad guys always think they're
smarter than everyone else."

Deana was listening to everything he said and processing it but got
distracted thinking about how Andy might have changed his appearance. She smirked, thinking his ego might make it difficult for him to
alter his appearance too much. It was impossible to imagine him disguised as a fat old man with a beard and glasses.

Ed pulled his chair over and sat down in front of her. He patted her knee and asked, "Hey, kid, are you okay?"

"What?" she said, and shook her head to get rid of Andy's face. "Okay? Yes, I'm okay. I'm furious. I was just trying to imagine Andy in disguise. I thought I was a good judge of people. He seemed normal, not perfect. He could be sarcastic at times, but he was always thoughtful and nice to me and my friends.

"I just remembered something else. Andy encouraged me to send the 'Having a great time, wish you were here' postcards to all my friends. He said I should send them right away, or I'd end up mailing them in Virginia. I sent cards to Cindy and to the ladies I met in a hunter education class. You're right. No one would expect to hear from me for at least a couple of weeks."

"Deana," Ed said, "I think your husband is a classic sociopath—a man without a conscience. Chances are this isn't the first time he's pulled off something like this. I've been dealing with the criminal world a long time, and I still have trouble spotting the really bad ones right off the bat. Appearing to be normal and lying are two of their specialties."

"Jim said the same thing," she said softly. "I know more about Andy than anyone. There must be something I can do to help. I can't just sit around and wait." With steel in her voice, she demanded, "Give me something to do."

Ed did not react to her rush of words right away. After a few moments of silence, he said, "Deana, I don't usually put my clients to work!" He smiled and continued, "Amateurs make mistakes, and those mistakes could get both of us killed." He stopped talking, letting her think about what he had just said. "However, this time I'm going to make an exception. You're upset, but you're not hysterical or grief-stricken. Am I right? Do I see anger and not despair?"

"Yes," she said calmly, "you see a very mad and determined woman, not a victim."

He slapped his knee and said, "All right. You will have to agree to do what I say and stay out of sight." Deana nodded in agreement.

Ed said, "There will be a lot of tedious checking on the computer and phone work. It would be a big help if you can take care of some of that work. Plus, you'll be close by, and I can keep an eye on you. Remember: we don't know where he is. Andy probably thought he had at least two weeks before your friends would start wondering about you. He managed to move the money out of the country, but he may have been counting on having more time to set up another identity. We don't know what he was up to. This could be a pattern for him. He might have done this before. He scored big on you. He might not target another victim for a while. On the other hand, if he finds out you're alive, we have to assume he'll be angry enough to come after you and finish the job."

Deana shuddered visibly.

Ed continued, "I'm not trying to scare you to death, just enough to make sure you stay alert and cautious. Remember what Lowell said: 'You're now the hunter, and he's the prey.' It's a sad part of reality, but if you're gone and there's no one to keep the case alive, it would get shuffled to the bottom of the pile.

"The good news here is that this means it is now a criminal case instead of a missing person's case. He married you under an assumed name. Based on that, you can get an annulment and press criminal charges. He never had legal access to your money."

Deana listened to Ed but got stuck on the words *good news*. Good news would be that she didn't have to press criminal charges because Andy had been mauled by a bear or ripped apart by wolves.

"Deana," Ed asked, "are you listening?"

She shook her head and pushed fantasies about Andy's demise from her brain. "Yes, sorry. Go ahead."

Ed explained that a lot of the investigative work might end up in dead ends, but one wouldn't know until one followed it to the end. "The devil is in the details," he said. Ed pulled out a copy of a form with personal information for the brokerage account. He pointed to the line asking for Andy's mother's maiden name. "People may be careful to fabricate a lot of things, but they tend to unconsciously tell the truth about their mother's maiden name." Andy had listed *Schneider* as his mother's maiden name. Ed suggested she start looking for a male born between 1950 and 1960 with the name *Schneider*. "It might help you narrow the search if we have an idea of where he grew up. Did he have any kind of regional accent?"

"The Midwest; he sounded like he came from Ohio, Indiana, Illinois—that kind of non-accent accent." He claimed to be from a small town in Indiana called Hamlet. Deana had never questioned it. He said there was nothing there but sad memories, and he never wanted to go back. "Uh, Ed ... I don't want to sound like I'm telling you what to do, but I don't care where he came from; I just want to find him. Aren't we better off focusing on where he is now?"

Ed laughed, obviously unperturbed by her suggestion. "Sometimes the past is the key to habits and patterns of behavior. Criminals are human, and just like everyone, they are creatures of habit. So far, he hasn't left much of a paper trail and no evidence of income. Scams like the one he pulled on you may be part of a pattern for him. Something in his past created the aberrant behavior. He may have ties to the past; he could still be in contact with a mother or father. It might be a way to catch him. In this line of work you just have to follow all leads and hope you get lucky. Tracking him down internationally could get too expensive even for you. If we uncover a trail of dead women, we'll be able to get some help from the big guys. I'd like to uncover at least one more suspicious death, and then I'll contact a buddy at the FBI. There probably is another victim out there."

"Okay, okay, sorry. I'm just anxious to catch him," Deana apologized. "I've been thinking. He did have access to money during the time we were dating. If you're right, his assets *may* have come from other victims and not his purported consulting business. As long as I can come up with the money, keep working as quickly as you can. There is also the small matter of the $2.5 million he stole. That alone is motivation enough!" She paused and looked at him. "I want my money back."

Ed said, "All right. You get started checking on his family. You told me Cindy met Andy through an Internet dating service. We'll actually have to go back to Virginia to get a court order to access the profiles of all the women he contacted. We'll contact all the women he might have approached. That's where your help will be appreciated. I'd like you to come with me for the interviews. They would be more at ease with a woman there.

"In the meantime, I'll get in touch with a friend on the force in Virginia. He's good on the computer. I'll ask him to compile a list of women who died within the first couple years of marriage. If they were wealthy, I'll ask him to get photos of the husbands for us. We'll start with Virginia. It will be time-consuming, but he owes me."

Deana didn't do a good job of hiding the skepticism she felt. Ed looked at her for a second and said, "Most criminals are caught as a result of boring, routine, painstaking searching. We have to cover all the bases and all the possibilities. If we can come up with at least one other suspicious death, we'll be able to get help from the FBI. How well do you know your neighbors?" Ed recognized the Alexandria, Virginia, address and knew it was in a neighborhood of quaint brick town houses that filled the history-rich area.

"I know my immediate neighbors and most of the block by sight. They're all Type A, working professionals. They rush out early and come home late."

"Give me a list of the neighbors who would recognize Andy. I'll get the police to contact them. We want to know if anyone has spotted him in the neighborhood. If they do see him, we want to know about it right away."

"I'll call them," Deana offered.

Ed said, "No, that won't work." He shook his head and drew his words out, "*Remember:* you're on your death bed in the hospital.

"He knows he runs a greater risk of being spotted if he tries to move items out of your town house. He may have just returned the one time for the computer. Tell me, why did your friend Cindy pass Andy on to you?"

"She thought she was doing me a favor?" Deana said, answering his question with a question and a shrug. "She said he was too outdoorsy for her; she said he was charming and a gentleman but a little reserved and not sophisticated. I should have been insulted when she told me that, but she laughed and insisted he was sophisticated enough for me and the good looks made up for a lot of things. Cindy is moving up at the National Art Gallery, and she wants an artsy-fartsy type to attend cocktail parties with her. She was born in three-inch heels, and you would never catch her hiking or skiing. Andy was definitely not her type."

"How much did she tell him about you?"

"She says she just told him we had a lot in common and that, worst case, he might be able to help me in the financial management area."

Ed groaned and nodded his head in agreement. "She was a big help," he said sarcastically and motioned for Deana to continue.

"She invited both of us to a cocktail party for a gallery opening. We were the only two there without body piercings. He suggested we sneak out early. We had a great dinner at a Thai restaurant in Arlington." Innocent memories about the start of a relationship she thought would be forever were replaced by empty feelings of betrayal. He had never been overly aggressive, letting her set the pace. And he seemed so nice and normal. She shivered at the memory.

"Did he bring up the possibility of a business relationship?" Ed asked, interrupting her thoughts.

"No. In fact, he claimed to be at a point where he said managing his own portfolio kept him busy full time. We now know that was all part of an act."

"Okay. Now, tell me a little about your friend Cindy. We'll know more about what Andy was up to when we get information on the other women he may have contacted. Cindy obviously fit the profile he was targeting. It sounds like she's another successful woman. What about family?"

Deana thought about her friend and realized that Cindy might have ended up Andy's victim instead of her. "Like me, she's alone. Her parents have been gone for years—a tragic traffic accident. She divorced about ten years ago and moved to Virginia to start a new life. We met at a professional women's group and hit it off right away. We've celebrated a lot of holidays together since we're both orphans."

"And you're absolutely sure," Ed said and hesitated for a second, "sure there's nothing between Andy and Cindy?"

She jumped up and said, "No! Absolutely not. I could tell. And besides …" She stopped talking and sat back down. The words *I could tell* hung in the air. Yeah, just like she could tell about Andy. The brief moment of doubt about the woman who was a good friend was over and gone.

"No. That's one thing I *am* sure about."

"All right," Ed said. "I had to ask. One more thing. You said you went to a Thai restaurant the night you met." He scratched his head and said, "Chinese, I'd say, okay; everybody eats Chinese. Thai is a little more worldly, and I thought you said he wasn't sophisticated."

Deana smiled and grimaced. "Well, *he* was the one who suggested Thai food. It surprised me, and I told him it was one of my favorites. I remember being pleased that he admitted asking Cindy what type of restaurants I like. At the time, I was impressed by his thoughtfulness." She finished the sentence with raised eyebrows.

Deana sighed and wrapped her arms around her body, hugging herself for comfort. She was beat, and Ed looked beat too. He pushed his chair back, stretched, and dropped to the floor, doing push-ups. Deana started laughing, "Hey, I thought you were beat!"

"Yep, I am," he talked through his push-up routine, "and you don't think straight when you're beat. And an old fart like me has to stay in shape to keep up with the bad guys. A gym isn't always handy, so I do push-ups and sit-ups." He stopped and looked at her. "The brain needs to think clearly too. Forget about it for the rest of the evening." He dropped right back into his push-up routine.

Deana had to laugh. Ed's weather-beaten face showed all his fifty years, yet he had more energy than men or women half his age. As fit as he looked, maybe the rest of the world could give up their gym membership and use his routine.

CHAPTER 8

Reality set in the next morning. Deana pushed the bright white cur-tains in the bedroom back to check the weather. It was a gray, gray day. No beautiful mountain views, no sun sparkling off the snow and ice. She got dressed, automatically plopping the wig on and checking in the mirror to make sure all the red curls were hidden. A walk to the bakery seemed a logical remedy for what was starting out as a gloomy day. She headed out with her constant companions, Bear and pepper spray. The houses that had looked quaint under yesterday's sun now looked sad and dingy.

The snowbanks piled along the streets were no longer white; they were gray and grungy. A few bars were already open, sad-looking charac-ters at home on bar stools knocking back their breakfasts. Deana recalled reading something about the high rate of alcoholism in Montana and Alaska. If they had a lot of days like this in Jasper, they probably had the same problem. Her blue mood lifted as soon as she opened the door to the bakery and was engulfed by the scent of yeast and cinnamon. If she lived in Jasper, her biggest problem would be the cinnamon buns, not the booze. Instead of AA, they would have to start a new rehab group, CBA—Cinnamon Buns Anonymous. Deana smiled and ordered a dozen.

Everyone was up when she got back to the house. They protested the cinnamon buns but greedily ate them. They all laughed when Deana proposed a CBA chapter in Jasper. Linda dismissed the theory about cold mountain towns and alcoholism. "Hey, we never go more than two to three days without being able to see our mountains. It's a million-dollar view, and we can put up with a few gloomy days in exchange for that. Honey, you can't buy paradise."

Ed looked at the last bite of his cinnamon bun, tossed it into his mouth, and chewed with a satisfied look on his face. "This is paradise," he declared, wiping the crumbs from the sides of his mouth and licking his fingers.

They talked about plans for the day and agreed to leave for dinner at Jack's around 5:00 p.m. Ed pointed a finger at Deana. "You're to stay inside from now on. No more early morning walks to the bakery!"

"Yeah, yeah," Deana said, flapping a hand at him. He would have been testier with her if he hadn't enjoyed the cinnamon buns so much.

Ed and Lowell had worked out the details behind the ruse of read-mitting Deana to the Jasper Hospital. Lowell had already released the article to the media claiming she was suffering from pneumonia and exposure. He couldn't commandeer a room in her name with a guard. The hospital *did* agree to transfer any calls that came in asking for her to Lowell's cell phone. Any visitors would be asked to wait while the receptionist alerted Lowell.

Ed warned Deana again to stay inside. This time his warning had more impact. There were no straggling sweet roll crumbs clinging to his chin, and the creases in his forehead showed real worry and concern. She gave him a simple salute and walked back to the bedroom.

Deana was dying to call her friends from the hunter education class. She couldn't help wondering if they wouldn't come up with a creative idea to help track Andy. She also wanted to tell them how unfortunately useful the class had been in helping her survive. But she knew Ed was right. She had to stay out of sight. At least she wasn't alone. The nights in the cave were long, not only because of the cold but because she was alone with the first niggling doubts about Andy. She remembered being disappointed and disgusted with his lack of planning and inability to fix her snowshoe. The possibility she hadn't wanted to consider was that Andy intended to abandon her. She had dismissed the idea as preposterous—something that happened to other people—and attributed the crazy thinking to fear.

The one recurring idea she had tried to suppress was that every time she closed her eyes it might be for the last time. Alone again with her thoughts, she was in a warm room, and in the next room were three people helping her. Now, her focus was on tracking Andy.

Ed's remark about the past being the key to habits and patterns made Deana think about Andy claiming to be from a small town in Indiana. What if he really was from Hamlet, Indiana, and had been using another name when she met him? Even if the phony name, *Andy Harris,* was a lie, there might have been some truth in his stories. It made sense. Ed was right. It would be difficult to stay within a completely manufactured history. If people keep their history and just change their names, they only have to remember one lie. Andy had talked about bowling and gym class and going to the Friday night football games. His words sounded genuine then. Replaying them in her mind now, they still had the ring of truth. She sat up straight. She hadn't been a great judge of Andy's veracity, but she had a feeling she couldn't shake that some of the unimportant details about his childhood were in fact true. Ed was on the phone. Deana decided this was a good time to see what she could find out on her own.

Deana's eyes opened wide when she read the high school students in Hamlet went to school in a town called Knox, the county seat. The information jumped out at her from the website on Hamlet. There really was a town in Indiana called Hamlet. Andy might actually have told the truth about growing up there. A memory of him on the edge of his seat at a performance of *Hamlet* now had a different meaning. He was enthralled with the performance. Now, she realized it was not the good but the evil truths Andy was absorbing. "Thus conscience does make cowards of us all" was one line from Hamlet that embodied Andy's actions. In his perverted thinking, a lack of conscience made him brave. There were plenty of lessons of villainy and deception in Hamlet. The little boy from the town of the same name—if that was really Andy's home—embraced all the dark lessons from the play instead of being enlightened by examples of hypocrisy and deception.

Something started pinging in her brain; she was on to something and couldn't keep the excitement out of her voice when she asked the receptionist at the Hamlet Junior High for the contact person at Knox High School. She tried to order old copies of the yearbooks. The school didn't have yearbooks that old but assured her the town library would have them. The friendly librarian was curious and wanted to know what she was up to. Ed's orders to keep a low profile flashed through Deana's mind.

The woman said, "Who is it you're trying to find, dear?" The voice seemed to be that of an older woman. Deana made a decision based on gut instinct to brazenly tell the truth. The librarian with the sincere sounding voice would either be moved to help or shocked and hang the phone up. It was a calculated risk. The chance of getting help from Mrs. Binkley, the librarian, would probably be better if she felt a little empathy for Deana. Deana calmly told her she had been left to die in the wilds of Jasper and asked if she could transmit a copy of the article in Jasper's paper covering the mysterious disappearance of her ex. Mrs. Binkley gasped and said, "Oh, my!"

Mrs. Binkley seemed to believe the story, but the written word would carry more weight than a verbal account over the phone. Deana waited ten minutes and called her back.

The librarian fussed about all Deana had been through and then got down to business. "You know, dear, it was during that time they merged two high schools. A small town next to Knox, Hamlet, was merged with the Knox school."

Deana's knee started pumping up and down as she waited for Mrs. Binkley to say how soon she could make copies of the old yearbooks. The nervous tic stopped when Mrs. Binkley said, "You won't have to wait for me to send copies. We may be a small town library, but we do keep up with what's going on in the rest of the world. All the years you're looking for are online. You can look through the pictures yourself."

Deana's heart skipped a beat. She was the one who was out of touch. "Thank you so much, Mrs. Binkley," she said. Now, she couldn't wait to get off the phone and start looking at the old yearbook photos. She had a feeling Andy's mug was in one of those books.

Fingers tapping on the desk top next to the keyboard, Deana leaned in and studied each photo of a young man. A picture of Andy was under the drumming fingers. She occasionally stared at it and back to an old yearbook photo if there was even a small possibility the student photo resembled the grown man's photo.

After going through four years of photos and not finding any matches, Deana's shoulders sagged. She sat back, deflated and discouraged. Then she realized they might be off by a year or two and turned back to keep searching.

Ed came into the room as she took a breath and was getting ready to go through more yearbook photos. She filled him in quickly. He listened with a hard look on his face and then hit his forehead with one hand. "Deana," he said, obviously trying to keep his anger in control, "I *told* you, you're supposed to keep a low profile."

"But, Ed, listen," she said.

"No, you listen. How do you know this librarian isn't your beloved husband's first cousin? Remember what I said about amateurs getting themselves killed?"

Deana groaned, "Sorry, I didn't think of that." She was properly apologetic and promised to not ever again do anything unless directly told by Ed to do it. He finally begrudgingly agreed that trying to track Andy through high school yearbooks was actually a good idea.

"Look, any harm is done. Send a photo of Andy to this librarian. Maybe she'll recognize him. Since she's now your bosom buddy"—he paused and raised an eyebrow—"she'll understand when you tell her it is important to keep quiet about this."

Deana shook her head in agreement. She was annoyed with herself for not having thought of sending Andy's photo to the librarian. *So much for gut instincts,* Deana thought, after searching through four more years of photos and not finding Andy. She had such high hopes they would find their first big clue to his background. Ed patted her on the back and told her again that there was a lot of slogging and what seemed like wasted time when trying to find someone like Andy.

Deana just nodded. Right now her mind was full of pictures of the faces of the young men she had been studying. Some looked scared, some smiled confidently, some were shy and looked anywhere but at the camera, and a few scowled. Unfortunately, a younger version of Andy wasn't in any of the pictures.

Deana sighed and turned her thoughts to the evening and Jack and returning home and learning to shoot a gun and living the rest of her life in fear. She scratched her scalp with both hands and grimaced. This keeping a low profile business was a pain in the tush. The wig was making her head itch. Then she had to laugh. Her life was in danger, and she was pissed because a wig made her uncomfortable.

"Get over it!" she said out loud.

Ed was sitting at the computer. He looked at her and said, "Get over what?"

Deana said, "We need to find Andy so that I can get my life back."

Ed smiled. "You can skip the wig tonight. It will be dark when you leave. I've already spoken to Jim. Get in the car in the garage before he opens the door. Lay down in the back seat. Jim will tell you when it's okay to sit up."

She nodded yes and then stopped the half-formed smile. The danger was real.

"Hey, you sure you won't join us tonight?" Deana asked.

"Naw, thanks. I think I'll head to Fritz's Bistro. I want to be close to the hospital in case we get a bite, and you never know what you might find out talking to the locals. Besides," he said and winked, "Linda says the hostess, Shelly, is someone I should get to know."

Jim's SUV struggled in 4-wheel drive up the steep climb to Jack's house. The mountain tops were bathed in moonlight, and the snow and ice sparkled like stars. Deana marveled at the beautiful scenery. It was much easier to appreciate the great outdoors from inside a warm SUV than from a ledge outside a cold granite cave.

A few days ago, she had looked out over the frozen lake and seen the beauty but also felt she might die there. Now, she not only admired the beauty but she had a special respect for the wild, rugged mountains. She had conquered a fear—multiple fears—and lived to tell the story. She leaned forward toward the window, taking in as much as she could of the landscape, looking for another wolf or sign of life. The area had gotten under her skin.

Jack came out to meet them, two large dogs in his wake. "Wow, great house!" Deana exclaimed before he could even say anything about the change in her appearance. His brow wrinkled, and he turned his head to the side to look at her. There was a question in his eyes but a smile on his face. Deana smiled back, pleased that he seemed to like the looks of the real her: unruly red hair, no glasses, and a healthy glow from sleep and food.

The house wasn't fancy, but it was beautiful. Natural stone bordered the base and deck. It was a majestic log chalet with a lot of glass overlooking the view of the valley. It was like its owner: down-to-earth and rugged.

They carried their drinks up to his second-floor studio. Jack and Linda talked about the light and paints. Jim and Deana admired different works in progress. It was amazing the number of sketches and unfinished pieces Jack had piled up along the wall. He pulled out a large black portfolio and spread out a series of drawings and half-finished water color renderings of views from the cave. Everyone oohed and aahed over the pictures. Even his sketches were powerful and captured the essence of the view.

Deana picked up one depicting the view from the cave. Unable to take her eyes away from it, she said, "Jack, you've probably figured it out already, but the wig and glasses are my disguise until Ed and Jim think things are safe."

"Understood," he said. "It would be tough to not leave an impression with your beautiful red curls."

He managed to pay the compliment without making her feel uncomfortable. She didn't want anyone flirting with her. She wasn't sure she'd ever be in the mood for flirting again.

Linda ruffled Deana's hair. The women were following Jack and Jim back into the family room. Linda winked at her. Deana stuck her tongue out at her friend and got a dignified look back in place just before Jack turned to ask if everyone was hungry. Jim and Linda felt Jack could be trusted and might be willing to help. Earlier that day, Jim had suggested Jack's house would make a great place for Deana to hide out. As she half-listened to Linda and Jack discuss watercolor versus oil painting, she looked around and realized Jack's house *would* be the perfect hideaway. No one knew about a connection between Jack and her, and his home was at the end of a dead-end mountain road. She had protested at the time, not wanting to be away from the safety of Ed, Jim, and Linda, and the idea was dropped. She felt some kind of kinship or attraction with Jack that went beyond him leaving a sleeping bag in a cave. She didn't want to even think about it now and was relieved they hadn't pursued the idea of dumping her at Jack's house.

Back in the large gathering room, Jack's paintings and a lot of earthy-looking pottery decorated the room. Deana moved closer to the painting hanging above the fireplace. It wasn't a rendering of the view from the cave, but it did depict a winter scene in the mountains. Snow covered the ground, tree branches drooped, heavy with snow, and the snow falling through the air was drawn so that the viewer was pulled into the painting. "Jack," she said quickly, "is that a moose?" Her eyes were focused on a corner of the wintry scene. The head of a moose with a large rack was staring back at her. "Is he smiling?" she asked in disbelief.

Jack laughed. "Yes, as a matter of fact, it *is* a moose, and he *is* smiling. Thanks for noticing. When I paint for myself, I like to remind myself to not take it too seriously."

Jim and Linda moved in to look at the moose. Jim said, "They're always out there watching us. Nice touch, Jack."

Dinner conversation flowed easily. Deana listened and asked questions while Jim, Linda, and Jack talked about local politics and problems. They knew a lot of the same people, and Jack seemed eager to catch up on all the local gossip. Jim mentioned another small lake in the backcountry that was particularly scenic. Jack jumped on an invitation to be taken to the lake. He said he would be out of town for a couple of weeks, and they made plans to hike to the lake next month. Jack turned to Deana and asked how much longer she would be in Jasper.

She hesitated, not sure how honest to be about her plans. Jim answered for her. "Jack," he said, "I hate to ruin what has been a wonderful evening by bringing up the unpleasant subject of Deana's husband, but I know we can trust you."

He explained Ed's plan to lay a trap for Andy at the hospital. "So, Deana has to stay out of sight until we know if he'll take the bait."

Jack nodded and whistled softly. He said, "Look, if there's anything I can do, please ask." He turned his head and looked at Deana with a half-smile and said, "Hey, maybe I should give you shooting lessons instead of curling lessons!"

Deana glanced at Jim, looked at Jack, and said, "I may have to take a rain check on the curling lessons." She pointed a thumb at Jim. "I'm supposed to stay out of sight, remember?"

Linda sat forward in her chair and said quickly, "Wait a minute! She *could* go to the curling rink." She looked at Deana and continued, "Deana, the curling rink is in a Quonset hut on the edge of town." She glanced at Jack, and Jim and continued in a calmer voice. "You wouldn't know to go there unless you were involved with curling. Plop that wig on, and we'll go to the arena tomorrow evening. Jack, you give her a curling lesson, and then join our team. We're short one tomorrow night. What do you say?"

Jim groaned and started to launch into a protest, "Honey ..."

Linda interrupted and pointed a finger at him. "And you can guard the only entrance to the arena."

They all laughed and looked at Jim.

"Oh, all right, unless Ed objects," he said. "Your husband has no known interest in curling, right?"

Deana assured him Andy wasn't interested in a sport if it didn't involve shooting something with a rack on it. Her attempt at humor was met with shocked looks instead of laughter, and she said, "Sorry, bad joke, poor choice of words." She quickly replaced the grimace on her face with a smile and said, "I would love to learn to curl. I've seen it on television but don't know anything about it." She did take a second to wonder whether Linda's motive was to recruit Jack for her curling team or to throw Jack and her together.

"Now that I think about it," Deana said, "I remember Andy coming into the room when curling was on during the last winter Olympics. He started laughing and said, 'What a joke. That's not a sport. It's just shuffleboard on ice.'"

Deana certainly knew how to stop conversation. The shocked looks returned, followed by a moment of silence. Jack and Linda both started protesting, and Jim broke out laughing.

Jack said, "It *is* a sport. And a challenging, engrossing one. That is to say, challenging and engrossing if you opt to play it well."

Linda interrupted, "Right on, Jack."

Jack continued, "Curling requires strong legs and good balance. Deana, you think you're in good shape?" he challenged her.

"Good enough shape for curling," she bragged, revealing that she might have actually agreed with Andy's assessment of curling.

"Okay," Jack said, motioning for her to stand up. "We'll see. Stand on your left leg, and hold your right leg in the air behind you." He looked at his watch and said, "Go!"

Deana assumed the one-legged bird stance and watched the three of them watching her. Her leg started shaking, but she managed to hold on to the stance.

Linda said, "Deana, you've got good balance. There's hope for you as a curler."

Jack looked up from his watch and said, "One minute. Very good. I predict you'll be a good curler."

"Linda," Jim said, "you have a key to the curling arena. Instead of worrying about watching the door to the curling arena during the public session, why don't you give the key to Jack? He can take Deana down there in the afternoon, come back here for dinner, and then go to curl with your team." He looked at Linda and Jack and said, "Sound like a plan?"

They both agreed. Deana wasn't too excited, but at least it would get her out of the house for an hour or two. She had to admit she was a little curious about curling, and spending a little time with Jack was not a hardship.

Jack said, "Deana, I'll be in Washington, D.C., in a couple of weeks. I hope you'll be safely back in Virginia while I'm there."

Deana thought, *The key word here is* safely. She couldn't shake an uneasy feeling that it would be a while before her life was secure and safe.

She couldn't believe it when he explained the reason for the D.C. trip was a show of his at the National Gallery. "Oh, do you know Cindy Prescott?" Of course he did; Cindy was in charge of the show.

"Deana, I hope you'll have time for dinner in D.C. I would love to see you there."

Linda kicked her under the table. Deana said, "Great! Sounds good. Ed will be with me in Virginia. I'll have to check with him." Either Jack was naive or Deana was a pessimistic paranoid. It was highly unlikely they would track Andy down within a couple of weeks, which meant she would not be traipsing around D.C. on dinner dates. She would more likely be taking Jack up on his offer of shooting lessons.

They helped Jack clean up and carried their lattes, made from his super-duper coffee machine, back into the gathering room. Something else she and Jack had in common: the coffee had to be good. Linda gave her a big smile.

Driving down the mountain, Jim's only comment was, "I really like that guy."

Linda agreed and teasingly said, "I think Deana does too! What was that business about checking with Ed?"

Deana explained Ed would want her to keep a low profile in Virginia and avoid being seen in her usual haunts.

"That's right," Jim chimed in, "and I don't think he'll want you running around town with or without Jack. Still, you could invite Jack to dinner at Cindy's place. Ed said you'll be staying at her apartment at the Watergate. Great security there."

Linda piped in, "No reason for you to not see Jack in Virginia. Hey, you said you were going to learn to shoot when you got home. Ask Jack to help you. Take him to a shooting range instead of joining him for dinner," she finished, laughing.

"Funny, very funny, guys," she said and thought to herself, *Funny the twists and turns life takes. Very funny.*

The funny turned to anxiety when she saw Lowell's RCMP vehicle parked outside Linda and Jim's house. Lowell and Ed were waiting inside the car.

Lowell explained, "A woman showed up at the hospital this evening after visiting hours and asked to see you. The aide on duty asked her to have a seat and left the area to call me. When she got back, the woman had disappeared. At least we have a decent description of her. The hospital security camera picked her up too. We've issued an alert for her. The problem is we don't know what type of vehicle she's driving. We'll canvas the area again tomorrow and see if anyone recognizes her." He passed a photo taken from the security camera to Deana, but she didn't recognize the woman. Deana let out a breath, relieved to see that it was not her friend Cindy.

She didn't want to admit it, but she had been afraid to even think about whether Cindy was somehow involved with Andy. She took a second to be disgusted with herself for doubting her best friend. All the warm, fuzzy feelings built up over a pleasant evening evaporated. The danger was real. She gripped the photo in both hands and stared at the woman. Was she a friend of Andy, a lover, or someone he hired? All of a sudden, the room was freezing. Now, she had to worry about not just Andy but one or even more people.

Ed added, "We can assume she was the woman who picked Andy up outside the hotel. We know we have to protect you from at least two people now. Promise me you won't leave the house."

Deana groaned and agreed.

CHAPTER 9

Ed was waiting for everyone at the breakfast table the next morning. "Any news about the woman?" Deana asked.

Ed shook his head and said, "No, not yet. Lowell is still passing her photo around town." He rubbed his forehead. "She could have gotten into town and walked around with a disguise. That would explain why no one recognizes her." He looked up and asked, "Hey, how'd it go last night? I mean, before you found Lowell and me waiting for you."

"Great, wonderful evening. That is, it was a wonderful evening until we got back and found out your trap at the hospital worked. How about you?"

"Interesting evening. I like this town. Had a very nice dinner at Fritz's. Shelly and I went to the Whistle Stop Pub after Fritz's closed."

Deana thought about how bizarre her life had become. Breakfast conversation jumped from innocuous, polite "what did you do last night" conversation to catching a killer. She was starting to accept the frightening reality that living with danger was now a normal part of her life. Listening to Ed talk, she realized his job had taught him to be able to move back and forth between the normal and the criminal. He couldn't be emotional about the violence, or it would cloud his judgment and decision making. The same thing was happening to her; she wasn't paralyzed with fear or too scared to think.

She tuned back to Ed. "She introduced me to a few people, and one of them turned out to be a shuttle bus driver. Turns out the train from

Edmonton got in really late the other night. The driver dropped a bus-load off at your hotel and was sitting in the bus doing paperwork. He looked up and saw a man leaving the hotel with his bags. A jeep pulled up, the man threw the bags in, and they took off. It struck him as odd that someone would be checking out and hitting the road that late. I showed him Andy's picture, but he couldn't identify him. He thought a woman was driving a car that fit the description of the Jeep you and Andy had rented."

Ed's news didn't make Deana break into a fear-induced cold sweat. Instead, she felt a tingle of anticipation. The fact that Andy had been spotted and that they knew for sure he had an accomplice made it feel like they had an edge on him. Deana said, "You *did* have an interesting evening! You think it was the same woman who came to the hospital looking for me?"

"Yep. It explains why we haven't found a trace of him. The woman had a car, and they transferred to her car. Your rental will show up. Another question. Actually, Shelly brought this one up. Why didn't you two stay at the famous Jasper Park Lodge? It certainly wasn't a matter of not being able to afford it."

"Andy said he wanted to be right in town."

"I think he wanted a hotel from which it would be easier to make an exit. You would have been less anonymous at the Jasper Park Lodge—high ratio of employees to guests up there. Now that we know he has an accomplice, it may make it a little easier to track him. It's harder for two people to disappear than one.

"It's funny the things that stick in a person's mind. The shuttle bus driver noticed the car had Alberta tags and figured they were driving back to Edmonton or Calgary for an emergency of some kind. Tourists don't usually pick the middle of the night after a bad storm to hit the road up here. It's too dangerous. They might have just moved to another hotel. I'll call Lowell this morning and see if he can track cars rented to women traveling alone. They could have driven back to Calgary or Edmonton that night and flown out on one of the early morning flights. Or … he might have left town, and she stayed. Maybe he returned to town when word got out that you were still alive." Ed stared out the window, considering all the possibilities.

Still staring out the window, he said, "They figured out the hospital was a trap and are probably on the run. If I were him, I would figure you would head back to Virginia."

Deana looked at Ed but didn't say anything. She was thinking. She didn't want to hide in a hole and wait for Andy to find her. She wanted to continue being the hunter, not the prey. She was about to say, "Let's go after him!" but before she got the words out, Ed barked, "Get packed! We're on a flight out of Calgary this evening. We need to get back to Virginia, get a court order, and check out the dating service. In a couple of hours, I'll check with my buddy in Virginia to see if he has turned up any deaths of young women who fit the profile. Have you thought any more about a career or job Andy might have had? What's he good at?"

"Funny, he's at home outside in the great outdoors. Somehow it seems incongruous. I expect someone who loves the rugged life to be clean, honest, and straightforward. City slickers, country slickers. You find bad guys everywhere. Sorry, I'm rambling. To answer your question, he could have been a hunting guide or park ranger. He seemed to know the Shenandoah Park area outside of Washington, D.C., really well."

"Okay," Ed grunted, "that's something."

Deana spent the rest of the morning looking through old photos from the Indiana high school. It was probably futile but, according to Ed, "You never know ..." She didn't see anyone who resembled Andy. The name under a young woman's photo did catch her eye. It was *Jean Schneider*. She was part of the freshman class. Deana stared at the photo, looking for a resemblance to Andy, but didn't see it. It probably wasn't anything. Schneider was a common enough name in the Midwest. She marked the photo to show to Ed later.

After lunch, Deana sat down to review her portfolio and figure out how to finance her revenge mission. It was hard to concentrate. She found herself staring into space, thinking about being back in Virginia, finding Andy, and what type of job Andy might have had. She looked up to see Ed watching her. He had a Cheshire cat grin and was holding a piece of paper with a photo on it.

"Three years ago, a young woman—a young wealthy woman—died a tragic death while camping with her husband to whom she had been married only six months. They were camping in the Mount Rogers National Recreation Area in southern Virginia. Her best friend saw the news release about your nights in the park. It had Andy's photo next to the article. She contacted the sheriff who had been responsible for the investigation in Virginia. The sheriff tracked Lowell down and called him this morning."

Deana's heart stopped. She knew before Ed spoke that Andy had something to do with the young woman's death.

"The husband's version was that she got up in the middle of the night, presumably to tinkle, wandered off, and fell over a precipice."

She locked eyes with Ed. "I know the Mt. Rogers area. Did this happen at Grindstone Campground?"

"Yep, it says here Grindstone Campground. He didn't take you there, did he?"

"No, but I think I'm beginning to understand why he never wanted to go hiking in Mt. Rogers."

"He would have been recognized there. It turns out he had been working there as a park ranger for about a year. He met Stephanie Randall when he was asked to conduct a day hike for a small group. His name then was Stuart Hudkins."

Ed flipped the sheet of paper around and held it in front of Deana's face. "Here's your boy in his park ranger get-up. They were married just three months after meeting, and he kept his job after the marriage. She kept her home in Bristol; her mommy and daddy left her a bundle after their private plane crashed. Weekends she and Andy would take turns getting together in Bristol or at his cabin in Mt. Rogers."

Deana fingered the photo of Andy in his park ranger uniform. Her instincts had been right. He had worked for a park service. If someone had shown her the photo a month ago, she would have thought, *Wow, that's one handsome man.* Now, she looked past the pressed uniform, the muscular arms, the ramrod straight posture, the neatly combed straight black hair, the face with perfectly proportioned features, and concentrated on the eyes. She shook her head. She still couldn't sense the evil that lurked behind those eyes. She handed the photo back to Ed.

"Lowell told the sheriff to expect a call from me. He was more than willing to share that he was always a little uneasy about the case. There wasn't anything he could do at the time. He told me there's usually a family member or friend pushing to prove foul play; in this case, there didn't seem to be any family. The woman, Stephanie, had a friend who came down from northern Virginia and tried to convince him it wasn't an accident. That's the woman who called him when she recognized Andy from the press release. Andy, calling himself Stuart, seemed to be properly distraught; there were empty bottles of wine, and he claimed to have fallen asleep. He called the locals for help when he couldn't find her in the morning. The mountain was socked in with fog, and they couldn't start searching 'til almost noon. His story fit. If you took the wrong turn from the bathrooms, you *could* walk over the edge of a cliff and fall about a hundred feet onto a rock face. It was midafternoon by the time they found the body. The sheriff said they now have a railing at that spot. Didn't do Stephanie much good."

"Huh," Deana snorted, "Andy—Stuart—whatever his name is, he would have found another cliff edge. Her life ended when she met him."

"Well, according to the sheriff, she had a high blood-alcohol content reading in her body, and the story was tragic yet plausible. They were in the middle of a meth investigation at the time, and his small department was stretched pretty thin. He suggested we talk to her friend in northern Virginia. Here's the name and contact number. We'll get in touch with her as soon as we get back to Virginia."

"What about Andy? Was Stuart Hudkins his real name?"

"We'll do some background checking. The sheriff agreed to get a copy of his job application at Mt. Rogers. I'll call his boss there after he paves the way for me. He said it was the least he could do."

Deana showed the old yearbook photo of Jean Schneider to Ed. "Luck and hard work," he said. "She may be a relative." He would follow up on Jean Schneider and asked Deana to start searching for information on Stuart Hudkins.

She shut down the computer after a disappointing yet not surprising search. It wasn't a surprise to find out Stuart Hudkins was as dead as the real Andy Harris. The disappointment was that they still didn't know Andy's real name. A Stuart Hudkins had graduated from Indiana University with a degree in park management; he died in a car accident right after graduation. Andy had picked wisely. A search showed the degree had been awarded, and he was qualified on paper for a park services job.

Deana was headed down the hall to tell Ed about the tie-in to Indiana when her phone beeped. Her eyebrows went up. It was the sweet librarian from Knox calling. The woman had shown Andy's photo to her husband. He recognized Andy as "that Irwin kid." Her husband had taught biology at the Catholic school in Knox. Deana grimaced when she heard the news. They had only considered the public school. He remembered Greg Irwin as a bright boy who was a loner. His dad was in a nursing home in town, but the mother was dead. Greg graduated from high school and worked for the State Forestry Department. He had married a young woman who died in a tragic accident the first year of their marriage. Greg left town shortly after his wife died. She said her husband was sure the man in the photo was Greg Irwin. The young woman he married was Meredith Givens. They were a handsome couple, and everyone thought it was nice they got together because Meredith had lost both parents to an automobile accident and was alone. Deana couldn't help thinking Andy/Stuart/Greg certainly seemed to be together with a lot of people who were alone.

Deana stood in the hallway for a minute, taking in all the librarian's information. She was getting a headache, and her stomach was going into spasms. Two cases of young women's lives ending in tragic accidents, married to the same man living as two dead men. Deana was the third one—the lucky one. She let out a breath, and her stomach unclenched. A feeling of sadness swept over her when it dawned on her she might not be the third one. There could have been others before her. She breathed in and out slowly. In just a few days, she had been transformed from a trusting soul to a jaded, suspicious one. *About time,* she thought.

Ed's reaction to the librarian's news was, "Well, well, well, there's a rotten ear in our Indiana corn. Andy's first wife, Meredith, had probably inherited a little something from her parents. It looks like we now have two young women with money and no family who lost their lives within a year of marrying Andy. You narrowly escaped being the third." He paused and looked at her, watching for a reaction. "You okay?"

Deana said, "Makes you wonder if we'll uncover another one, doesn't it? He has to be stopped."

Ed said, "We'll find out more about the accident that took Meredith's life, but it looks like his MO is to stage an accident and avoid getting his hands dirty. That puts him in the category of Bluebeard killers: interested and motivated by profit rather than lust or sadism. See what you can find out about his Greg Irwin alias. Let's get you back to Virginia as planned. I'll feel better if you're settled at Cindy's apartment. I'll fly out to Indiana by myself. This will be enough to convince the FBI to get involved. It looks like two possible murders and a third attempt. I told you, you just never know. Check articles in the Culver paper about the first wife's accident, call the librarian back, and see what you can find out."

Ed paused, raised his eyebrows, and winked at Deana. "I don't have to tell you what to do; you're getting pretty good at this. Tell her I'll be in Culver next week and will want to talk to her and her husband. I'll stop by the nursing home and see what I can find out about the father and who is paying the bills. Your Andy may have had enough of a conscience to pay for his dad's nursing home stay."

Deana cringed and said, "Please, Ed, do not refer to him as *my* Andy. How can you use the word *conscience* in conjunction with a murderer?"

"Sorry," he answered with the proverbial sheepish grin on his face. "Maybe his dad has money, and Andy is waiting for him to die. There may be some attachment to his father or the town he grew up in to bring him back there. Any contact he might have had with his father could help us find him."

She sat down to work on tracing the bad guy who wanted to end her life. She had to smile. Life used to be pretty dull. Cooking for friends and her husband, occasional consulting work, hiking, biking, movies, reading, and French classes to prepare for a trip to France—Andy's first trip out of the States. She had taken a break from the consulting work after their marriage. Andy had wanted them to spend as much time together as possible. At the time, Deana thought it was sweet. Now, she figured it was part of his calculated plan to isolate her. If no one saw her, they wouldn't miss her, and they wouldn't look for her. They would all assume she was wallowing in marital bliss with the accordion-playing Romeo.

She hadn't known a single policeman before this trip. Now, she was on speaking terms with an honest-to-god Mountie, and her sidekick was a retired FBI agent. Linda, Jim, and Jack were three new friends she hoped to have in her life for a long time. She just had to get that life back. To do that meant devoting all her energy, money, and cunning to capturing Andy.

Deana slapped her forehead, remembering Jack's invitation to give her a curling lesson that afternoon. She left a message on his phone explaining that she and Ed were going to take off that evening.

"Call me in Virginia," she said. "I might want to take you up on your offer of shooting lessons. Give me a rain check on the curling!"

CHAPTER 10

The gentle beauty of the Blue Ridge Mountains was a warm and inviting sight from the tiny airplane window. The window framed a picture that kept moving and changing as the plane made its approach. Deana's shoulders dropped, and the tension slipped out of her body. She stared out the window and smiled, thinking about the contrast between the jagged granite peaks of the Rockies and the soft, rounded mountaintops spread out below her. The Rockies took your breath away and made you feel like a teensy tiny part of the universe. The Blue Ridge made you feel like snuggling into a comfortable old couch. Home—home sweet home at last. It was home sweet home, Virginia, but it wouldn't be home sweet home in her own bed.

She glanced at Ed. His arms were folded, eyes closed. His head rested on a pillow sandwiched between his cheek and shoulder. He looked peaceful and harmless. Sleep removed the impression of energy and drive he carried when awake. Ed's words went through Deana's mind as she watched him sleeping. "Do *not* make the mistake of thinking he'll stop trying to kill you." Ed insisted she maintain the disguise they had concocted in Jasper: a brunette wig with shoulder-length straight hair and bangs, glasses, baggy jeans, and a cheap, no-name puffy black ski jacket. The wig made her scalp annoyingly itchy. Her biggest worry was that one of her more aggressive scratching fits would displace it. She patted her head to make sure everything was in place and reminded herself that an itchy scalp was really the least of her problems.

Cindy had insisted they stay at her Watergate apartment. The Watergate was a super-expensive luxury condo building overlooking the Potomac River, just down the street from the State Department, the White House, and across the street from the Kennedy Center. That, as much as the river view and marble floors, attracted the rich and powerful. Ed's response when Deana told him about Cindy's offer to put them up was, "The Watergate? Perfect. They have tight security."

She had looked at him with raised eyebrows and said, "They might not let me in looking like this. They'll think Cindy's running a shelter."

They didn't talk much on the way from the airport. Deana was alone with her thoughts and Ed with his. She used to poke fun at Cindy for living in a yuppie stronghold. The Watergate offered its residents the security and safety that would satisfy the most paranoid celebrity or public figure. Cindy lived there to be close to the wealthy and powerful. They were valuable contacts in her job. Deana wouldn't poke fun at the Watergate anymore. She was thankful to have a safe place to sleep while they continued the search for Andy.

The evening traffic was backed up on the highway, but their taxi flew down the HOV lane. Deana hunched forward, looking out the window, and started drumming her fingers on the car door. The sense of rush and urgency that was part of the rhythm in the bustling city she called her home made her forget how tired she was. She considered what it would be like to live in a small town instead of the busy city she knew. Yet, in barely a week in supposedly peaceful Jasper, she had experienced more excitement and danger than in a lifetime in Washington, D.C. People talked about chucking the city life for the slower pace of small towns. Linda, Jim, and Jack had done just that. No one ever said, "I'd like to chuck it all in and move to New York or Washington, D.C."

She sat back in the seat and closed her eyes, considering it was people and their kindness that made you want to be in one place versus another. In spite of the scary nights in the wilderness, any bad memories of Jasper were edged to the side by warm memories of time spent with Linda, Jim, and Jack. *Ah yes, Jack,* she thought, sensing a little ping in her heart or brain. She wasn't sure what she was feeling but shook it off. No time for romance now.

Ed didn't want her anywhere near her neighborhood, but she wanted to see her home, even if it was from the back seat of a cab. So much had happened and changed in the last week. She had a strong need to know that some part of her world was stable. She had lived there for years before marrying Andy and was confused about whether the bad memories associated with him would be too much for the many good pre-Andy memories. Ed finally agreed to drive by the town house before they crossed the river and headed to Cindy's apartment.

The cab pulled up in front of what Deana once might have thought of as a safe place—her historic Alexandria town house—close to people, restaurants, theatre, music, and shopping.

"Here we are, Ed. Home sweet home," Deana said in a flat voice. She gestured to the front gate. Light from gas lamps cast a soft glow, which had always seemed nostalgic and homey. Now, the flickering light from the old-fashioned lamps gave her goose bumps. Andy could be hiding in or around the house. The red brick walls and the solid wooden door had lost the promise of hidden safety and warmth. Looking at the door, an image of the opening to the cave flashed through her mind. She shivered inside the warm cab.

Ed asked the cab driver to pull into a space across the street from Deana's town house. "I just want to check something," he said and asked for the house keys. "You stay in the cab. The brown hair and baggy clothes might work in an area where he isn't looking for you. Around your own home, he would recognize you."

He told the driver to lock the doors. Deana and the taxi driver watched Ed walk around the side of the front steps and jump onto the landing from the side. After a few moments, he jogged back to the cab and instructed the driver to take off.

"There's a surveillance camera focused on your entryway. You know anything about it?" he asked.

She shook her head no. She immediately understood Andy had beaten them to the house.

Ed looked at her and said, "Later." They would talk about the camera at Cindy's.

From the street, the Watergate looked like any other high-rise office building. Inside was a different story. The doorman wore a tailored black suit. He opened the door to a lobby with marble floors, sparkling chandeliers, and oriental rugs. It had the feel of an elegant living room. There was no hum or buzz of activity in the air. A young woman dressed in a black pantsuit and crisp white blouse stood up behind her antique desk. If you listened carefully, you heard the sounds of a piano recording. It wasn't Muzak; it was Bach. To her credit, she welcomed them without a withering toe-to-head appraisal and said Cindy was expecting them.

Deana figured the Watergate residents probably didn't entertain many guests looking as scruffy as the two of them. They were not sporting designer clothes or designer haircuts and wheeled cheap black canvas carry-on suitcases with squeaky wheels.

As they turned to leave, the door behind the receptionist opened. Deana got a glimpse of a wall of video screens that showed locations within the building. The man who came through the door was big and burly. His head was shaved, and his black suit flapped open to reveal a handgun. Normally Deana would have found him scary. Now, his appearance was so comforting she wanted to run up and hug him in spite of the fierce scowl that looked like it was a permanent part of his face. The luxury oasis of peace and gentility had a scary-looking protector who was more comforting to her than all the plush surroundings.

Cindy greeted them warmly at the door. She snatched the wig from Deana's head and said, "That's better." She put her arms around her friend and pulled her into the apartment.

As soon as they stepped into the apartment, Ed whistled and walked over to a wall of windows that looked over the Potomac River. His eyes ran over the brightly colored modern furnishings. He turned to Cindy. "Deana's lucky to have a good friend like you."

She met his gaze and said, "She'd do the same for me." She had set up a large banquet table in one of the guest rooms. There was a phone, desktop computer, printer, and office supplies neatly arranged on the table. "I thought you could work here," she said.

Cindy looked at her watch and left for a dinner event. Ed and

Deana sat down at the worktable. He confirmed her fear that Andy was responsible for the surveillance camera at the town house. "He beat us here. He doesn't know me, and I think I avoided the camera. It was set up to capture the front door. He probably has it configured to transmit to a TV monitor. He could be anywhere, but I'll bet he's close enough to react quickly once he knows where you are. We'll talk to the detective about it. We may be able to lure Andy into the house if he thinks you're there." Deana left Ed to get settled and collapsed on the bed.

Ed was at the kitchen table finishing a plate of eggs when Deana strolled in around 9:30 in the morning. He updated her on his plans for the day. He had already spoken to Jack.

"I know Jack is coming out here in a few days. I told him I would get you set up with a gun. He agreed to help you with shooting lessons when he's here. I'll be in Indiana when Jack gets here, so that will work out perfectly." They had a meeting with the detective assigned to the case. Ed wanted to get the ball rolling on the court order. After that, they would drive out to Culpeper and buy a gun from a man named Snooky who sold guns out of his basement office.

Deana looked at him and asked, "Snooky? He doesn't live at Deer Ranch, does he?"

"Yes, as a matter of fact, he does," Ed said, disbelief creeping into his eyes and voice. "You don't mean to say you know Snooky?"

"Well, not exactly," she answered. She told him about the hunter education class and Kimberly's dad's invitation to hunt with them *after* she took shooting lessons from Snooky. "I didn't really think I would get interested in hunting, but I did want to learn how to handle a gun." She rolled her eyes and, in an attempt at sick humor, said, "Now, it looks like I will be hunting my ex-husband."

"Deana, this is for your protection," Ed said sternly. "You are not hunting down your ex-husband. Understood?"

She held both hands, palms up, and saluted Ed to show she did understand. She shrugged her shoulders and couldn't help adding, "I just can't believe I'm buying a gun from a man named Snooky."

"Hey," Ed said, "you mentioned Andy used an indoor shooting range in Chantilly. This is legal and safer for you than standing around in a busy gun store and running into Andy by accident. Snooky's a retired cop. We worked together on a case, and he helped us set up a successful sting operation. We caught the killer, but Snooky ended up on disability. Now, he sells guns and teaches people how to use them safely."

They drove back across the river to Alexandria to meet with the detective assigned to the case.

"I'll be honest with you," Detective Kate McAdams said, "we don't usually work with private investigators. You checked out. We do work with the FBI, and Randy Doran said you were okay." She hesitated. "Well, actually more than okay. He said your client is a lucky woman," she finished, extending her hand to shake hands with Ed.

Deana didn't alter the complacent expression on her face, but she thought if one more person told her how lucky she was, she would scream.

Kate's shiny black hair was cut short. The gelled, spiky style had the same effect as Ed's military buzz cut. They were two peas in a pod: efficient, no-nonsense investigators. The wrinkles on Kate's forehead and around her eyes made Deana guess her to be in her mid-thirties. Her pale white complexion was set off by her clothes: black slacks, black turtleneck, black shoes. Her only concession to glamour was the chunky gold earrings she wore. The other accessory, a shoulder holster holding her 9mm gun, looked as comfortable on her as a gold necklace might have looked on another woman.

She looked as fit as Ed and shared his confident manner. They didn't waste time on small talk or grabbing a cup of coffee. Ed talked, and Kate asked questions about the case.

Their conversation made it clear they were very serious about the threat of Andy surfacing to arrange another accident. Ed's comment, reminding Deana of the danger of becoming a forgotten victim, played in her head: "Deana, investigations die when there is no one pushing the case. So far, we suspect Andy of two other murders. Any serious investigation of those murders died with the victims. They may be on the books as cold cases, but nothing will happen unless someone calls attention to them. Andy knows that."

Kate and Ed agreed to work on several fronts. Armed with a court order, Kate would go to the offices of the online dating service. She agreed to let Ed and Deana follow her to the offices, but they could not go inside with her.

"We don't want to risk contaminating the chain of evidence," she explained. "If this goes to trial, it could create problems if the victim was present during interviews. It could raise suspicions that you tampered with the evidence."

Kate agreed with Ed that Andy's master plan for meeting women might yield valuable information to help them catch him. She had no objection to letting Ed and Deana continue some of the grunt work involved in researching women Andy might have contacted.

Ed told Kate about the surveillance camera aimed at Deana's front door and his idea for a sting operation. Kate said, "Great idea! We'll set it up right away."

She hesitated and leaned forward. If a twinkle in the eye could be described as steely, that was the look in Kate's eyes. She obviously was getting a kick out of the idea she had. She glanced at Ed with a smile and then at Deana.

"You'll go in your house with another woman, one of our police-women. She'll stay, and you'll exit in her clothes and the same wig she'll wear going into the house." She looked at Deana with a raised eyebrow. Deana nodded to show she understood. "Kind of corny, but we'll use his trick to catch him. I think we can rig up a couple of cameras in the fence that will pick up anyone coming through the front and rear doors. Then we wait for Mr. Harris to make a move. When the policewoman gets in, she can check for listening devices and disable them."

"Okay, it sounds good to me," Deana said and looked at Ed.

He said, "Good plan, Kate. I like it."

Kate wanted to continue looking for suspicious deaths of other young brides. She would contact the police in Indiana and Mt. Rogers to get copies of any official police reports. She had already requested a court order through a circuit court judge to access payment records at the retirement home where Andy's dad was living. Ed started to tell her he wanted to meet and talk to Stephanie Randall's friend Michelle Grant.

Kate held up her hands and said, "Don't tell me about it. I can't take you with me on calls, and I can't control what you do on your own. I just ask you report to me any relevant information you're able to uncover. As of right now, Michelle Grant's case is not part of your case. If you find something that helps build the case for probable cause, that's great, but be careful."

Ed looked at Deana and said, "Let's go, Tonto." She rolled her eyes but had to admit to a twinge of excitement to be in on the hunt.

They followed Kate's car to Arlington, a suburb of Washington, D.C. It was in the wealthiest county in the United States, next to the nation's capital, but it looked and felt like a seedy, run-down neighborhood. Trash was blowing around in the streets, and boarded-up windows on the second floor of the building contrasted with the smiling faces of smartly dressed professionals on the company's Web page. Ed's only comment while they waited for Kate was, "The wired world sure does make it easy to deceive people. From the Web page you would never know it's a two-bit operation."

Kate came back out after only a half hour and motioned for them to follow her. She led them to a more upscale part of town where they found a table at a coffee shop.

"The headquarters for the dating service is staffed by exactly two people. I'm surprised they even bothered with office space. They could have run the business from their kitchen tables. The young man and woman were eager to help. They want to avoid bad publicity for their business."

Kate had a copy of Andy's registration and password to the dating service, giving her access to all the women he had contacted. She now also had the addresses and phone numbers of the women who had responded to Andy's initial email to them. Kate planned to interview all the women. She showed the list of names to Deana and asked if she recognized any of them. Deana pointed to Cindy's name.

Kate's eyebrow went up. "The woman who introduced you to Andy, right?"

Ed answered the question. "Yes, she did. We're staying at her apartment at the Watergate. I know what you're thinking. Cindy's okay. She's not involved with Andy."

Kate made another face. "Maybe you shouldn't be staying there. If she went out with him, he knows where she lives."

"You're right," Ed said, "he knows where Cindy lives. He's never been in the apartment. If he shows up there, I'll be ready for him."

"Your call," Kate said, but she didn't sound convinced it was a good idea. Kate returned to her office and left them with a promise of keeping them informed.

Ed and Deana returned to the makeshift office at the Watergate. "Deana, Kate has her hands full, and she'll do a thorough job; however, I still want to snoop around Andy's home town. We may find out more from talking to people in person. If Andy had been in trouble as a juvenile, those records would have been destroyed by now. The only way to find out if there was an indicator of his aberrant behavior is to talk to people who knew him.

"I'd like to find out what kind of accident caused his first wife's death. See what you can dig up on that, and I'll check in with Snooky. I thought we'd pick up your gun this afternoon. Snooky has a covered range on his property. I told him about Jack and the shooting lessons he conducts in Jasper. Between the two of them, even if you're not completely comfortable handling a gun, you'll hit your target and not your foot." He winked and slipped off his jacket.

"Have you had that thing on all day?" Deana asked, pointing to his shoulder holster and gun.

"Yep. I feel naked without it. It's when you think you don't need it that you need it."

"I thought we were safe here?"

"I don't want to take that for granted. If someone can talk their way past the front desk, you're not safe." Ed paused. "See what you can find out about that accident in Indiana."

Deana said, "Yes, sir," and saluted him. "First, I need to take about thirty minutes to organize what's left of my investments. You want to get paid, right?"

Ed took over the office Cindy had set up for them. Deana sat down at a desk in the bedroom with her laptop. She called the realtor in Florida and told her to sell the oceanfront condo in Sanibel Island, Florida. Deana gritted her teeth as she listened to the realtor's dismayed response.

"Deana, no, you love that place. It may sound crazy for a realtor to talk a client out of a sale, but I hate to see you lose it. Could you rent it out—anything to help you hold on to it?"

"Thanks, Ginger. Please don't make this any harder. I'll explain everything some other time."

Deana was surprised at how much the property had appreciated. It was a relief to know the realtor expected it to sell quickly. One million dollars would take care of all the money problems. *What a stupid schmuck,* Deana thought. *Andy settled for $2.5 million.* She felt another twinge of relief that she found out about him sooner rather than later. A loss of $2.5 million was a small price to pay to still be alive.

Deana smiled at the sound of Ed's voice talking on the phone. It was a comforting background noise. She turned to her laptop to see if there was anything online about the alleged accident in Indiana. She started with a Google search on Andy's first wife, Meredith Givens. The idea of Google searches made her squirm. It felt like an invasion of privacy, but she knew Ed was right. If they established a profile for women Andy targeted, it could help lead them to him. And it was personal. Deana wanted to know why he had picked her and what she had in common with his other victims. She entered the maiden name of Andy's first wife, Meredith Givens, and waited for a response. Ed insisted that leads to cases were usually from "a shot in the dark." The more they knew about the women in Andy's life and the circumstances of their deaths, the easier it would be to understand his MO. Deana shivered, considering the possibility young Meredith might have been his first victim. She tilted her head to one side and stared out the window for a second. It was only fitting that she, Andy's most recent target, was doing research on the woman who was possibly his first victim.

There was nothing on Givens. She did find a newspaper article about the caving accident in which Meredith Irwin died. At the time, it caused an uproar over the difficulty of the cave for amateur spelunkers. The cave was subsequently closed. Ed would be able to get more information when he got to Indiana. Deana stood up, stretched, and headed for Ed's make-shift office to give him an update when the phone started ringing and the doorbell chimed. She reached for the phone and heard Ed call out, "I'll get the door. Stay in your room."

It was Lowell on the phone. He just got out the words *We've found your rental car,* when she heard a muted pop, something heavy falling with a thud, a loud bang, and then silence.

Deana dropped the phone and scrambled to push away from the desk. "Damn," she groaned. She had rammed her shin bone on the edge of the desk. Rubbing it, she stumbled to the open door. The sight made her forget the aching shin.

Ed was flat out on his stomach, a gun next to his hand. Deana was frozen for a second. She screamed, "Shit!" and moved toward Ed. Her foot caught on something. She fell to her knees. Her mouth opened but nothing came out. A body, a woman's body, was face down next to her. Deana was so close she could smell the blood pooling around the small hole in the back of the woman's head.

Cindy's going to kill me, flashed through her mind at the sight of the blood soaking into the white carpet. Deana's hand was inches from the gun that lay next to the woman. She started to reach for it and pulled her hand back. She wasn't afraid of the gun. An instinct she didn't understand but listened to warned her that it wouldn't be a good idea for her fingerprints to be on the woman's gun.

"Ed, Ed, no, no," tumbled out of her mouth as she scrambled to Ed's side. She knew Ed had saved her life. The woman shot Ed to get to her. She didn't hesitate to put her hand on Ed's wrist. There was a pulse. He was still alive.

Deana's eyes were fixed on the back of Ed's head. She touched his back and bent her head next to his.

"Hang in there, Ed. Help is on the way." Maybe he heard her and maybe not. She pushed herself to her feet and pounded the intercom button that connected the front desk to the condo. Staring at the blood that transferred from her hand to the button, she gulped and screamed, "Get an ambulance here right away! Two people have been shot. Get up here right away. I need help!"

The expression on her face hardened as her gaze went from Ed to the woman. She forced herself to step back to the woman, knelt down, and put her fingers on the side of the woman's neck. There was no sign of life.

"Dead, she's dead." Deana murmured, yet she felt nothing for the woman. Instinctively, Deana knew this was the woman helping Andy. Deana turned back to Ed. Without thinking, she knelt down and pushed and pulled him onto his back. "No blood," she said out loud.

Then she saw the hole in his chest and just a small amount of blood coming from the hole. Ed's eyes fluttered open and closed. Deana was frantic. She couldn't think of anything to do but remain at his side and talk to him.

"Hang in there, Ed," she whispered, hanging on to his warm arm for a second and getting comfort from his pulse. "Help is on the way. Hang in there."

She felt helpless and useless. She didn't know anything about first aid. It looked like Ed was going to die trying to save her life.

Deana was holding on to Ed's hand when the security guard from the front desk entered the room. He had his gun drawn but quickly holstered it when Deana spoke.

"Please do something."

He looked at her as if he wasn't sure whether she was a threat or not. "Are you hurt?" he asked, pointing to the blood smeared on her hands.

"No, no," Deana answered and gestured to Ed and the woman's body. If she tried to say any more, the tears would start.

The guard checked Ed's pulse and then the woman's for signs of life. He called the police. Deana heard him talking as if he were a million miles away instead of in the same room. She closed her eyes after he told the police the scene was secure, and one gunshot victim was alive.

He turned the phone off, looked at the woman's body, and a garment bag on the floor. "Crap. That's the woman with clothes from Neiman Marcus for Ms. Prescott. I called the apartment, and a man answered. I told him I was sending her up with the clothes."

Within a few minutes police were at the apartment, but there was no sign of medical help. Deana gently put Ed's hand down and stood up. "Where's the ambulance? He's dying." She started shaking, arms hanging at her side, fists clenched.

The officer who appeared to be in charge motioned for her to be quiet and told another officer to call in the paramedics from the staging area. "Ma'am, we have to make sure the scene is secure before we bring in the paramedics."

The man who gave the orders pulled Deana aside, and everyone started ripping out gloves and putting them on. The scene was surreal and busy. Deana half heard fragments of conversations. An officer said, "Nine mm Luger with a homemade muffler silencer." She turned to look. He was pointing at the gun next to the woman's body. Another voice said, "I found the second bullet, fired from the Glock. Looks like a Hydra-Shok bullet."

After a few minutes, the paramedics arrived, secured Ed's body to a backboard, hooked up an IV bag, and took him to the hospital.

"I want to go with him. Where are you taking him?" Deana insisted. The man she thought seemed to be in charge stepped toward her and identified himself as Detective Wheeler. He was a big, beefy guy wearing a wrinkled brown suit, a once-white shirt—now yellowed with age and washing—and an out-of-style wide brown tie with blue stripes. His belly hung over his pants. There would have been no hope of buttoning the suit jacket. He looked sloppy, but his eyes told a different story. They were alert and cunning. He led Deana into the dining area, keeping his eyes directed at her face, watching her reactions.

Deana sat down at the table, expecting him to do the same. Instead, he rested his backside on the edge of the table and gave her a steely stare.

Deana didn't say anything. She closed her eyes and hid her face in her hands. He was trying to intimidate her, but she was too worried about Ed to be angry. Detective Wheeler saw two gunshot victims and a woman with blood on her hands. That was all he knew. In his eyes, she was a suspect.

"I need you to tell me what happened," he said, eyes narrowed and unfriendly.

Deana explained the bizarre sequence of events. She heard her voice as she answered his questions. It was the voice of a robot—dead and empty. When he asked why someone would want to kill her, she told him to call Detective Kate McAdams.

At the mention of Kate's name, Detective Wheeler looked at her with his dark brown unruly eyebrows raised in a question. "Detective McAdams? You're a friend of hers?"

Deana started to explain. Wheeler put up the palm of his hand, indicating she should stop talking.

"I'll ask her myself." He called Kate's number. In a less than friendly voice Deana heard him say, "McAdams. Wheeler here. You know a Deana Harris?"

He kept his eyes on Deana as he listened to Kate. After a few minutes, he moved into the hallway out of earshot.

Deana looked at the blood on her hands. Some of it was from the woman, and some of it was Ed's. She knew she should wash the blood off, but she didn't have the energy. She wanted Wheeler to come back so that she could get to the hospital. Wash your hands, she ordered herself, and walked into the kitchen.

Detective Wheeler walked back in as she was watching the water, tinged a light red, running down the drain.

"What are you doing?" he barked.

"I ... My hands were covered in blood. I had to wash them."

Wheeler shook his head. He looked at her with a knowing smile. He gestured for her to move back into the living room. As she walked back to take a seat, she heard him say, "A little water clears us of this deed. How easy it is then!"

Deana stopped and turned to look at him.

"Lady Macbeth," he said.

Deana was shocked. She stared at Wheeler, thinking she needed to hold her tongue and not say what she was thinking: *I know it's Macbeth. I'm surprised someone with your charm and sensitivity knows Shakespeare.* His comment meant he wanted her to know he didn't trust her. He had just finished talking to Kate. What had Kate told him? Kate knew Deana wouldn't have done anything to hurt Ed. She refused to rise to Wheeler's taunt.

He read from his notes and said, "The first sound you heard was the woman firing the gun with a silencer. You heard Mr. Robbins' body fall and a loud bang. Mr. Robbins was face down; you turned him over." He stopped and fixed his eyes on her. "You shouldn't have done that." He let that sink in for a couple of seconds and continued. "What I don't understand yet is how Mr. Robbins was shot in the chest and ended up on his stomach."

Deana looked at him and naively asked, "Why? Why not?"

"Ma'am, the chest shot would have thrown him back and he would have landed on his back."

"But he might have rolled over to pull out his gun and shot from his stomach," she said slowly, thinking it out as she spoke. She was getting the sinking feeling that Detective Wheeler did consider her a suspect. And Kate, what did Kate really think?

He took a step toward her, leaned over quickly, and sniffed her arms like a dog.

"What, what are you doing?" she asked. Before the words were out, it clicked; he was checking for the smell of gunpowder on her clothes. That's why he was so angry about her washing her hands. She stood up and shoved both arms under his nose. "Here—take a good smell. I didn't shoot him!"

"Okay, okay," Detective Wheeler said. "Calm down. We'll confirm the sequence when we talk to Mr. Robbins." He flipped his pad shut and looked at Deana with a face devoid of emotion.

She had the uncomfortable feeling he still didn't believe her, but she was more worried about Ed. "Will Ed be okay?"

The detective shrugged. "He was alive when they carried him out of here, and they are very good at handling gunshot injuries. Unfortunately, they get a lot of practice in this town. I'd say he has a good chance."

He saluted Deana with his pad and turned to walk away from her. Then he did what can best be described as a Colombo maneuver. Pad still in hand, he turned and asked in a soft voice, "Why would someone you don't know want to kill your friend?"

"I … I don't know," Deana stuttered. "I think she was after me. Didn't you talk to Kate?"

"Yes," he said, again in the same quiet voice, "but I wanted to know what you think."

Deana just shook her head; now she felt sure she was a suspect. Without Ed, it was just her version of events. She wanted Ed to recover because he was her friend and protector. Now, she needed him to recover to corroborate her story.

Standing in a corner, arms wrapped around her body, Deana watched the police finish up their crime scene work. Her eyes followed the police as they carried the woman's body out of the apartment. She groaned when she remembered she had left Lowell hanging on the phone. Then there was the small matter of explaining the whole mess to Cindy. Her stomach tightened, and pains shot through it when she thought about Cindy and realized her friend could have been shot. She shook the thought out of her head and forced herself to listen to Detective Wheeler. He asked if she recognized the woman.

"I don't know," Deana answered tiredly. "I haven't seen her face."

"Well, ma'am, that's a problem. Your friend, Mr. Robbins, was shooting Hydra-Shok bullets. They are designed to do a lot of damage when they exit." He paused, "I'll put it this way, there won't be an open coffin at her funeral."

Cindy arrived in time to convince Detective Wheeler to let them stay in another apartment in the Watergate. In the first sign that maybe he didn't consider Deana a suspect, he looked at Cindy. "All right. They have tightened up security at the front desk. No deliveries will be allowed to the units. However, whoever is doing this could try to get to Deana through you, so I need to warn you to also be careful."

Cindy gave him a curt nod and moved to put her arms around her friend. Deana pulled away and moved to look through Ed's papers. She found the photo of the woman looking for her in the Jasper Hospital and handed it to Detective Wheeler. "Is this her?"

Detective Wheeler agreed it did look like the woman on the surveillance tape at the front desk. Her identity remained a mystery. He explained they would run her fingerprints and hope she was in the system.

Deana gathered up the computers and research material and followed Cindy to an apartment on another floor. The Watergate kept furnished apartments available for visiting dignitaries. This one was furnished with an elaborate security system that covered every room in the apartment. The manager helped them set the security codes. Now, they had to figure out how to shake off the evening's horror.

Cindy surprised Deana. Her beautiful home was a disaster and her life disrupted. She put her hands on Deana's shoulders and said, "Deana, I'm just glad you're alive. I'll admit, I thought you and Ed were a little over the top in worrying about Andy. I figured he got the money and was long gone. Please do exactly what the police advise from now on, and don't go off on your own trying to solve this."

CHAPTER 11

"**C**indy," Deana said, "I can't stay here. It's too dangerous for you. I'll move to a hotel."

Cindy smiled at her friend, walked over to the table, and opened her designer leather tote bag. She turned, holding a small gun cradled in her right hand.

"There are a few things you don't know about me, girlfriend," she said, eyes twinkling. "I can take care of myself. I don't advertise the fact that I'm carrying a gun, but I always have it with me. I'm alone a lot at night in the museum and driving home late. Years ago, I decided to be prepared. My dad taught me to shoot when I was a kid. If I want to, I can go out with your buddies from hunter ed and bring dinner home. I don't like to advertise—conflicts with my image." She removed and held up her three-inch heels.

The next morning, Deana woke up feeling lousy. She and Cindy had dealt with the bizarre situation in an admittedly juvenile way by drinking too much and eating their version of comfort food—pizza and ice cream. Cindy couldn't stop saying, "It's all my fault. I'm so sorry." She felt guilty for introducing Deana to Andy. Deana kept apologizing for exposing her to life-threatening danger, bullet holes and blood in her apartment. To these she added displacing her and upsetting her life and work.

Deana gulped a cup of coffee and headed to the hospital to check on Ed. There was no ex-wife or family to rush to his side. That meant there wouldn't be anyone holding his hand when she got to his room. No one to look up and stare at her, resent her for putting him in the hospital. Ed wouldn't blame her, and that made her feel even worse.

Deana poked her head around the door to Ed's room. The voice of a man speaking softly made her stop and listen. "Hang in there, Ed. You're going to be okay. Remember that time I got shot, and you tore up the shirt you were wearing to make a tourniquet? Then you complained I owed you a new shirt. You get better, and I'll buy you any shirt you want."

Deana smiled and waited to hear Ed's response. There was no sound. She closed her eyes, let out the breath she was holding, and forced herself to step into the room. Randy was putting on his coat. "You must be Deana. Randy Doran. Ed and I go way back."

Deana didn't acknowledge his greeting. Her eyes were on Ed's still body, moving from the breathing tube to his usually ruddy face. His face was now drained of color. *Like a corpse,* Deana thought, and shivered. Finally, she glanced at Randy and then moved to touch Ed's hand.

"He'll make it," Randy said. "He's a tough old bird."

She forced herself to turn and meet Randy's eyes.

"I'm so sorry," she managed to say.

Randy's clothes looked like they had been thrown on in a hurry. A baggy Nationals sweatshirt and jeans hung on his skinny frame. He had rushed to the hospital after a call from Kate. Deana shrugged. It had been an act of kindness for Kate to get in touch with Ed's old friend. There really was a heart beating under Kate's tough-girl demeanor.

Randy told her Ed had lost a lot of blood and would be unconscious for at least twenty-four hours. Once his condition stabilized, the breathing tube would be removed, and he would be able to talk. Surgery had been done to determine the extent of the damage to his chest. He had been very lucky. He was alive and would recover. There wasn't anything Deana could do for him.

Randy spoke quietly. "Ed told me all about the case and his suspicions. I've set up a meeting with Detective McAdams later this afternoon." He touched her shoulder. She let him guide her to the door. "You can come back later. I'll drop you off at the Watergate."

Deana noticed Randy checking the car mirrors as he drove. She remembered Ed had told her Randy started out with the FBI twenty years ago in the Washington office and ended up being a bureau chief, responsible for tracking money laundering. After growing tired of government paper fraud cases, he requested a transfer from Washington to Richmond. Ed had chuckled when he said Randy thought middle America was a better breeding ground for interesting cases than D.C. After hearing about Randy's track record, Deana expected to meet a fit, stern-looking, prototypical FBI agent with a bud sticking out of his ear.

Ed's old friend was a small, wiry guy with an easy, open manner. Alert eyes took in everything from behind steel-rimmed glasses. The clue to his background as an agent was the way he drove. He took what she knew was not a direct route to the Watergate, making last-minute turns without signaling. They arrived safely in spite of the fact that Randy's eyes seemed to be looking behind and around them instead of on the road in front of them. His head swiveled around one more time before he opened the car door for her. One hand on her elbow, he escorted her to the entrance and turned her over to the big burly security guard.

He asked the guard to make sure Deana got to the apartment safely. To Deana he said, "Kate will be in touch."

Deana thought, *Yeah, sure, you and Kate will keep me filled in on all the latest developments.* She slid the dead bolt in place and thought about what to do over the next few days. Jack would arrive from Jasper that afternoon. She hoped Snooky would still be willing to let them come out to practice as planned. And Snooky would now know how important it was for her to be able to protect herself. Someone had to let Snooky know about Ed's condition. The unpleasant task had fallen to her.

Her first call, however, was to a lawyer. It was the lawyer who had drawn up her will and handled real estate transactions. Deana asked him to start the annulment proceedings. He wasn't a friend, just a business associate, but he couldn't help saying, "Deana. Don't get married again."

Chastising herself for putting off giving the bad news to Snooky, she punched in his number. Snooky didn't say anything for a few seconds after Deana explained Ed's condition. When he finally spoke, Deana heard a slight southern drawl in the deep voice. "We'll get you set up with a gun. I'll come in to see Ed after we take care of you. That's what Ed would want."

Deana decided Ed would want someone to go to Indiana. If she went, she could stay in touch with Kate on her cell phone, and Kate wouldn't know where she was. It would require Cindy's cooperation, but Deana knew she could count on her friend.

Deana reached for the phone again to call the librarian in Indiana. This time, she explained the whole sordid mess to her. The woman's reaction was, "You poor thing. My husband always said there was something funny about Meredith's death."

The librarian was eager to help. Deana asked her to collect any newspaper articles about Greg Irwin and Meredith Givens. Deana told her she would be there in a couple of days. Crossing her fingers, she explained that Ed was sick and wouldn't be able to make the trip. Sick was an understatement.

Deana grimaced at the thought of Ed fighting for his life in the hospital. He would be pulling tubes and wires out of his body and stumbling out of the hospital if he knew she was planning to take the trip to Indiana by herself. She remembered the gun education conversation with Ed. "Learning to handle a gun doesn't make you qualified or capable of conducting your own investigation. You're not a trained, experienced professional. Don't get a false sense of security and don't go off by yourself."

Deana thought, *Just sit here and do nothing?. Not in the plan.* At least she would have a gun and shooting lessons before traveling to Andy's home town. It would mean driving to Indiana instead of flying if she wanted to have a gun handy. After all that had happened, pepper spray was no longer her weapon of choice.

Deana's eyebrows lifted in surprise when she saw a call coming from Kate. Maybe she really would keep her up-to-date.

"Deana, the rental car was found in a long-term parking garage in Calgary. It had been wiped clean, and they weren't able to pick up any fingerprints. On this end, Detective Wheeler found the taxi driver who dropped the shooter at the Watergate. He picked up the fare at Neiman Marcus. The garment bag has the store's name on it, but none of the clothes had tags on them, and no one in the store recognized the woman as a recent customer. The silencer on the gun was homemade. I'm assuming Andy put it together. The woman was probably planning on doing the job and slipping out and into a taxi or just walking away. We're running her fingerprints. We'll know within a couple of days if she's in the system."

Deana absorbed all the information. "What about the undercover agent in my town house?"

"No developments there. She didn't find any other cameras or recording equipment inside. We'll pull her out of there tonight."

Deana sighed. "Thanks, Kate. Thanks for letting me know what's going on."

"You're welcome. Oh, Detective Wheeler wanted me to tell you he's sorry for being a little rough on you. You were his best suspect at the time." Kate chuckled. "That's pretty big coming from Wheeler. I don't think I've ever heard him apologize to anyone."

Deana said with deliberate sarcasm, "Please tell him no hard feelings. Kate, are you going to send anyone to Indiana?"

"It's a good idea, but I can't send someone out there. There is no justification. Meredith Givens Irwin's death was recorded as an accident. An autopsy was not performed, and we can't request one unless we can uncover probable cause."

"An autopsy? Isn't it too late for that?" Deana asked.

Kate sighed and answered the question. "It depends on the type of trauma or injury. An autopsy can distinguish between accidental and deliberate trauma. The medical examiner and police may have had suspicions but not enough solid evidence to order an autopsy. If there is a strong enough pattern to establish probable cause, we can order one. Like I said, right now, Andy's first wife's demise is not a high priority. We need to establish a relationship between Ed's shooter and Mr. Harris. We also need to take another look at Stephanie Randall's death." She stopped talking, and there was silence. Deana figured Kate was having second thoughts about wasting time explaining police procedure to an amateur.

"Enough," Kate finally said. "Ed would want you to stay put at the Watergate, and that's what where we want you too. Let us do our job."

Deana thanked her and sat down to think. Kate had just given her another reason to justify a trip to Indiana. A little investigation might uncover the evidence needed to initiate an autopsy. There was work to do to get ready for the trip down the dark road to Andy's past.

Deana answered a call from Cindy. "Hey, girlfriend! I must say, you sure don't waste any time!"

Jack had called Cindy and turned down an invitation to dinner, excusing himself on the grounds that he wanted to check with Deana first. Deana's protests that she and Jack were just friends met with "Yeah, sure!"

Cindy finished her teasing with, "Well, he is definitely a nicer human being than Andy. I never said anything, but I always thought there was something off about that guy."

Deana thought about Jack and wondered how comfortable he would be in her world. Andy was never interested in spending time with her friends. He always said he wanted to keep her to himself. She had the feeling Jack would fit in anywhere. She had planned to take both Ed and Jack to dinner and to show them around the city. Now, she would be alone with Jack. She was looking forward to seeing him again but was a little nervous about being alone with him. Right now, she needed a friend, not a romance, in spite of Cindy's encouragement and her own feelings for Jack.

Thinking about Jack reminded her she owed Jim and Linda a call. She knew Kate had been in contact with Lowell. Jim and Linda probably already knew about Ed, but Ed was their friend, and they deserved to hear everything from her. As soon as she heard Jim's calm voice, she pictured the kind man with a nasty scar running across his face and burst into tears.

Jim let her cry until the sobs turned to sniffles. He said, "Jack called us. We know what happened. We're just glad you're all right. Don't worry. Ed will recover." Deana promised to keep them up-to-date on Ed's condition.

Deana drove south out of the city in a rental car and relaxed once she was past the heavy traffic that surrounded Washington. Snooky's directions led her to his farm outside the town of Culpeper. The last time she drove south out of northern Virginia was to attend the hunter education class in Madison, a few miles south of Culpeper. It was just a few months ago. A lot had happened in those few months. Deana knew she had changed in that time. No longer naïve and stronger than she had thought she was, she knew she could get through anything.

The interstate turned into a sleepy four-lane highway surrounded by fields covered with a dusting of snow. The exit for Snooky's house put her on a narrow country road. She slowed down, looking for a mailbox covered in a camo paint design. Snooky had said, "It's a camo mailbox on the right. You can't miss it."

"You can't miss it" usually means you do, Deana thought. But this time, she spotted it. She turned onto a gravel driveway and drove through a heavy metal gate pushed open on either side of the driveway. She hit the brake when she saw a large orange and black "No Trespassing" sign hanging on one side of the gate. On the other side of the gate there was a small hand-painted sign that said "Deer Ranch." Deer Ranch didn't appear to welcome unwanted guests. She continued another five hundred yards and pulled up in front of a ranch-style home dwarfed by the low structure next to it. The muffled gunshots meant it had to be the shooting range. Deana shook her head and walked up the sidewalk to the house.

The door opened. A tall man with a completely bald head peered at her from over the top of his reading glasses.

"Deana, come on in," he said. "I'm Snooky." He waved her into the house without shaking her hand. He wasn't fat, but he had a little paunch, which, combined with the reading glasses, made him look more like a grandfather than a retired cop with his own shooting range.

She didn't notice Snooky's disability until they sat down to talk. He picked up his left hand and placed it on the desk. Her gaze lingered a second too long, and he offered, "Lost my hand in the last case I worked. That's where I met Ed. This one's just for show." He smiled, "But I haven't lost my mind, and I can still shoot."

Deana told him about Ed's planned trip to Indiana. She asked him to explain how, after ten years, an autopsy could show Meredith Givens' head trauma was not an accident. He pointed to the metal edge of a gun safe and said, "If I shove your head onto that hard surface, the injury will be different from the injury you receive if you slip and fall on it. You said she suffered a head injury from a fall in a cave. The autopsy might end up showing deliberate trauma."

If an autopsy showed Meredith Givens's death was not an accident, it would be enough to get the FBI involved in the case. Deana wondered if Stephanie Randall's body had been cremated or whether exhuming it would yield further evidence of another murder disguised as an accident.

She left carrying a 9mm resting inside a case and a box of shells. She laid the gun and shells on the back seat and picked them up again. Turning to Snooky, she asked, "Uh, should I put this in the trunk? Is it okay to drive around with a gun in the car? I mean, I don't have a license or anything."

"Deana, there's no gun registration law in Virginia. The gun has to be in a case, but the case doesn't have to be locked. The gun can even be loaded, but I don't think that's a good idea until we get you comfortable handling it."

He said he planned to drive in to see Ed in a couple of days. "There's no point in hanging around his bed now. I'll wait until he's able to talk intelligently and tell me what's going on. I might be able to help." He told her she and Jack were welcome to come out and practice shooting any time and gave her the okay to return the next day with Jack.

Kate and Randy Doran were leaving Ed's hospital room when Deana turned the corner. Hands on hips, Kate said with a steely look, "I thought I told you to not leave that apartment in the Watergate."

Deana met the stare with one of her own determined looks and said, "Cindy dropped me off. We left from the underground garage. I stayed down in the seat until I got out of the car at the hospital." Deana paused and, in a friendlier tone, asked, "How's Ed?" She suppressed a grin, thinking about Kate's reaction if she knew Deana had driven out to see Snooky.

"He's tired and a little groggy," Kate answered. "The first thing he wanted to know was whether you were okay. Go ahead in; we'll wait for you."

At least Kate was willing to give her a few moments alone with Ed. Whatever Ed told her must have convinced her Deana was not to blame for the shooting. It didn't help Deana breathe any easier. Her body felt cold and heavy as she forced herself to go into Ed's room.

She walked on tiptoe to the side of his bed. His eyes were closed. She stood still for a minute, watching him, not sure whether to wake him up or not.

He groaned, and his eyes opened. "Deana," he whispered. She had to lean close to him to hear his words.

"Deana, I'm sorry. It was an amateurish mistake on my part." Deana winced on hearing him use the word *amateurish,* remembering his warning when he decided to let her work with him: "Amateurs make mistakes, and those mistakes could get both of us killed." Deana told him she was just glad he was alive and to expect a visit from Snooky in a few days.

"Good, good," he managed, "Snooky can help."

She finally let her breath out and relaxed. Ed was going to be all right. "Ed, you wouldn't be here if it wasn't for me. Don't even think about apologizing."

Deana joined Kate and Randy in a quiet corner of a hospital lounge. Kate gave them a brief update on the status of the interviews with the women from the dating service. It turned out that Andy did not pursue women after the first contact if they either had a child or at least one parent or family member still alive. It was just as Ed had surmised: Andy was looking for someone who was pretty much alone in the world.

Kate said, "We have four women to contact tomorrow. There's one in D.C. with an out-of-service number. I drove by the address on my way to the hospital. It's an up-scale, short-term-stay apartment building. According to the bio on the dating service, she's a financial consultant. And …" Kate paused and looked at them with a satisfied glint in her eyes, "she has a record. The name is Sandra McDonnell. Unlike Andy, Sandra didn't bother trying to create a false identity. She's served time for embezzling from her employer."

Kate paused again and said with a knowing look in her voice and on her face, "She worked at an Internet dating service. She got out of prison and listed herself on the same dating service Andy was using. I figure she was trolling for suckers—just like him." Kate sighed. "No violent crimes in Sandra's past. Unlike Andy's targets, Sandra's lived."

Deana leaned forward and asked. "Are you thinking she may have been the shooter?"

Kate nodded. "It's a strong possibility. The apartment building is in Detective Wheeler's territory. He's going to meet me there later, and we should be able to confirm if Sandra was the shooter."

Randy looked at his watch. "I've got to get back to Richmond. My office will be looking into the Mt. Rogers case." He looked at Kate, not Deana. "I'll be in touch."

He turned to Deana and said, "Stay safe. We will stop this guy."

The police were through with Cindy's apartment. Deana and Cindy moved back to Cindy's condo. Jack called from the hospital. Deana got over her reluctance to see Jack alone when she heard his voice and agreed to meet for dinner.

She had the rest of the day free to finish the travel plans for the drive to Indiana. She stood at the window with a cup of coffee in her hand, staring at the view of the Potomac River. She sighed and watched the sun sparkling on the river. It was a breathtaking view. Unfortunately, she had to stop appreciating it and make herself consider the possibilities for Andy's next move. There was always the chance he could go back to his home town and not be looking for her at all in Virginia right now. He still didn't know they had discovered his real identity. Deana reasoned Indiana would not be a safe place for him. He would be more likely to be recognized there, and he hadn't visited his father since his wife, Meredith, had died. Even if he were in Knox, he wouldn't be expecting her, and she would be on the lookout for him. And this time, she would be armed. Andy tried to stage a fatal accident for Deana, Stephanie Randall supposedly fell to her death, and his first wife died in a caving accident. Andy didn't like to get his hands dirty. He concocted simple yet believable scenarios that would end officially as accidental deaths. The attack in the Watergate was a break in his pattern. It wasn't a carefully planned accident, but it was a carefully planned murder. Ed's presence and actions made the attempt a failure.

She would have to wait until Ed was better to ask him what he thought. Andy might have been angry and frustrated that the plan to leave Deana to die in Jasper didn't work and changed his tactics. The woman he used at the Watergate attempt was now dead. She knew even Andy didn't have an unlimited supply of women who would succumb to his charms and be willing to commit murder for him.

That evening, Jack picked Deana up in the underground parking garage. The man who got out of the car to greet her was a citified Jack. His Jasper uniform of jeans and a thick woolen sweater had been replaced by a pair of corduroy pants and a tailored tweed blazer. His hair was still a little unruly, as if he had just run his fingers through it. Jack looked a little anxious, probably wondering the same thing Deana was worried about—was the attraction still there? Any hesitation or misgivings dissipated as soon as Jack's face broke into a big smile. He stepped toward her and took her hands in his.

"Deana, it is so good to see you."

She fought back tears. Instead of talking, she put her arms around him and buried her head in his chest. She had been giving herself pep talks about staying strong and tough. Just having Jack there to support her and feeling the warmth of his arms around her gave her courage. He awkwardly pushed her away and kissed her lightly on the forehead.

She stayed out of sight in the back seat until they got to the hospital. The good news was Ed's condition had improved. The hospital wanted to release him in a couple of days. Snooky and his wife had invited him to stay with them in Culpeper until he was back on his feet again.

Deana gave Jack the ten-cent tour of Washington on the way to dinner. He was suitably impressed by the views of the city from the river and the background of the highlighted monuments. They were dramatically lit up at night, and the day-time dirt and congestion weren't there to detract from the beauty.

Jack said, "The power center of the world; it looks pretty good for the tourists. What happens when we move over a few blocks?"

"Yeah, well. It's the same all over the world, isn't it? What you see here is man-made beauty. Not like Jasper—"

Jack spread his arm toward the twinkling lights and said, "This has its own beauty. I've never had the chance to see it in the evening and through the eyes of an expert tour guide." He paused and turned to look at her. "Deana, you look great. How are you handling everything?"

"At this point, I'm more angry than scared. I keep thinking that if Cindy had been home, the woman might have shot her as well as Ed." She paused and said in a shaky voice, "I don't want anyone else to get hurt."

Jack touched her arm and said, "Deana, let the police do their job. They'll catch him. Don't worry." He looked her in the eye and continued, "Deana, I'd like to put my arm around you, but I don't want to scare you. I know this isn't the right time. I just want you to know if you need me, I want to help."

He paused and looked away. "Look, this is awkward." Then he smiled at her and said, "True confession? I'd like to do more than put my arm around you. There's something between us, and in spite of living on opposite ends of the continent … oh heck. Deana, I really like you. Let me help. That's all I want to say."

She took both of his hands in hers and said, "Jack, I really like you too, but right now, it looks like anyone that spends any time with me could be in danger. Ed almost died. If Cindy had been home, she might have been killed." She dropped his hands and said in a sure voice, "Teach me to shoot. That's the best way to help me."

Jack's exhibit opened the next day, but he insisted Cindy would take care of the details. Shooting lessons for Deana were a top priority. If they got started early the next day, he would be back in time to check the exhibit before the late-afternoon opening. He invited her to join him at the gallery and stay for dinner. She had her excuses ready. "Jack, you'll be the center of attention. And Ed would not be happy if he found out I was gallivanting all over town."

Jack's response was perfect. "You're right. I wanted you to see the exhibit and forgot about the danger. We can sneak you in for a private tour later this week."

Deana nodded in agreement. She would be halfway to Indiana by the time the gallery opening was over. Plenty of time to come up with an excuse before then.

Jack picked Deana up early the next morning. They headed out of town to meet Snooky. When they stopped for gas at a busy intersection outside of Warrenton, Jack insisted she stay in the car. "Ed's orders," he said, "and I'm locking you in."

"Okay. Just bring back a chocolate doughnut and coffee, and I'll be happy," she called to him.

She watched him turn and point the Smart-key at the car and heard the locks drop down and the beep-beep-beep signaling she was locked in the car. When he walked into the gas station store, Deana relaxed back into the seat. Her head turned to the right, and she screamed.

She locked eyes with the man getting into a car two cars down. His hair was blond, but it was Andy.

Deana couldn't move. She stared as the man quickly formed a pistol with his finger and pointed it at her. Her mouth dropped open. Then she fumbled with the seat belt, screaming, "It's him! Stop him!" The windows were closed. No one could hear her cries.

She reached into the back seat for the gun case and dropped it on the floor, cursing the Virginia law that said the gun had to be in a case. She grabbed her phone and tried to take a picture of Andy. His car was already moving. She turned quickly and tried to open the car door. It wouldn't open. The button to unlock the doors was on the driver's side. She scrambled into the driver's seat and found the button for the central unlocking switch. Opening the car door from the inside triggered the screeching high-pitched alarm. By the time she got out of the car, opened the gun case, and grabbed the gun, the man she was sure was Andy was gone. She had only caught a glimpse of a beige sedan.

Jack came out of the store with the doughnut and coffee. "What's going on? Deana, put the gun away!" Mercifully, he turned off the alarm.

She was attracting frightened stares. The sound of approaching police sirens warned her she was probably the reason for the sirens. Someone would have called the police to report a woman screaming and holding a gun. A state trooper pulled into the parking lot, lights flashing. Everyone moved as far away as they could get and still watch the action.

By then, she had placed the unloaded gun back in its case and explained to Jack that she was sure Andy had been in the parking lot. *Oh no,* she thought as the state trooper approached—*not another Detective Wheeler.* The reflective sunglasses made it impossible to see his eyes. The combination of the black leather boots and his hand resting on his gun as he walked toward her made her realize she was in real trouble.

"Are you the woman with the gun?" he asked.

Deana told the state trooper she purchased the gun from the owner of Deer Ranch. She was on the way there for shooting lessons. At the mention of Deer Ranch, the reflective sunglasses came off.

He said, "You know Snooky?"

The next second, he was on the phone to Snooky. Whatever Snooky said kept the trooper from handcuffing her and hauling her off to the local jail.

He said, "Snooky's on his way. He'll be here in ten minutes."

When he arrived, Snooky confirmed Deana was not a crazed murderer. He managed to convince the state trooper that she was in fear of her life. Snooky was so convincing in her defense that a chill ran through her as he described the danger she was in.

"Curly," Snooky said, and Deana wanted to cover her eyes and cry, realizing her fate was being discussed by two men with nicknames. "She had the gun in the case as required by law. She purchased it because she's in danger. Her husband has already tried to kill her once. She's trying to do this right. She was on her way to see me today with this gentleman for shooting lessons. That gun wasn't even loaded."

Deana cringed when he told Curly to call Detective Jackson. Now, Kate would find out she was not working away inside the Watergate.

"Snooky," Curly interrupted, "you know I could confiscate that gun and write her up for brandishing a weapon."

"Yeah, yeah, I know, Curly, but you know me. Haven't I always been straight with you?" He stopped until Curly reluctantly nodded. "Well, you know the law. If she is in fear of her life, she has a right to defend herself. If this lady says that was her ex, then that was her ex. Let them follow me to my place, and let's forget about this."

Deana held her breath while Curly decided. He removed his stiff, broad-brimmed gray hat and wiped his brow. So much for descriptive nicknames. Curly was bald. He put his hat back in place, hitched up his pants decisively, and stared her down. Deana decided this was not the time to win a staring contest. She let her eyes and head drop down.

"Ma'am," he said, "did you get a license plate number?" She had to answer no. His next question was, "Make and color of the car?"

"I'm sorry," she said. She meant it with all her heart. "It was some kind of sedan. Tan or beige, but I don't know the make. I was too upset to pay attention."

Curly turned his head to look at Snooky. Snooky shrugged but didn't say anything. Curly turned back to Deana and put on his reflective sunglasses before deciding to address her.

"Snooky is right. If you are in fear of your life, you are allowed to remove your weapon from the case and defend yourself. If I charge you and you get a lawyer, the case will be thrown out. We'll forget it. I'll check the station's surveillance cameras. If I can pick up the car and identify the plate, I'll be in touch."

Snooky interrupted. "He'll ditch that car and pick up another one and be on the move before you even get started."

Curly called Detective Jackson. As soon as they finished talking, Deana's phone rang. Kate demanded to know what she was doing in Culpeper. Deana held the phone away from her as Kate's voice raised in volume. Kate couldn't get any madder, so Deana decided to just tell her the truth.

In as calm and soothing a voice as she could muster, Deana said, "Just listen before you say anything." Deana explained about Jack's visit, Snooky's relationship with Ed, and Jack's role in helping her learn to shoot a gun.

There was silence on the other end of the phone when Deana stopped talking. Kate sighed and started talking slowly, drawing out each word. "Deana, it is a very bad idea for you to be running around with a gun." She paused. Deana could sense through the phone Kate was trying to control her temper. Her voice, sounding a little less exasperated, continued, "At least you're trying to do it the right way and are learning from a professional. Still, if you will just stay in one place, you won't need to use a gun."

"Kate," Deana said, "I wasn't safe in the Watergate even with Ed there. I need to be able to defend myself with something more than pepper spray."

Deana wasn't sure if Kate believed it was really Andy she had seen. Kate asked twice, "You're sure it was him?" Deana figured Kate thought she was frightened and seeing Andy everywhere.

But it was him. He had dyed his hair blond, the same predictable disguise Ed had warned against using. He would change that right away and would switch vehicles. He knew Deana was in Virginia, and he would be on the move before law enforcement could begin to identify him and the car. She hoped the store had surveillance tapes that would confirm her story.

If Deana had any doubts about learning to shoot and walking around like a gunslinger, seeing Andy turned doubts into resolve. Seeing him reminded her of a few things—stance and how to hold a gun—from the time Andy had tried to teach her to shoot. She hadn't been a good student for him. He said she looked ill at ease with the gun. Of course she looked ill at ease. She almost shot her foot off the first time she handled the gun.

Snooky stood by while Jack started the lesson with instructions on safety. His teaching approach was the opposite of Andy's. Andy had left out the basic safety instruction. An idea flashed through her mind that Andy might have planned a gun accident for her demise if she hadn't refused to continue practicing. She no longer felt ill at ease. She had the best reason for being a good student. Her life was at stake.

Snooky and Jack practiced on either side of Deana until her hand was tired. Snooky explained and demonstrated the importance of stability. "If you do have to defend yourself, it will probably be at close range. Don't flinch. Be committed to the shot. The more you practice, even dry firing or in different positions, the more proficient you will become."

He led them to a metal shed the size of a trailer. Jack and Deana looked at the door and stopped. As if on cue, they looked at each other and grinned. Deer antlers framed the length and top of the door. A hand-painted wooden sign at eye level read "Deer Ranch Clubhouse—No Trespassing." The deer whose antlers graced the door would have appreciated the clubhouse being named after him and his family.

Deana thought they were going into the clubhouse to talk, but Snooky continued the lesson. He moved quickly from walls to tables and chairs, standing, kneeling, and taking aim at imaginary targets with his gun. He grunted a couple of times when he moved from a kneeling or prostrate position, but the arm holding and pointing the gun was always steady. "Pop," he said each time he took an imaginary shot.

"When you're in a *situation*," Snooky said, emphasizing the word, "assess quickly, and figure out your best opportunity for stabilizing your gun." He looked at Deana and pointed at her gun. "Now, you try it."

She felt a little self-conscious. This had to be a guy thing. It seemed like a real-life video game.

"Snooky," she said, her voice drawing out his name, her attitude showing how silly she thought this exercise was. One look at Snooky—hands on hips and eyes dark and challenging—and she said, "Okay. I'll try."

And she did. Her first attempts were reluctant, but she could feel her body change as she started to concentrate. Snooky barked out the direction of the threat, and all her senses went on alert as she dove between chairs or under the table. After five or six sequences, she was starting to sweat, and her gun arm was shaky. It was mentally and physically exhausting.

"Enough!" Deana said. "I get the idea. I'll practice. I promise."

Snooky slapped her on the back. "Ed told me you were sharp. That was real good, Deana."

She smiled at him and said, "Annie Oakley lives again?"

Jack looked impressed and said, "Thanks, Snooky. I couldn't have taught her any of that." His face clouded over, and his voice dropped. "I'm just a hunter and don't have to worry about returning fire." Jack glanced at her. "Let's keep Deana out of any situations in which she might have to worry about it."

Snooky said, "In the perfect world, she wouldn't have to know how to shoot." He gestured toward the door, and they followed him outside. "But this ain't a perfect world."

Kate called just before they got back to Washington. She had interesting news on Sandra McDonnell. According to the hotel's records, Sandra had stayed there for a few months.

Kate said, "The clerk told me Sandra called in a few weeks ago and said she wouldn't be back, to just throw away whatever she had left in the apartment. She said there were family problems.

"He also said Sandra was out a lot in the evening, but he did recognize Andy's photo. He remembered seeing him come in with her a few times. He didn't know if he was her boyfriend or someone else's husband.

"Deana," Kate continued, "we showed him the photo from the dating service. He confirmed that it's Sandra."

Relief that they had at least identified one of the bad guys evaporated at Kate's next statement.

"However, Sandra isn't the Watergate shooter. It looks like Andy was getting help from more than one person."

At the news that there was probably yet another person in Andy's little band of desperadoes on her trail, Deana crossed her arms and folded them in front of her body. She wasn't sure if a shrink would identify the gesture as one of comforting herself or steeling herself for more bad news.

In spite of what Kate had told them about Sandra's criminal history, Deana felt a twinge of something for her—maybe sympathy, maybe fear. Yeah, she was a con artist, but there was more than money at stake in a relationship with Andy. Sandra's life was now as much at risk as Deana's.

CHAPTER 12

Deana wiggled her fingers to relieve the numbness. She noticed her fingernails were ragged and needed attention. That was the least of her worries right now. *Breathe,* she told herself and relaxed her grip on the steering wheel. She was tired and stiff, and her growling stomach reminded her she had forgotten to eat lunch. But she was halfway to Indiana, and she wasn't turning around.

This trip was very important. It was a feeling she couldn't shake. The information that would lead them to Andy was in Indiana. One of Ed's tenets was that you had to talk to people who knew the jerk you were after. *Jerk* was her word. Ed would have used the word *perp.*

The sun slipped into the horizon behind a hotel billboard. Deana took it as a sign and headed to the hotel. She pulled into the parking lot at a crawl, sweeping her eyes from the parked cars to the rearview mirror. No one had followed her off the exit ramp, and the parking lot was quiet. A few cars and trucks were parked for the night, their windshields frosted over.

Deana surveyed the sterile, quiet hotel room and relaxed. It was the perfect spot. Her hand lingered on the dead bolt after she slid it into place. The solid clunk made her feel safer than she had in a long time, but two scenes kept replaying in her head: two shots, a dead woman, Ed's wounded body, and locking eyes with Andy at the gas station. She could still feel Ed's sticky blood on her hands. She moved to the sink to splash water on her face. One glance in the mirror told her she looked as bad as she felt. Eyes bloodshot from lack of sleep and one bout of self-pity-induced crying created the impression of a plain Jane who had just finished a night of hard drinking.

The predictable hotel noises were oddly comforting: low sounds coming from a television in the next room, a voice echoing in the hallway, the hum of the heating unit, and the murmur of highway traffic. A cup of hot tea would take the chill out of her bones. She started the hot water in the hotel coffee pot and looked for a tea bag. Hands cradling the hot cup of tea, she inhaled the steam from the tea, closed her eyes, and sat down on the bed to think. She had gone straight from the surreal scene with Andy to the shooting lesson. Smiling to herself, she remembered she had started out shaky and scared but got stronger and steadier with every boom and recoil.

Jack had put his hands on her shoulders and said softly, "Relax, relax. Breathe out and relax." He turned out to be right. When she finally relaxed, she hit the targets and at some point realized she actually enjoyed shooting. She picked up the gun and felt its heft. It felt good and solid in her hand. Snooky had told her to practice dry firing. Now was as good a time as any. Moving quickly around the hotel room, she assumed different positions and softly said "pop" each time she took aim at an imaginary target—all of them with Andy's face.

Then she caught a glimpse of her own face in the mirror. She stopped and stared at the woman, arm extended, gun pointed at her reflection. It was the coldness in the eyes that shocked her. The memory of Ed's words, *Be prepared to shoot to kill,* drove all the warmth out of her body again. The eyes staring back at her were capable of shooting to kill.

Deana let her arm drop to her side and placed the gun gently on the night stand. She shook her head and half smiled at the realization that Andy would be surprised to see the cold and determined look in her eyes.

A knock on the steel door cut through the silence. She bolted up as if someone had slid a block of ice down the back of her sweater.

"Room service!" a woman's muffled voice called, followed by another knock.

Deana didn't answer. Her first thought was what kind of room service—the bathroom had plenty of towels, and the hotel didn't have a restaurant. Half expecting someone to use a hotel pass to open the door she reached for the gun and walked softly over to the pin-sized peephole. A woman with a coat on and long blond hair stood outside her door. The face was distorted through the peephole. The smile looked like a creepy leer.

Breathe deeply, she told herself, trying to ignore her pounding heart. Andy could be out there next to this woman. Time to just get this over with. "Now," she whispered and threw the door open.

Her gun was pointed at the chest of a woman whose hand fell away from holding her coat shut to reveal a black see-through negligee.

"Don't shoot, don't shoot!" the woman shouted. She was obviously not offering the typical type of room service. She stammered and backed away down the hall, stopping for a second to remove her man-killer heels. Then she took off at a dead run.

Deana didn't say anything. She just slammed the door shut, slapped the deadbolt in place, and braced herself against the wall. Her whole body was shaking. She had just pointed a loaded gun at a woman and had been prepared to shoot her point blank.

Another problem flashed through her mind. She relaxed and sat back down on the bed as she realized it would resolve itself. The woman couldn't call the police because she had been illegally plying her trade. Deana hadn't watched to see which way the woman went, but she heard footsteps pounding down the hall to the side exit—not in the direction of the reception area. And some good might come out of this. Maybe the woman had been frightened enough to realize she should change professions.

Deana was up early the next morning. The hotel bill had been slipped under her door. *Good,* she thought, *I can slip out the back exit and not see anyone.* The temperature dropped steadily, and more snow appeared on the ground as she drove from Virginia to the Midwest.

She pulled over and got out of the car to stretch her stiff back and knees. The snow-covered farms stretched out over land that offered a view uninterrupted by trees, hills, or homes. The size of the open fields, where the nation's corn, wheat, and soybeans were grown, made the small, scenic Virginia farms look like hobby farms. Deana breathed the crisp, cold air. She sat on the hood of the car for a few minutes to marvel at the quiet and solitude. Relieved to see that the Ohio farm land was in a working cell phone area, she read a text from Kate.

The surveillance camera at the gas station store had captured the man Deana thought was Andy but not a clean shot of his face. Kate wanted her to come in and view the footage to confirm that she still thought it was him. It defied all logic, but Deana felt better lying verbally than committing a written falsehood. Maybe it was because one could still cross one's fingers when speaking a lie.

Deana dialed Kate's cell. When she heard Kate's voice, she crossed her eyes and fingers and said, "I didn't sleep all night. I think it's the flu."

Kate quickly agreed to send a copy of the video to Deana's phone. Deana knew the excuse was a good one when Kate continued the conversation on the phone instead of asking her to come in for a meeting. No one wanted to catch the flu.

Kate said, "We interviewed Stephanie Randall's friend Michelle Grant. Turns out that Michelle is a high-powered corporate attorney and knew Stephanie and her family through work she had done for them. Like you." Kate hesitated, as if she knew she might have said the wrong thing. "Uh, Stephanie Randall was introduced to Andy by a friend who met him through a dating service."

Kate paused, giving Deana a chance to say something. Deana didn't speak; she just shook her head. It was confirmation that she wasn't the first and only victim. She wasn't the first and only one to fall for Andy.

Kate went on to recite the facts: "Michelle met Andy through a dating service; he was using the name *Stuart Hudkins*. After a couple of casual dates, she invited him to escort her to a Christmas party at Stephanie's house. Before arriving at the party, she explained that her best friend's parents had just passed away. The next day, he called to tell her he felt a kinship with Stephanie and wanted to ask her out. When she didn't even feel a twinge of jealousy, she knew he was definitely not the guy for her. Michelle became concerned when the relationship moved very quickly. Stephanie and Andy were married after knowing each other for only a few months. Michelle hadn't been able to convince her friend to get a prenuptial agreement. She said Stephanie was a real sweetheart but thought that Michelle's concern was motivated by a wee bit of the green monster. So Michelle stopped pushing. After the wedding, Andy monopolized her time."

Deana quietly shuffled her feet to keep warm while Kate continued to relate her conversation with Michelle. "Michelle had been suspicious about the circumstances of her friend's demise. Stephanie was not a big drinker. Michelle didn't believe Andy's version of events. Unfortunately, he was next of kin and executor of her will. He had Stephanie's body cremated, put on a sad look, and claimed he was too devastated to live with Stephanie's memory all around him. He sold the house quickly at a below-market price and liquidated all her accounts. He seemed to be in a hurry and knew a lot about financial matters for someone who was a park ranger. Michelle had tried to get in touch with him, but he left no forwarding address, and his phone number had been disconnected. She suggested he might have moved money to an offshore account to avoid leaving any trace."

"Deana, are you there?" Kate asked when she didn't get a response to her report.

Deana said, "I was thinking, at least he didn't get the chance to cremate me!" She was also watching a tractor-trailer truck approaching on the highway and timed the whoosh of the truck with covering the mouthpiece on the phone.

"Deana, you are something else! You were married to a really bad guy, and you're cracking jokes. I'm impressed."

Her praise made Deana wince. Kate wouldn't be so impressed if she knew Deana had lied to her. But all she said was, "Yeah, right. What's next?"

Kate said, "I'll talk to Randy Doran this afternoon. We have enough to get the FBI involved. The best way to catch Andy is to follow the money trail. The FBI can issue a subpoena to a judge requesting access to your brokerage accounts. If he has in fact moved funds to offshore accounts, we'll need to have solid evidence of crimes he's committed to get cooperation from authorities in other countries."

"That's it? You talk to the FBI, and they take over?" Deana asked.

"Basically. I'm still waiting for the information from Indiana in case we have a third death to add to the case. They're digging up the reports. None of the cases was entered online, and the files are in storage. I should have something from them in a couple of days."

"You mean the police in Indiana are just going to copy old files and send them to you? No one's going to talk to anyone?" Deana asked ingenuously. Just in case Ed's hunch was right and boots on the ground were better than dead pieces of paper, she was making a point with Kate that would mitigate some of Kate's anger when she found out about Deana's excursion.

Kate didn't catch the hint of sarcasm in Deana's question. She continued, "Right. With cases this old, it's time-consuming to track all the parties. Some have retired; some have moved or died." She sighed. "And we just don't have the staff. We're putting our resources on the two suspicious deaths, attempted murder, and possible illegal money transfers."

Deana focused on the last few words—*money transfers*. "What about my money? Can the FBI get it back for me?"

Kate said, "Yeah, if we're lucky and he moved the money to an account in the Caymans. That's another reason we need the FBI involved. The Caymans won't give me the account information, but they'll cooperate with the FBI. If Andy moved the money to a Swiss account, you'll never see it again. The Swiss don't bend to pressure from anyone. The FBI office in Richmond will pick up the case in Mt. Rogers. It's another piece of luck for you; since Randy works out of the Richmond office, it looks like he'll be assigned to the case."

Deana wished people would quit telling her how lucky she was. There was nothing lucky about anything that had happened so far. She said good-bye to Kate and got back in the car. She was getting closer to Andy's home town, and that meant it was time to don the latest disguise. She'd been busted in the brunette wig; Ed said no blond hair, and red was her natural color. That left black and gray. Cindy had picked up a wig with short, straight, black hair. Checking herself in the mirror as she tugged the wig into place, she thought, *Dangerous—I look dangerous.* Her curly red hair had doomed her to being cute. The straight black hair made her look and feel hard and tough.

The center of the small town was dominated by an old-fashioned courthouse built from local stone. The requisite Moose lodge, advertising bingo, was across the street. A bowling alley anchored a corner on the main street. Deana parked in front of a shop selling ice cream and sandwiches. The parking meter took nickels instead of the quarters required in big cities. Peeking through the window of the store, she saw that it looked pretty busy and figured at least the food had to be okay.

When Deana entered the store, all conversation stopped. Heads turned to see who the newcomer was. She managed a small nod of her head that included the whole room. High-backed turquoise vinyl-clad booths were occupied by people dressed in the heavy green work shirts, pants, and overalls favored by farmers or jeans and thick flannel shirts. Heavy winter jackets hung from metal hooks at the end of the booths. At first, it felt eerie, like stepping into a store from the 1950s. Then a phone rang, and Deana saw the familiar Smartphones and iPhones in people's hands. The little town wasn't quite the throwback it appeared to be.

Deana kept her head down, letting the straight black hair fall across her face and avoiding eye contact with any of the customers who might still be sizing up the outsider. She couldn't help thinking she should have found a McDonald's on the highway. On one hand, it was nice to know that in a small town the entrance of someone new was interesting enough to get people to break their connection with an electronic device. On the other hand, she stood out in this local joint. In a fast food stop on the highway, no one would have noticed her.

Keeping her voice low, Deana ordered a sandwich at the carryout counter from a young woman who looked fresh out of high school. Her blond hair was cut in a stylish short wedge, longer in the front than the back. A red streak had been expertly applied across the front. The look was edgy, even in the big cities. In the little restaurant in the middle of

Indiana farm land, it was positively revolutionary. Her wholesome smile and sweet voice contrasted with the trendy big-city hairdo.

"Are you visiting?" she asked, after taking Deana's order. Once again, the outsider's business seemed to be more interesting than the electronic connection. The buzz in the air dissipated as everyone waited for the answer.

"Yes," Deana started to say and swallowed the word with a cough. "No, just passing through. I needed to get off the highway." The whole restaurant was listening to everything. There was no need to keep her voice down. She might as well speak loud enough so that everyone got the same story. If she didn't, she figured everyone would just ask the young waitress as soon as she left.

Deana thought she shouldn't take a chance that Andy might have spies or a connection that would tell him where she was. Low profile, low profile. No one should know she was ever there.

"Oh," the young woman said. "How far are you goin'?" Her interest seemed genuine, but Deana was starting to feel nostalgia for the snippy, snooty waiters in Washington. Of course, she was interested in a strange woman dropping in off the highway. She probably had her own dreams of heading down the highway. Time to turn the tables on her.

"How about you?" Deana asked with smiling eyes. "You from here? Looks like a nice town."

"Yes, lived here all my life," she answered, emphasizing the "all" with a sigh. In a more upbeat tone, she added, "I'm going to cosmetology school and then ..."

Before she could finish, a customer yelled, "Carly, we need a refill of your leaded over here!" Carly mumbled a disappointed "Sorry," gave Deana a wizened look that said more than the "sorry," and hustled off to her other customers.

The library was a small but sturdy-looking brick building sandwiched between a laundromat and an honest-to-goodness old-fashioned hardware store. There was no glitz calling customers to stop and look at the display of goods, but the simple, unadorned, useful objects on display caught Deana's eye. She lingered in front of the windows. One window displayed metal piping, hammers, hinges, and building materials. The other side was crammed with small appliances, dishes, and kitchenware. It was a mini-Lowe's. It looked like it had been there forever. If she couldn't get what she needed at the library, the hardware store might be more than a source of tools. It might be a source of information on families that had lived in the town a long time ago.

A bell tinkled when Deana pushed the heavy door of the library. She glanced up to see a real bell attached to the hinge. No electronic warning systems, no metal detectors here—just the nostalgic metallic tinkle to let the librarian know she had a customer.

Deana looked around. The hush and silence of the small-town library felt like someone wrapping arms around her. The door thunked closed solidly into the frame. One final little vibration from the bell gradually disappeared into the heavy silence of the room. Deana let her breath out and breathed in the comforting smell of furniture polish instead of the musty book smell she expected. A woman walked toward her through the book stacks.

"Hello, are you Deana?" she asked. "We don't get many strangers here. I figured it had to be you." She wrapping her hands around Deana's extended hand. If anyone looked the part of a librarian, it was Dorothy Griffin. Her silver hair was pulled back in a bun, and a very sharp pencil poked out of one end of the bun. Deana quickly found out Dorothy was very efficient. She had collected and copied files of the old newspaper articles about Meredith Givens and Greg Irwin.

She had everything from the short announcement on their wedding to Andy's mother's death and Meredith's death. Dorothy pushed the half-glasses hanging from a cord around her neck up onto the bridge of her nose and tapped a finger on the wedding announcement. She explained that Andy's family had lived in the town for fifteen years when the mother died. Everyone had liked the mother; no one knew the father well. He was a roofer and worked alone. He kept busy and supported his family, but other than showing up for his jobs, he kept to himself.

Dorothy shifted in her seat and became serious. She said, "My husband is good friends with the man who was sheriff then and some of the other old-timers. We'd like you to have dinner with us tonight."

Deana sensed more to this than small-town hospitality. If Dorothy wanted her to meet the sheriff, it must mean there was more to the history than what appeared in the newspaper articles. Deana eagerly accepted the invitation. She told Dorothy she had left the impression in town that she was just passing through. She didn't want word to get out about her interest in the Givens and Irwin families.

"Don't worry about me," Dorothy said and winked. "If anyone asks, you were tired of driving and wanted a quiet place to read." She pointed to a comfortable chair. "I'll say you nodded off reading a newspaper."

Deana glanced back down the street toward the sandwich shop. Everything seemed so innocent and honest in this small town, yet it had been the home of a man who turned into a killer. Young Carly, the waitress, had lived here all her life. Chances are her parents were from Knox and grew up with Andy. She might not ever see Carly again, but she knew if she needed more information, Carly would be eager to help.

Deana found the hotel Dorothy recommended and settled in to read the pile of newspaper articles. She paused to sniff the cup of coffee brewed by the little machine in her room and was relieved it actually smelled like coffee.

The first time Andy's family made the news was at the time of his mother's death. She had died in a carbon monoxide accident when he was fifteen. Father and son told the same story about returning home from hunting to find the wife/mother dead on the kitchen floor. A gas leak in the kitchen was blamed for her death.

"Whoa!" Deana yelled when she read that Jean Schneider, a niece who lived with the family, was not home at the time. *Schneider:* the name Andy used as his mother's maiden name and the name of the young woman in the high school yearbook. Ed had planned to follow up on Jean Schneider on his trip to Knox. Just like he was fond of saying, "A little luck, a little hard work."

Deana was too excited to sit and paced the room as she read. If Dorothy and her husband knew Andy's family, they knew Jean Schneider.

The first words in the next article sent a charge through Deana that was better than caffeine. She sat up and threw her legs over the side of the bed. It was the headline, "Newlywed Dies in Caving Accident," that made Deana clench the paper.

The article was about Meredith's death in a caving accident. The eighteen-year-old woman and her nineteen-year-old husband, Greg Irwin, had only been married for six months. They were on a caving trip in southern Indiana and rappelled into a cave. The husband went to get help after his wife fell, breaking her leg. She hit her head and was unconscious when he left her to get help. By the time he returned with a rescue crew, she was dead. The reporter described the young husband as distraught. Deana knew what the newspaper writer didn't: Greg Irwin killed his wife. She let out a deep breath and closed her eyes before finishing the article. Andy missed his real calling. He should have hopped a train to Hollywood and become an actor.

The reporter devoted the rest of the article to the number of accidents related to spelunking. Meredith's death had been preceded by several other successful rescues of injured spelunkers and was the impetus needed to see that restrictions on spelunking were tightened. Meredith herself was forgotten.

Jim, Ed, and the sheriff from Mt. Rogers had all said the same thing. If the victim's friends or family didn't push for attention on the case, the easy explanation was accepted. And energies quickly shifted to newer or more sensational crimes.

Meredith's "family" was also her killer—Greg Irwin, aka Stuart Hudkins, aka Andy. Andy's victims may have been forgotten at one time but not any longer. Deana was determined to find out the truth behind the deaths of Meredith and Stephanie.

A tall, thin man answered the door to Dorothy's home. He was dressed in John Deere green pants and a green work shirt with the sleeves rolled up. Long underwear peeked out of the collar and sleeves. Dorothy had said her husband was a farmer. The clothes and weather-beaten face certainly made him look the part. The worn work clothes were clean and pressed. He looked solid and honest, and there was a concerned look in his eyes when he reached out his hand to greet her.

"You must be Deana. I'm Sam Griffith, Dot's husband."

Sam introduced Deana to his friend Sonny Wilson, the retired sheriff. Sonny's khaki shirt and pants were probably the closest he could get to the uniform he had worn for years. Sonny's open collar also showed the requisite long underwear. Both men wore their wrinkles well. They looked like they also went to the same barber. Their salt-and-pepper hair was clipped short in the same style.

Dorothy insisted that what she called "serious discussion" be saved until after dinner. "This young lady needs a break from her sleuthing," Dorothy said and winked at Deana.

Deana started to sit down at the table. She quickly stood up when she saw Dorothy, Sam, and Sonny were standing behind their chairs, heads bowed. Sam said a short prayer of thanks. Deana's head was down, but she peeked at her hosts while Sam spoke in a deep, sincere voice.

The grace before dinner wasn't a common practice among Deana's Washington friends. She had to admit it was nice. They enjoyed a quiet dinner with talk about the local high school sports, the weather, and the crops. Then they moved into the living room for the conversation that was the reason for her visit.

Sonny's story confirmed Ed's hunch. Suspicious deaths were part of Andy's life. Andy and his father were each other's alibis in the death of the mother. They collected on an insurance policy, and the case was closed. Sonny didn't have enough evidence to get an order for an autopsy. It looked like an accident.

"What about the niece? How did she fit in?" Deana asked.

Sonny proceeded to relate a chilling tale. "Mr. and Mrs. Irwin moved here in 1972. She was pregnant and gave birth to a son, Greg, shortly after they moved here. Four years later, she was away for a while and came back with a baby girl. No one really knew them well enough to tell how long she'd been gone. She claimed it was her brother's baby and that the parents died in an accident. This is a small town, and people do notice things and talk. There was a rumor at the time that it was actually Greg's mother's baby, and Greg's father wasn't the father.

"What I'm about to tell you is off the record. Juvenile records are

destroyed after seven years, and there is nothing left in the files to corroborate the history. When the girl started school, social services and
my office were called in. We had good reason to believe there was sexual
abuse of the girl. The brother and the father were the likely suspects. The
medical evidence was strong enough to put the girl in a foster home. She
wouldn't talk, and the family insisted it must have happened at school."
He shook his head and continued. "It was a long time ago and a different time. The parents took the boy out of the public school and put him
in the Catholic school. The girl, Jean, graduated from the public high
school and left town. I don't think her foster family ever heard from her
again. The father had a stroke and has been in a nursing home outside
of town. You won't get any information from him. He isn't able to talk."

"Who pays the bills?" Deana asked quickly.

"Good question. Your detective in Virginia can request the records,
but I'll tell you what I know. He moved into the facility, and there was a
bank account managed by a local lawyer. The account has been depleted,
and he is now officially a ward of the state."

"What about Meredith's aunt? Is she still alive?" Deana asked.

"No, I'm afraid she passed away. We were friends, and she came in
to talk to me when Meredith died. Meredith had inherited a little money
after the death of her parents. The aunt wanted her to take time and
grow up before settling down. She said she always felt there was something odd about Greg. She thought he always seemed to be playing a
part—the part of a love-sick young man. His arm would be hanging over
Meredith's shoulder, but it was rigid, not relaxed. The aunt suspected
he was more interested in Meredith's money than in her. She worried
he might break her niece's heart one day but never thought he would be
desperate enough to kill her."

Sonny hesitated and then said, "There's something else. The year
after Meredith died, a body was found in the woods bordering the town.
It was a young girl, Leslie Thompson, who had disappeared four years
earlier."

He explained that young Leslie—only sixteen at the time—disappeared after winning the jackpot at the church's monthly bingo night.

She rode her bike home, carrying $300 in cash, and was never seen alive again.

"Bingo!" Deana couldn't help blurting out in disbelief. "You've got to be kidding."

Deana's face turned red as she realized from the pained look on their faces that she had just made fun of what was obviously an accepted activity.

"I'm sorry," she said, leaning forward. "I just meant I couldn't believe someone would get killed over an innocent game like bingo." She sat back, relieved at the smiles on their faces. Bingo was obviously still a big part of small-town life. She remembered passing through small towns on the way to Knox and seeing signs advertising the bingo jackpot.

Sonny said, "Her family didn't report her missing until the next morning. She was one of eight children on a farm. No one gave a thought to the possibility of foul play. She hated the farm and the work involved. Everyone assumed she had hit the road with the money and would come home when it was gone. Most of the town had been at bingo that night, and a few folks remembered seeing her grab the money and jump on her bike. The case was treated as if she had run away from home. The department did everything it normally does in the case of a runaway. There were no leads, and it remained a mystery until her body was found.

"It took a while to establish her identity once we found the body. We assumed she was the victim of a robber/murderer passing through. The case remained unsolved, but it always bothered me. She had to ride her bike past the Irwin house to get to her farm. They were neighbors. The Thompson girl's murder and the death of Greg's wife seemed too coincidental to me. People don't kill each other here."

He half-smiled and continued, "If you piss someone off around here, they'll slash your tires or put sugar in the gas tank. Drunks will start swinging at each other, but we haven't had a homicide in twenty years. The mother's death made three deaths, two of them accidents. It bothered me, but Greg left town right after Meredith's death, and I convinced myself Greg was one of those people who just can't catch a break." He blew out his breath and stared at the floor, as if ashamed to look up. "I should've listened to my gut instinct."

It was so quiet the proverbial pin dropping would have sounded like a fifty-pound weight hitting a tile floor. Deana figured they were giving her a few minutes to put the three deaths together. She said slowly and quietly, "I think you're suggesting Andy—Greg to you—had something to do with all three of these women's deaths, starting with a sixteen-year-old girl." She looked up at Sonny, and he met her eyes.

He nodded his head up and down and said, "Yes, yes, I am. Just too many coincidences for a quiet little town."

Deana looked at the coffee cup on the table and willed herself to pick it up. If she could pick up the cup with a firm hand, it would mean she could handle the latest shocking news. Her hand circled the cup, but the shaking threatened to spill the coffee all over Dot's polished coffee table. That seemed a worse sin than just admitting she felt like an elephant had stomped on her chest. Using both hands, she carefully set the cup down. She closed her eyes and pushed the heels of her hands against her forehead. The rustle of Dot's shirt was the only sound hanging in the air as she moved over to sit on the arm of Deana's chair and put her hand on Deana's shoulder. Still, no one spoke, for which Deana was thankful. She could only think about the wasted lives of two young women and the horrific possibility that Andy had contributed to the death of his own mother.

Finally, Deana touched Dot's hand and said, "Don't worry. I'm okay. Well, not exactly okay, but I'll live and that young girl didn't. I just feel terribly sad for Leslie. Her luck at bingo ended up making her a target. And his wife, Meredith. Both so young."

Deana kept her next thought to herself. Andy had certainly hit the jackpot with her. The $300 prize he probably stole from the young bingo winner was small potatoes compared to the $2.5 million he stole from her. She was immediately ashamed of herself for thinking about the money. Leslie lost not just her bingo earnings but her life.

There was a little throat clearing from the men, and Dot gently laid her hand on Deana's back. Deana couldn't shake the image of an excited young girl racing home with her bingo winnings. Whatever dreams she thought she could make come true with her money never had a chance. They had to catch Andy and stop him. That wouldn't happen unless she finished what she came to Knox to do. She shook her head and gently removed Dot's hand from her back.

"Excuse me, but this is important," Deana said. She retrieved her briefcase and pulled out the Watergate surveillance photo of the shooter. She handed it to Sonny. "Do you recognize her?"

Sonny held the picture out at arm's length, pulled it in close, and slid his reading glasses out of his shirt pocket. He studied the photo, tapped it with his finger, and said, "Well, I'll be damned. She's a dead ringer for Mrs. Irwin." His fingers gripped both sides of the photo, and he studied it intently. Without looking up, he said, "Wait a minute. This could be Jean Schneider, all grown up. Where did you get this?"

Dot snatched the photo from Sonny's hand and murmured, "Oh my, it does look like Jean."

Deana said, "That's the woman who tried to kill me a couple of days ago. I told you Ed was sick, but the truth is he was shot trying to protect me from her."

Deana told the story of the Watergate shooting. When she got to the part about seeing Ed on the floor, the memory of the blood coming out of a hole in his chest was too much for her. Her voice started to shake.

Dot didn't say anything. She just moved to sit again on the arm of Deana's chair. She wasn't a big woman, but the thin arm she draped over Deana's shoulders transferred the warmth in her heart. Deana took a few seconds to steady her breathing; with her hand holding on to Dot's, she finished the story. She explained that she had spotted the name *Schneider* in the high school yearbook but hadn't associated the grainy yearbook photo with the surveillance photo of an older Jean captured by the Watergate camera.

Deana looked at Sonny, Sam, and Dot and said slowly, "Thank you. You have been a tremendous help. I'll call the detectives in D.C. tonight, and someone will be in touch."

Reaching up to scratch her head without dislodging the wig, she decided she was now in the company of people—friends—who knew her worst fears and figured they might as well see the real Deana. She pulled the wig off and ran both hands through her hair. "This wig is driving me nuts!"

"Oh!" Dot said, "I couldn't tell it was a wig. You have beautiful red hair." She wrinkled her brow and said in a voice full of concern, "A disguise. You poor thing. You're wearing that wig as part of a disguise."

Dot's next words made Deana whip around to stare at her.

"You know," Dot said, "I remember little Leslie had beautiful curly red hair. Just like yours."

"Dot!" Sam said. "You're scaring her."

Dot apologized quickly. "Honey, I'm sorry. I wasn't thinking."

Deana *was* thinking—thinking about the irony of Andy's first and most recent targets having something in common besides money. She couldn't help asking, "Freckles? Did she have freckles?"

Dot answered, "Why, yes. She did."

Deana shook her head without speaking. She thought to herself, *Red hair and freckles—just like me.*

Deana thanked them for their help and returned to the hotel. She remembered Ed's insistence that the best way to solve a case was to collect as much information as possible. He had a gut feeling about the trip to Indiana, and he had been right. Talking to real people instead of sifting through old files had unearthed the most important information they had found on Andy and his past. They now knew who the Watergate shooter was. Kate's official request for records related to Meredith's death would not have told them anything about Sonny's suspicions of the Irwin family.

Deana knew Kate would scream when she found out Deana was in Indiana. Kate didn't disappoint her.

Deana quickly pulled the phone away from her ear when Kate demanded, "You're where?" Kate calmed down when Deana told her they could identify the shooter and quickly explained Sonny's suspicions about the other deaths linked to Andy.

Kate said in a stern voice, "Listen, Deana, we still don't know where

Andy is, and we don't know whether Sandra McDonnell is helping him or might be his next victim." She reminded Deana to not go anywhere near her own home. Randy Doran would meet with them in his office as soon as Deana returned to the Washington area. The FBI was now stepping in to take over the lead in the case.

Deana called Ed's room. The phone just kept ringing. She tried his cell phone and didn't have any luck. She shrugged. He was either out cold or taking the required daily walk down the hall. Looking at the phone, she realized how much she missed talking to Ed. It was Ed's opinion she had learned to respect. She wanted to hear him say he was proud of her for taking the trip to Indiana and making some real progress in the case.

CHAPTER 13

The springs in the bed poked Deana's back when she collapsed on the hotel mattress. She was exhausted but knew sleep wasn't in the cards. She groaned, sat up, and started to pull off her coat. Immediately changing her mind, she shrugged the coat back on and walked to the thermostat to turn up the heat in the room. The feeling that she would never feel warm again was back. This time, it wasn't the temperature in the room that chilled her blood. It was the snapshots in her head of Jean Schneider, Meredith Thompson, young Leslie, and finally, Andy—the loving husband and the man whose real job was planning and implementing the death of women in his life—that made her shiver.

Her face hardened as feelings of sadness for the innocent dead women turned into anger. The memory of Andy's smiling face was quickly replaced by Andy's leer and his arms reaching toward her through the bars of a jail cell. A grim smile of satisfaction replaced the morose expression on her face when she pictured his head surrounded by flames. She let the desire to strike out at Andy subside. A cool head, not one moved by rash action and revenge, was needed to outwit and catch a killer. Deana looked at her phone and thought about Ed waiting in the hospital for news. It was late. She didn't want to risk waking him up. The good news she had for him would have to wait until morning.

There were two messages from Jack and a text from Cindy. Jack's first call was full of concern for Deana's stomach problems. She grimaced. She didn't like deceiving Jack. His voice in the second message was stern, and his words were deliberate. "Deana," he said, "I know you're in Indiana. I brought flowers to the Watergate, and Cindy told me the truth. Call me right away."

Cindy's text was short. "In meetings. Call Jack ASAP."

Deana sat for a minute, considering the excuses she could give Jack to explain why she had lied to him: she didn't want to put him in danger, he was busy with his exhibition, and it was her problem, not his. She wanted to be ready when he answered the phone.

Jack's voice sounded tired and heavy. He started out saying, "Deana, sit down." She sighed and rolled her eyes, thinking he was taking the trip to Indiana a bit too seriously until she heard his next words.

"Deana, Ed is gone. He ..."

"Gone?" she interrupted. "What do you mean? He was barely walking."

Jack let out his breath. "Ed is dead. He passed away this afternoon."

"But, but," Deana insisted, "he was fine the last time I talked to him." Deana clutched her stomach. This time the pain was real. She closed her eyes, seeing Ed and hearing his last words to her: *Deana, I'm sorry. It was an amateurish mistake ...*

Jack said in a whisper, "Deana, are you there?"

"Here, I'm here," she said, dragging out the words. "I'm here."

After a few seconds passed, Jack spoke slowly and calmly. "Deana, I'm so sorry. It looked like he was going to be okay. He couldn't wait to get out of the hospital. He passed away quietly. It happens sometimes with a serious injury. When the person rallies, the heart just stops."

The heater in the room was going full blast, but the news about Ed left Deana shaking like she was back in the cave. The drone of the cheap hotel heating system was the background to the thoughts running around in her head: *Ed can't be dead. I had so much to tell him. Wanted to ask him about Leslie Thompson and the other women who died because of Andy. It's too late. I can't ask Ed anything.* She clenched the phone so hard she cried out in pain.

Jack didn't say anything. He waited patiently while Deana dealt with the news of losing her friend and protector. "It's my fault," Deana said and squeezed her eyes shut to stop the tears.

"Listen to me, Deana," Jack said. "Jim and Linda asked me to check on Ed in the hospital. I was the last person to talk to him before he passed away. Ed didn't blame you. He blamed himself. You should have heard him. He really thought the world of you. He thought you had a lot of courage to take off for Indiana." Jack paused, and Deana heard him laugh. "Ed said you made a hell of a detective. Said you had good instincts but were a little naive about the risks you took."

Jack couldn't see Deana's face relax into a smile. She dried her damp face with a sleeve. Ed had been proud of her. That was enough to keep her strong. She wouldn't let Ed's memory down.

"Ed made me promise to keep an eye on you," Jack said. "Snooky had agreed to fill in for Ed until he recovered. Now, you've got both Snooky and me keeping tabs on you."

Deana said good-bye to Jack and slid under the covers fully clothed. Jack didn't have to get this involved in her life. Now, he had changed his own travel plans and was staying in D.C. until she returned. She grimaced, knowing she should appreciate his gallantry. It made her nervous. She didn't want to like Jack too much and depend on him. There was no time for romance in her life. Just being around her exposed Jack to the risk of being collateral damage in Andy's campaign to get rid of her.

On the other hand, his friendship was a lifeline. Jack and Cindy were the only two people she could really talk to while she stayed in hiding. Yes, she could talk to the police, but they were just doing a job. Cindy and Jack were friends.

Jack didn't know the complete history of Andy's victims. He was just concerned with *her* safety. Sixteen-year old Leslie, Andy's mother, Meredith Givens, Stephanie Randall, and now Ed—all dead because they came in contact with a psychopath. Andy wouldn't stop killing. There would be other victims fooled by the handsome man who looked you in the eye when he talked to you and made you trust him. Thinking about Ed and the justice he deserved, she threw the covers off and walked into the bathroom. She grabbed the Kleenex so hard that half the contents came out of the container and scattered on the floor. Deana wiped the tears away, forcefully crumpled up the tissues, and threw them into the wastebasket. She grabbed the edge of the counter in the bathroom and looked in the mirror. Staring back at her was a woman with eyes swollen and red from crying, hair sticking out like she had climbed out of a dumpster. There was no point in trying to sleep. She started driving back to Washington, D.C.

Kate reached her as she was approaching the Watergate. She told her Randy Doran was now officially assigned to the case. They wanted to talk to her as soon as she returned. The Randy who picked Deana up for the meeting with Kate was not the concerned, smiling guy she had met in Ed's hospital room. Ed's death changed everything. Randy had lost an old friend, and his mood was somber. She knew he had every right to blame her for Ed's death. His greeting told her he didn't. He extended his hand and held on to hers, not letting go. Deana forced herself to look in his eyes.

"Deana, I know you think Ed's death is your fault," Randy said. "It's not. We're going to get the SOB who's responsible."

Randy was quietly alert on the way to Kate's office. He checked the mirrors and took a roundabout way to get there. He didn't stop the slow turning of his head from side to side until the car passed into Kate's building.

There were four beat-up, wooden chairs around the table in Kate's office. Randy and Kate sat down. Deana hesitated for a second, looking at the fourth chair. Ed would have been at this meeting. She shook her head and sat down.

Randy started off by referring to the new information Deana un-covered during her trip to Indiana. He said, "Sounds like a special psy-chopath serial murderer."

Deana blinked her eyes in surprise. Randy threw the term out in an almost chipper tone of voice instead of a sinister one. He could have been talking about Andy's major in college instead of his chosen career of a murderer. Randy's professional interest was piqued in the way a scientist would be excited by a rare specimen.

Deana tuned back in to hear Randy say it would take a couple of weeks to get approval from a judge to access Andy's brokerage accounts.

In the meantime he would run Andy and all his aliases, as well as Sandra McDonnell, through the National Crime Information Center (NCIC) database.

He said, "We already know Sandra has a record. It looks like she limited herself to embezzlement and hasn't been tied to any murders. I agree with Kate. Sandra may have been using the dating service to contact targets for embezzlement and hooked up with Andy. She could end up being his next victim. Right now, she's a good cover for him." He paused and grimaced. "You can bet he'll find a way to get rid of her if she's a liability."

Randy leaned forward in his chair. "The FBI will ask for a warrant to be issued if there's probable cause; it normally takes a couple of months, but in this case I can speed it up. I'm going to get in touch with the police in Indiana."

He turned to look at Deana. "Thanks to your snooping, we have enough for an exhumation order on Meredith Givens. Your ex is a high risk for leaving the country, and I need to get busy tracking the money transfers ASAP. We want to concentrate on figuring out his next move. The big problem is we don't know who he is now. He's established a pattern of living under false identities. We have to assume he's picked up a new one."

Randy explained that Kate would be the detective from Deana's jurisdiction to coordinate contact with the police in Indiana, Mt. Rogers, and Canada. He said the TV crime dramas made it look like the FBI swooped in and took over criminal investigations. In fact, the local police ran the investigations and sometimes asked for help or advice and resources from the FBI.

Kate said, "Randy and I worked together last year when he helped us out with a mini- serial murder in northern Virginia."

Deana raised her eyebrows. "Mini?"

"She says *mini*," Randy explained, "because the perp only managed to kill two people before she caught him. The official FBI definition describes a serial killer as someone who has killed at least three people. Kate saved some lives by contacting us for help before the official definition was met. A lot of the time the police wait too long to contact us."

Deana stared at the floor, trying to make sense of how or why some-one would kill once in a while, over a period of time, and not get caught.

Randy asked, "Hey, are you okay?"

"Yes," she said. "I heard your definition of a serial killer—someone who has killed at least three people—but what makes them do it, and how do they pull it off without getting caught? I just don't get it."

Randy proceeded to explain the psychology of serial killers and what made Andy so prototypical and yet special. He fit a lot of the commonly accepted ideas about serial killers: loner, started young, was very charm-ing, picked same type of victim and same method of killing (in Andy's case, staged accidents), and killed more than three times. What seemed to make Andy more intriguing than the typical serial killer was that he didn't engage in lust or violent killings. Randy explained that serial killers usually killed for the perverted pleasure they got from the sadistic killing. Andy was the special, organized psycho who spent time planning various ways of staging accidents. He didn't actually get his hands dirty or stick around to watch his victims suffer.

Randy said, "Officially we would classify Mr. Irwin as an *expedience killer*. He kills for profit. He shares some of the common characteristics we find in serial killers: is extremely manipulative, has no successful long-term relationships with women, works to continue to perfect his skills, and kills in a predatory, premeditated, and deliberate manner. Serial killers usually do not use firearms for their crimes.

"He planned well in advance to stage your murder and that of the previous wife, Stephanie Randall. The fact that he has the intelligence to plan and organize will make it difficult to find him. Serial killers are often obsessive and thorough in their planning, but their backgrounds are often quite different. The better we understand someone, the greater chance we'll have predicting their behavior. The best way to catch a serial killer is to think like him or her," he said, looking at Deana, as if trying to gauge her reaction. He didn't take his eyes off her. "Deana, your knowledge combined with the circumstances of the other suspected murders, will help us develop a profile to catch Mr. Irwin."

Deana looked down at her fiercely clenched hands. Randy's

description of serial killers made her realize how lucky she was to have survived. Andy didn't want to get his hands dirty; he didn't get off on a rage killing. It was the planning and fantasizing that gave him a thrill. Being a victim of the for-profit expedience killer was the only piece of good luck she had had in this whole crazy saga. She survived because he underestimated her.

Kate asked, "What about trophies? The case you helped us on last year was prosecuted on the basis of trophies the perp kept in his home—in a saxophone case, to be exact. Would Mr. Irwin be likely to have trophies stashed somewhere?"

"Right. It's like a baseball player who wants to keep a home run ball or golfers who collect golf balls from different courses and actually display them on the wall. Serial killers keep trophies of their accomplishments—undetected, meticulously planned murders—to remind them of their success. They will collect photographs, body parts, underwear, jewelry—anything they can use later on to remind them of their victims."

Kate turned to Deana. "The agent searched your town house and didn't find anything. Is there any hiding place we might have missed?"

Deana said, "There's a small gun safe in the garage. He kept it locked at all times. There's no key; it's a combination lock."

"We'll pick it up and take a look," Kate replied.

Randy reminded Kate that Andy had been to the town house. "I'll bet the safe is empty. He had a chance to remove anything from it when he went in to pick up his computer. Any trophies would be a top priority for him to keep with him. If he has to transport them, they'll be small, maybe photos."

They wanted Deana to come up with any hiding places Andy might have used. She kept thinking about what type of trophy he might have collected from his victims and what he had squirreled away to remind him of her. Remembering the photos he took on the fateful snowshoe hike sent a shiver down Deana's spine. Andy probably had a small quirky, sick album of photos of all his victims. If he had put her photo in the album, he was going to have to take it out. Randy's characterization of serial killers being organized and careful planners coincided with

Andy's personality. His desk was always neat, the file drawers were always locked, and he shredded everything. With a queasy feeling, she realized now that his need for secrecy was not related to his clients' accounts. They were fictional. The obsessive attitude toward his files was related to his crimes and victims, not to a real need for security and privacy. Randy was right. She had been carefully manipulated and groomed to accept Andy's reality.

Kate and Randy discussed catching someone in the tone of voice you would use in trading questions to solve a tricky crossword puzzle. There was no emotion in their voices. They were motivated by the intellectual aspects of the chase. Deana knew they wanted to prevent any more deaths, but, to a listener, they approached the challenge without sentiment. It was a job to them. It was personal to her—very personal.

Given Andy's background and interests, Randy felt Andy was more likely to lie low in the U.S. or Canada. His knowledge of the outdoors indicated he would stay in remote areas and not head for a big city. Randy explained that everyone had comfort levels. In times of stress animals sought out their definition of a fuzzy woolly blanket. Andy's seemed to be woods, lakes, mountains. If he had to, he could survive for a long time in remote areas with little human contact. He probably had cash stashed in bank accounts under false names. They couldn't count on finding him through the aliases he had used.

Kate agreed with Randy that Sandra could very likely become Andy's next victim. Randy suggested they focus on her home town. Flipping through the file on Sandra, Kate chuckled, saying, "According to the file, she graduated from a high school in Erie, Pennsylvania. No wonder she turned to a life of crime. Probably the only way out of Erie."

Randy laughed, "Careful, Kate. I grew up outside of Erie. It has a variety of ethnic neighborhoods, and that means good food. It is a great place to grow up. We spent the summer on the water and the winter playing in the snow." He sighed at the memories of his happy youth and quickly got back to business. "As soon as we have the subpoena, we can start tracking the money. In the meantime, we don't want to waste time. If Sandra is still alive, she's probably helping him." Randy rifled through the file on his desk and pulled out the photo of Andy in his park ranger uniform. He turned it around and held it up for Kate and Deana to see.

Kate said, "The crime scenes/accidents have all been outdoors, in woods and forests, from Indiana to Canada to Virginia. I'm betting he'll end up in another rural, woodsy area. He has a sidekick now, and it's harder to for two people to travel undetected than one person. I would think he'd avoid hotels. What's your guess?"

Randy said, "My guess is he'll look for a cabin in a state park instead of a hotel. He could lay low with the cover story that he and the little lady want to do some fishing."

Kate practically snorted when she asked, "Fishing? In the middle of winter?"

Randy laughed and said, "Yes, fishing. Ice fishing is popular in the north, and there are always cabins available around the lakes. Get their photos out to all the east coast parks. Most of the groups renting cabins this time of year are groups of men. A man and woman will stand out in someone's memory."

Randy wanted to hold off releasing photos of Andy and Sandra to the press for a few days. He was afraid it might endanger Sandra's life.

Kate said, "If only Sandra would use her cell phone and get in touch with someone, it would be easier to track them. Our best bet is to track the money; at some point, he'll need more cash. He's probably smart enough to have already transferred a large sum and set up another identity. If we're lucky, Sandra will do something careless to help us find them before Andy kills her too."

Kate filled them in on what her team had found out about Sandra McDonnell. "Nice little Catholic girl from the bad side of town. Her dad had been a small-time bookie; Sandra got caught embezzling from the local insurance office and served a light sentence at the women's prison. She was a model prisoner, took all the computer classes they offered, and got out early—an example of the powers of rehabilitation." She looked up and smiled a crooked smile, "And the reality of recidivism."

Kate told them Sandra ended up working in the IT department for an Internet dating company. She was allowed to work from home, which gave her plenty of time to work out her own scam. Kate looked at her notes and said, "She's been married three times. She met lonely men who didn't ask for a prenup, married them, and divorced them within the year, walking away with half their assets." She looked up with a wry smile and said, "No history of violence, just good old-fashioned breaking hearts and scamming."

"Do you think she's in on the plan to kill me?" Deana asked, thinking out loud.

Kate frowned and said, "Good question. From what my guys learned about her, it doesn't sound like it. She has no history of violence; however, the stakes in her three marriages were a lot smaller than the money involved in your case. Johnny, one of my investigators, talked to her sister and her mother." She looked at her watch. "I asked Johnny to join us. He should be here any minute."

Right on cue, a short, burly man with a big man's swagger entered the room. Deana couldn't help but smile as she sized him up. Johnny was about thirty and looked more like the hard-nosed law enforcement prototype than any of the other more experienced professionals she had met so far. Kate asked Johnny to describe his interview with Sandra's mother and sister.

"Well, the dad is back in jail again for running numbers. I swear the mother, Edie, was hitting on me. She's a real charmer. If Sandra's anything like her mom, I can understand how she was able to get all those men to marry her. Anyway, there's no history of violence on her father, mother, or Sandra. If Sandra's a violent criminal, I'd be surprised. Sandra and her family are the types that get away with what they can, using their wits, but they don't use weapons or violence. Edie and the sister, Debby, were genuinely worried about her when they understood the seriousness of the situation. They tsk-tsked and said Sandra was always a sucker for the good-looking guys, not the nice ones.

"Edie told Debbie to tell me everything, and she revealed that Sandra had called a week ago from DC, telling her she was about to score big and not to worry about her new baby—she would be sending Debbie money for the baby and for a lawyer for their dad. And she told them she was in love.

"All hell broke loose, and Edie started yelling, 'What do you mean she was going to score? I thought she had a real job. She'll end up in jail again.' I reminded them she was in real danger, and they both started crying. Too much drama for me." He shook his head and rolled his eyes.

Randy interrupted Johnny. "Do they have a way to get in touch with Sandra?"

Johnny said, "Sandra told them they wouldn't be able to call her. She promised to be in touch soon. Hinted she might actually be in Erie and asked if the house key was still hidden in the same place."

Randy got up and pulled out an atlas of the east coast, which he attached to a display board. He pointed to Lake Erie. "You know, Sandra's probably familiar with the U.S. side of Lake Erie, and that's a lot of unpatrolled, open shore line. It would make sense to head north and try to cross into Canada. Everyone who grows up on the Erie shore sneaks over to the Canadian beaches at some point. We would take off in a boat, run across, party, and fish. It was impossible for the Coast Guard to patrol the shore line. In those days, no one worried about it too much. Sandra may have done the same thing."

Johnny added, "She sure did. When I asked Edie and Debby to tell me about Sandra and what kind of things she liked to do, they laughed and answered, 'Party and shop.' I asked about boyfriends, and they showed me a photo of Sandra when she was about eighteen. She had her arms around a young guy holding a string of fish. Debby said he was a fisherman, a Canadian she met when they ran out of gas in the middle of the lake. Debby said they used to sneak across the lake and party with the Canadians. She mentioned Long Point and Turkey Point as the party areas. Edie said Lake Erie's more dangerous than the Bermuda Triangle, and she didn't want Sandra jumping on a boat to hook up with a guy who cared more about perch fishing than Sandra. Debby said Sandra really liked him, but it ended at the end of the summer. I tell you, those two are something else."

Randy said, "Good work, Johnny. Sandra's familiarity with the easy lake access to Canada may give Andy the idea to cross into Canada. We'll keep that in mind and get their descriptions out to the border crossings and harbor areas. Andy will keep her alive only as long as she's of use to him. That's why I would still like to keep Sandra's disappearance out of the news. He will think he's safer traveling with her as a couple. It will give us a little bit of an edge."

Randy stood up and asked Johnny to put Deana in a cab for the ride back to the Watergate. He put both hands on his hips and made eye contact. "Deana, you learned a lot on your trip to Indiana. But you put yourself and potential evidence at risk by involving yourself in the investigation. I'll need to talk to you. You have valuable insights that may help us catch your husband; however, I need you to stay in a safe place. For now, I agree with Kate that it's still dangerous for you to return to your town house. Stay with your friend at the Watergate as long as possible."

Deana nodded in agreement but knew it would be impossible to sit still and not try to figure out where Andy was. She couldn't continue to live her life looking over her shoulder, checking the rearview mirrors in the car, scanning rooms, worried Andy might be close. She also knew she needed to keep those thoughts to herself. Head down, she followed Johnny out of the room.

"Johnny," she asked, making conversation, but really wanting to know the answer, "how do you know if someone is following you?"

He stopped walking and asked quickly, "You think someone's following you?" His tone was not disbelief but concern.

She shook her head and said, "I haven't actually seen anyone. It's just a feeling. Ever since the incident at the gas station in Culpeper, I have the uneasy feeling someone's watching me."

Johnny looked at her in his no-nonsense way and said, "Lady, my advice is to follow your instincts. He might have you in his sights now. He used one woman to try to get to you. Sandra McDonnell's still out there. She might be doing his dirty work for him now. Listen to Kate and Randy. Do not go out on your own."

He slammed the door of the taxi shut and directed the driver to the

Watergate. "You speak English?" he asked the driver. The driver, who probably had a doctoral degree in his home country, assured him he did. "Okay. Sorry, buddy. I'd appreciate it if you would open the door for the lady and escort her to the entrance when you get there."

Johnny's hand slapped the roof of the cab, and it pulled out into traffic. Deana turned in the seat. Johnny stood on the sidewalk, his head scanning the street. He was watching to see if he could spot anyone following the cab.

CHAPTER 14

Deana looked out the window of the cab taking her back to what she considered a prison cell in the Watergate. The overcast day was starting to match her mood. She would follow Randy's warnings up to a point. He told her to go straight to the Watergate, but she wanted to make a scouting trip through Alexandria before returning to Cindy's apartment. Randy said it himself—she knew Andy—and knowing him meant she would recognize him by how he moved, the shape of his body, or whatever made her realize at a glance who someone is. The police would try to recognize Andy from a photo; Deana could see through a disguise.

Johnny's orders had made an impression on the driver. It took a little convincing with a twenty and her most charming smile and persuasive voice to get him to make a detour before going to the Watergate. Deana directed him to drive slowly down the street her town house was on. Shrinking into the back of the seat, she tugged at the zipper to open her jacket. She was sweating—sweating from fear, wondering if Andy was doing the same thing she was doing. They could both be circling the old neighborhood, trying to spot each other.

At the end of the street her shoulders dropped in disappointment and relief. Everything looked normal. It was unreasonable to expect to end the ordeal by spotting Andy from the safety of a cab. Deana shook her head at her own naiveté. What did she think, anyway, that she would spot Andy disguised as a repairman or dog walker, speed dial Kate, and sit safely in the cab watching Johnny grab Andy and put him in hand-cuffs? Very naive. The street was as peaceful and quiet as it should be.

The cab stopped at the light on the corner next to the neighborhood bookstore. Deana leaned forward and told the driver to pull over. The bookstore made her think about Andy surrounded by travel books and maps when he planned their hiking and camping trips. The books he had used were in the town house. She couldn't go there, so she would have to buy new books. Randy was right. She knew Andy and his habits. A memory of watching him bent over topo maps with a pencil in his mouth flashed in her mind. For one nanosecond, the image of Andy concentrating on maps brought back a warm memory of a time with her husband. Deana shook her head and reminded herself that any tender moment shared with Andy had not been real. Andy had told her he was scouting out wilderness areas for hunting. Now she knew it was far more likely he was looking for a hiding place for himself or a spot to leave one of his victims.

It took another twenty to squelch the driver's reluctance to let her get out of the cab. Deana put her hand out to push open the door at the bookstore, stopped abruptly, and spun around to scan the sidewalk. She rubbed her neck, but it didn't make the suspicious tingle that someone was watching her go away. She shook her head. Silly. Of course it felt like someone was watching her. The cab driver was leaning against the cab staring at her. Deana gave him a sarcastic smile and scanned the sidewalk one more time. It was just a normal, busy scene full of shoppers and tourists going about their business.

The bookstore was huge—three levels, with a staircase running through the middle of the store. She started walking up the stairs to the travel section on the top level but still couldn't shake the feeling someone was watching her. She stole a quick glance over her shoulder. A man was just starting up the steps. He was bundled up in a hat and coat. Couldn't be Andy—he moved like someone much older.

The realization that she knew the man stopped her dead in her tracks.

"Snooky!?" she demanded. "What are you doing here?"

Deana immediately cringed at her own stupidity. She had done exactly what she wasn't supposed to do—called attention to herself. She grabbed Snooky's arm and pulled him to a quiet area with a couple of chairs.

"You scared me," she said in a half-whispered voice. "What are you doing here?"

"Ed was worried about you. He said you aren't real good about taking orders. He was always afraid you would be an easy target if Andy was stalking you." He looked a little embarrassed. Deana calmed down when she realized why. "I guess my surveillance techniques are a little rusty. How'd you spot me?"

She sighed and said, "I don't know. I just knew it was you. I was starting to get paranoid, sensing someone was watching me. Now, I'm relieved it was you."

"Well," Snooky said. "Not just me." He gestured to a man looking at books on a shelf next to them. "Uh, Deana," he said, looking a little sheep-faced, "I'd like you to meet an old friend of mine, Frank Cosner."

A man about Snooky's height, but with scraggly light brown hair escaping from the edge of a Red Man cap, nodded to her, put the book he was pretending to read back on the shelf, and walked over to shake her hand. He was wearing jeans and a red and black flannel shirt with a pack of cigarettes peeking out of the front pocket. In spite of the work boots he was wearing, he moved quietly and gracefully.

He removed his cap and said, "Nice to meet ya'. I understand you know my daughter."

Deana looked from Frank to Snooky, confused. Frank said, "Kimberly. You took the hunter education class with my youngest daughter, Kimberly."

"Oh …," she said and looked at him for any resemblance to Kimberly. Kimberly was a rosy-cheeked cheerleader type. Her dad had small eyes and barely any eyebrows. His face was irregular—too long for the different parts—but there was something in his walk that reminded her of Kimberly. She had the long legs and moved like a cat, just like her dad.

Deana felt less paranoid. It was clear why the back of her neck had been tingling. There was a veritable parade of protectors following her, maybe more protectors than people trying to stop her. She looked at Snooky expectantly..

He said, "Deana, with Ed gone, I asked Frank to help me keep you safe. He's the best hunter I know, and he was willing to take a couple days off work to help." He paused to let that sink in and continued. "Frank won't take any money for this. Kimberly was quite taken with you, and any friend of hers is a friend … you know what I mean."

Yes, she knew what he meant. Snooky wanted to avenge Ed's death and wanted to protect her, but there was still the risk helping her would only expose more people to Andy's madness. Instead of arguing, Deana threw her hands up. She suggested they all go back to the Watergate and brainstorm about tracking Andy.

The cab was idling outside the store. The driver jumped out when he saw Deana walking toward the cab with two men, neither of whom looked particularly prosperous or respectable. He watched them warily, shrugged his shoulders, and got back in the car when Snooky opened the door of the cab. Deana started to get in but turned and, choking back tears, said, "Snooky, I'm so sorry about Ed."

Before she could tell him it was her fault, he put his good hand on her shoulder and said, "Ed saved my life once. He probably didn't tell you that. I owe him."

Deana thought about Jack. He would be miffed when he found out she had met with Snooky and Frank and hadn't asked for his help. The thing was, in addition to her wanting to see him, Jack would actually be a logical person to help them figure out what Andy might do to hide or escape. He was an outdoorsman, and he was smart.

Jack answered his phone on the first ring. Deana explained the situation. Jack's voice sounded amused when he responded to her request to join the brainstorming session.

"I thought you'd never ask," Jack said. He volunteered to pick up Chinese carryout for everyone on his way.

Deana blinked quickly, trying to get rid of the pang of disappointment that flashed through her mind. She and Jack wouldn't be working alone. A rueful look crossed her face. She didn't want to delve any further into analyzing that disappointment. There were two old sayings she repeated to convince herself she wasn't putting the three men in danger: there's safety in numbers, and lightning never strikes twice. A killer had maneuvered her way into the apartment and killed Ed. Deana was sure of one thing. That particular bolt of lightning would not strike again.

Snooky spread Deana's purchases out on the dining table: books on national and state parks on the east coast and maps. It was clear right away that Snooky and Frank would be a big help. Deana suggested calling the parks in Virginia that rented out cabins, but Snooky knew all the Virginia campgrounds and park cabins would be closed through the winter.

"The only places open will be around ski resorts. Pennsylvania or West Virginia might be a better bet." He laughed. "Virginians are fair-weather adventurers. Pennsylvania and parts of West Virginia have a lot of rough winter weather, and folks there will hunt, ice fish, and even camp through the winter. Besides," he added, "this Sandra McDonnell's from Pennsylvania. She may know a spot that would be a good hideout."

"Hey," Deana said, "I remember two of the women in the hunter education class, Lorna and Linda, were getting ready for a hunting trip to Pennsylvania with their husbands."

"That's right," Frank said and pulled the Pennsylvania map in front of him. "Never could talk my wife into anything like that. Little Kimberly's been buggin' me to take her ever since she heard about Lorna and Linda goin' up there," he continued, pointing to a spot on the map. "Allegheny National Forest, 516,000 acres of wilderness. This is where Lorna and Linda are headed with their husbands." His fingers rested on a small town on the southern tip of the wilderness area. "But if you want to disappear, you'd head up here." He pointed to an area in the middle of the forest.

Frank pushed his chair back and paced around the room, rubbing the stubble on his chin and tossing a cigarette lighter from hand to hand.

Snooky looked at him and asked, "What are you thinking, Frank?"

Frank stopped his pacing and said, "If he's tryin' to keep from getting caught, the best camouflage might be to hide among other people instead of tryin' to disappear in a wilderness area."

He pulled the map in front of him and ran his hand from the middle to the northeast part of the forest. "The only roads accessible by car here will be one or two the forest service will pack down to get to snowmobilers who run into trouble." His finger pointed to a spot on the map labeled Pymatuning State Park. "This is closer to the interstate. There's a large lake and a reservoir that goes for at least sixteen miles. Best fishing I've ever seen. And there are a lot of cabins and a big campground in the state park. It will be more crowded than the forest. You can pick up a snowmobile and ice fish."

Noisy snowmobiles and waiting for a fish to bite under the ice didn't sound like Deana's idea of a good time, but what Frank said made sense.

"I'd go here, just like Lorna and Linda and their husbands," he said, pointing to the forest. "I like peace and quiet when I'm fishing, but this guy might figure he'd stand out less in a crowd, ya' know what I'm sayin'?" He cocked an eye at Snooky.

"Frank, you may be right," Snooky said. He nodded at Deana, "Greg told Deana he thought Andy might head for Canada across Lake Erie. Pymatuning is pretty darn close to Lake Erie and the highway."

Jack traced a line on the map from the Allegheny National Forest to Erie and across a dotted line in Lake Erie delineating the Canadian border.

"Hard to patrol this border," he said. "I had an aunt who lived in Port Rowan. We visited once when I was a kid." He pointed to a harbor on the Canadian side, on a straight line from Erie, Pennsylvania. "There wasn't much there then: a large marsh, a lighthouse, and a few old shacks on the beach. There probably hasn't been much development since then. It would be a good spot to cross into Canada."

Snooky pulled out a map of Ontario. "Look at that," he said, "barely thirty miles across the lake from Erie to Long Point, Canada."

"That's one of the towns the detective who interviewed Sandra's family mentioned," Deana said. "The sister told him Sandra would sneak across the lake and party around Long Point and Turkey Point."

They all leaned in to study the map. Long Point Provincial Park and Turkey Point Provincial Park were both highlighted on the maps. Deana barely heard Snooky say, "It makes sense. A short drive from the northern tip of the forest and they're at Erie and a short boat ride into Canada. It makes a lot more sense than trying to hide in the States."

Deana wrinkled her nose, picking up the reassuring masculine smells from the heads just a few inches from hers. She kept her eyes on the map and fought to keep her emotions in check. It wouldn't do to lose it and start crying because the smell of Old Spice, sweat, and starched work shirts made her feel safe among friends. If they thought her courage or resolve was waning, they would smother her with concern. Even worse, Snooky might insist he stay with her, and that would restrict her movement too much. Her thoughts were racing, but she forced a benign expression to stay in place. She didn't want to miss the opportunity to be there when they caught up with Andy. That thought scared the sentimental, weepy feelings away, and she focused on the map.

An uneasy sixth sense nagged at her as her eyes slid north and south between Long Point and Pennsylvania. A straight shot north through Virginia and Pennsylvania would pass through small towns in run-down areas. Another guy dressed in camouflage would not be noticed. Sandra, on the other hand, might leave an impression. Andy would dispose of her before the tried to sneak into Canada. A premonition Deana couldn't keep to herself made her say, "He'll kill her, won't he?"

"Yep. He'll have a better chance traveling quickly and undetected without her," Snooky said. "It may already be too late." He paused and took a breath, "Okay. He could find a cabin on a website, or he could just rent a snowmobile and find an unused cabin for a night or two. Let's get to work. It doesn't matter if he broke into a cabin or rented one. If he's far enough away from civilization, he won't have electricity. He'll have to burn wood or use a generator, and someone will notice. Kate can get the Forest Service to help. They'll know if someone's in one of the remote areas. We can help her by doing some of the grunt work."

They called, emailed, or faxed every possible cabin rental they could find in the Allegheny National Forest and the Pymatuning State Park.

Snooky's orders were to just find out about cabins and snowmobiles for rent. He warned that it was Kate's job to ask for help in identifying Andy and Sandra as renters. After a couple of hours, they had put together a short list of cabins for rent in the winter.

Snooky and Frank checked the hallway and relocked the door. They headed to the guest bedroom, stifling yawns as they walked down the hall. Deana watched them and thanked her lucky stars they had her back. She was as tired as their drooping shoulders told her they were.

The room was very quiet. Deana and Jack sat comfortably in the silence. Deana was exhausted and unconsciously let her eyes close. She blinked them open quickly at Jack's touch. He put his hand over hers.

"Deana, when this is over—and it will be over soon—it would do you good to get away. Promise me you'll come back to Jasper for a long visit." He teased, "The Park Service offers a great course on wilderness survival skills." He smiled mischievously. "You could teach the class. You can ski through April; Linda will teach you to curl."

His voice grew softer. "Linda and Jim are your friends. Remember, Jim saved your life. You are part of their life now. They want to make sure you stay in touch."

Deana was afraid she would burst into tears. She didn't risk saying a word. She just looked at Jack and nodded.

"And Jasper promotes healing," Jack continued. "You'll need a peaceful environment and friends once all this is over."

"My last visit wasn't all that peaceful!" Deana protested. "But if getting over this is like getting back on a horse, I want to retrace the hike to the lake, scramble up the side of the cliff, and paddle a boat around on the lake."

She looked into Jack's very kind face and had to fight to not collapse in his arms. She put her hands on top of his and said, "Thanks, Jack." She meant it from the bottom of her heart. She wanted to say they would all drink a toast to Ed but couldn't risk more than the two words, or the tears would start.

Jack nodded. He made Deana promise to stay inside and let Snooky be her eyes and ears. Jack would be tied up with his exhibit the next day but would call to check on her.

Snooky and Deana were up early. Frank was already on his way home. He had left Deana a message to call Kimberly when this was over. Snooky looked her in the eye and explained that he had told Frank to go on home because he knew she was now going to listen and stay inside the Watergate. Deana smiled and saluted him to show she understood.

She sent an email to Kate with the possible hideouts for Andy they had found in Pennsylvania. She was surprised to get an immediate response: "This is exactly the sort of grunt work that can turn up a lead. We'll send out a fax with photos of Andy and Sandra to everyone on your list. The fax will include a warning to not attempt to apprehend them but to contact my office immediately. If you want to stay at it, do the same for West Virginia and the Carolinas."

Snooky and Deana exhausted possibilities for snowmobile rentals and cabin rentals in West Virginia and the Carolinas. Finally Deana talked him into going home. Before he agreed, he looked at her sternly and said, "You'll stay inside, right?"

Deana sighed. She was getting a little tired of hearing that demand from everyone. She crossed her heart. Snooky took off with a promise of coming back the next day—or sooner if she needed him. Deana stood gazing out over the view of the Potomac River from the Watergate apartment. She remembered what Randy had said about serial killers. One of the characteristics was that they were often meticulous planners. Andy had known Sandra for several months. He had plenty of time to plan escape routes and would have had plenty of time to get to know her well enough to find out about her teen years in Erie. It wouldn't take a genius to figure out that crossing from Erie to Canada was possible. The more she thought about it, the more certain she was Sandra would meet with one of Andy's accidents as soon as she had served her purpose.

One thing she couldn't explain was why she cared about saving the life of a woman who might have been helping Andy plan her own death. Johnny's description of Sandra and her family made Deana think

Sandra was also a victim of Andy's powers of manipulation. He could easily have painted himself as the victim and Deana the villain to enlist her sympathy and help. She had to give Sandra the benefit of the doubt.

To kill time and keep herself sane while waiting to hear from Kate, she started searching the Web for information on the Canadian towns Sandra's sister and Jack had mentioned. The information on Long Point was fascinating. It was a twenty-three mile- long sand spit jutting out into Lake Erie, connected to land by a causeway. It looked wild and beautiful, a rare stretch of undeveloped beach, woodlands, marshes, and ponds. The waters around it were treacherous and had the nickname of "the graveyard of the Great Lakes." The dangerous waters had kept development away from the area. It was thousands and thousands of acres of protected marshland and home to a private hunting club. Deana's fingers started to twitch and wiggle over the keyboard. The more she learned about the area the more she realized that Andy would fit right in.

An image of her husband sitting in front of a glowing screen destroyed Deana's concentration. He was hunched over the keyboard, rapidly clicking and moving around the articles about Long Point. Deana wasn't superstitious, but she did have to admit to an occasional tinge of true extrasensory feelings. It was one of those fleeting feelings that she was trying to ignore now as she fought to push the image of Andy out of her mind. She didn't want to even consider that the two of them were reading the same articles.

Yet it made sense. Of course Sandra would have told him all about Long Point. Andy would have checked out the area—just like Deana was doing. He would have found it to be the perfect hiding place.

Randy was the one who had said Deana knew Andy better than anyone else. The idea that Randy was right and that she was now channeling a murderer's thought processes sent a small shiver through her. The ringing phone brought her out of the spooky daydream.

Deana saw it was Kate calling. She quickly grabbed her phone, hoping Kate had good news.

"Deana, we just got a call from Pymatuning State Park in Pennsylvania. The park ranger there saw the fax. Instead of responding that cabin rentals were closed in October, he took the initiative to call a little private cabin rental business that caters to ice fishermen. A couple rented a cabin for two weeks. The park ranger scanned the photos to the manager, and he was pretty sure it was Andy and Sandra. It looks like they're laying low for a few days. They checked in yesterday. We're putting together a team with the local Pennsylvania police, the state forest service, and our guys. We're headed up there in a couple of hours. This all happened about five hours ago. We have to move fast. He rented the cabin for a couple of weeks, but that doesn't mean anything. They might stay for a couple of days and keep moving."

"Yes! I can't believe it!" Deana screamed. She was on the verge of thanking Kate for letting her know. Kate didn't give her a chance.

"I'm calling you because we're going to need an article of Andy's clothing. The cabin is a mile from the parking area, and the only access is a snow-packed snowmobile trail. We're going to have to surround the cabin on foot. The local police have access to a bloodhound. Working with the dog would at least help us confirm it was Andy who got out of a car, got on a snowmobile, and headed to the cabin. So, how about it, is there still any of Andy's clothing in the house? Something we could use to give the bloodhound the scent?" Kate asked.

"Yes, clothes and shoes," Deana answered quickly.

"Okay. Johnny will meet you at the town house and pick up anything you think Andy might have been the last person to handle. Bloodhounds are pretty incredible. Their ability to pick up a scent and remember it is hard to believe. We'll FedEx the scent packages to the local officer who works with the bloodhound to be ready in case we have to use the dog."

Deana winced at the bad play on words, but she was so excited she didn't care. "Kate, it sounds like you're using a good dog to catch a bad dog. What in the heck is a scent package?"

Kate laughed, "Nice to see you've still got a sense of humor. The bloodhound's handler, Dave Stewart, captures the scent on a piece of gauze; he wipes down something the perpetrator would have touched, puts the gauze in a sealed baggie, and places the baggie over the dog's snout until he has absorbed it. Voilà, ole Jake is ready to track. It's pretty amazing to watch. Dave and Jake have been involved in a lot of important cases; we're lucky they're close by and available. Gotta go—I'm moving into a dead zone. Get a move on. Johnny will be at the town house in twenty minutes. We'll keep you posted; don't touch the clothes or shoes. Just be ready to point them out to Johnny!" she warned.

Deana sighed in relief. Her creepy premonitions about tracking Andy down in Long Point were examples of letting her imagination run away with her. A bloodhound would do the tracking. Kate's team would stop Andy before he left the States. Whistling, Deana quickly threw her things in a suitcase. She had to move fast to meet Johnny. She was already counting on being able to spend the night in her own home.

She paused at the door for one last glance around Cindy's guest room. A large (and, to Deana's eye, outlandish) modern piece of art was the focal point in the room. It looked like someone had thrown handfuls of red, black, and blue paint onto a white canvas. The room had everything a guest would need: desk, dressers, television. But it reflected Cindy's taste for everything sleek and modern. And it was a guest room, not home. Deana closed her eyes for a second and pictured herself ensconced on her own comfy gold sofa, feet resting on the matching ottoman, remote pointed at the gas fireplace. The roaring fire wouldn't provide the smell of wood burning. The smell of popcorn and hot chocolate would compensate. Yes, that was how she would spend the evening. After Johnny collected the scent package, her own home was where she wanted to wait for news that Andy was in custody, and the nightmare was over.

CHAPTER 15

Deana closed the solid hickory door of her townhome and rested her back against it. It was just after 5:00 p.m. Before she had a chance to enjoy the relief of being in her own home, her cell phone rang. It was Kate calling from Pennsylvania. Deana jumped up from the table as she listened to Kate's news. A car that met the cabin owner's description and the trailer for the snowmobile were parked at the trailhead in the parking area for the cabin. There were fresh snowmobile tracks leading down the trail.

An image of a smiling bloodhound, slobber dripping from its jowls, long ears flopping from side to side, popped into Deana's mind when Kate told her Jake had picked up Andy's scent in the parking area. A smile of triumph broke out on Deana's face when Kate went on to describe Jake's eagerness to head down the trail. They had Andy cornered.

Deana stood still. Her eyes moved around the table where she and Andy had shared many meals. She looked down. The hand not holding the phone had a death grip on the back of a kitchen chair. That chair had been Andy's chair. She pulled the chair away from the table and shoved it into a corner.

Kate heard the loud scraping noise from the chair legs being dragged across the floor. "Deana, what was that sound?" Kate demanded.

"It's okay. I shoved a chair to let off some steam. I should be happy and icing down a bottle of champagne. But I'm afraid even anticipating the celebration that this nightmare is over will jinx it. I won't be able to breathe until I know you have caught him. How much longer?"

"We've paired a local with each of our guys. It's too risky to approach through the forest at night. Any sounds would be magnified in the still night air. And any lights they need to find their way might give Andy enough warning to make an escape. We have to count on the fact that he may have night vision goggles. The team will start moving in on snowshoes at the crack of dawn. As soon as they let us know they've surrounded the cabin, I'll be out there on a snowmobile with the local sheriff."

Kate explained that early-morning snowmobile engine sounds would not necessarily alarm Andy and Sandra. Andy would assume a snowmobiler had taken the wrong trail. Instead of the "sound of music" filling the hills, the hills in the area were filled with the loud, whining sounds of snowmobiles all through the day.

Deana sat quietly after she ended the call with Kate. Then she deliberately walked into the kitchen pantry, found a bottle of champagne, and put it in the refrigerator. There was no joy on her face or in her movements. She had an uneasy feeling about Andy really being trapped. But she had enough hope to make the gesture of chilling the champagne.

She walked through each room, checking again to make sure every window was locked. Her cell phone was in her pocket. The gun and holster were still hanging around her shoulder. Standing in the doorway of the master bedroom, she stared at the bed she had shared with Andy. No way would she crawl into that bed. Instead, she padded up the stairs to the guest bedroom. Her hand moved to the light switch, but she pulled it back. No reason to let anyone watching the house know where she was. Even now, knowing Kate would have Andy in custody within a few hours, she felt like she was in hiding in her own home.

She sat down on the twin bed fully clothed, took a deep breath, and laid her head on the pillow. Her eyes closed, but her thoughts kept her awake. She imagined Kate's team sneaking into place around the cabin and the look on Andy's face when he realized they had caught him. She finally fell asleep with the image of Jack, Snooky, Kate, even grouchy Detective Wheeler, toasting Ed's memory and Andy's capture.

Deana was settled in front of her fireplace in the den with her morning coffee and the newspaper. It was the first day she felt safe enough to walk down the street to grab the papers. She had gladly shed the gun and holster and left it on the table before leaving the town house. The only sign of her nervousness was the constant picking up of her cell phone. She stared at it, willing it to ring. Kate finally called a little after 9:00 a.m. Deana answered with a smile, which disappeared as soon as Kate started talking.

"I'm sorry. He *was* here. It looks like he rented the cabin and left right away. There were no signs it had been used at all. We found the abandoned snowmobile in another parking lot used by snowmobilers. We're trying to figure out if he stole another car or truck or had one pre-positioned. We'll know by the end of the day if a snowmobiler shows up, and his vehicle is missing. Get back to Cindy's apartment. It's the safest place for you until we know which way they're headed."

Deana groaned. "Shit! We'll never find him, will we?" she demanded.

"We were close this time. I made a mistake. I didn't think he'd keep moving. I was so sure we would catch him in the cabin. We've got an APB out on him. Someone may recognize him. He has to stop for gas; he has to buy food. Call me when you're safely back at Cindy's apartment."

Deana settled back in her chair, disgusted, and looked at the gun and holster resting on the table by the window. Sighing, she got up and walked to retrieve them. Looked like she would be Annie Oakley for a few more days. As soon as her back was turned, she heard a sound she had learned to recognize in the last few days—the click of a gun hammer. Deana immediately recognized the woman holding a gun on her.

"Sandra McDonnell?" she asked.

"Nice to meet you," Sandra responded coldly. "Sit down. Nice little fire you got goin' there." She walked over to the table and picked up Deana's gun. Keeping her gun pointed at Deana, she dropped a pill into the coffee cup and stirred it a few times.

Deana took a long, slow breath. She remembered everything Johnny had said about Sandra. She wasn't supposed to be a violent criminal.

"Sandra, talk to me. Where's Andy? What are you doing?"

"Honey, there's nothing to talk about. You will drink that and fall asleep. I'm going to close this room up tight and you'll die peacefully." She glanced at her perfectly manicured nails and smiled at Deana. "Drink up, like a good girl, so I don't have to shoot you. Now!" she ordered.

Sandra's eyes darted around the room nervously. "Are you alone?"

Deana realized if Sandra wanted to shoot her, it would have already happened. Sandra had to use both hands to hold the gun up, and it looked to Deana like her hands were shaking.

"Yes, I'm alone. How did you get in?" Deana tried to keep her voice low and soothing.

Sandra decided to answer that question. "Used a glass cutter on the panel in your back door." She seemed to be proud of herself. "You didn't hear a thing, did you?"

"No, I didn't. You did a good job." Deana figured the irony of her praise was lost on Sandra. She just wanted to keep her talking. There was a slim chance she could talk Sandra out of killing her. "Sandra, you're not a killer. Don't do this. As soon as Andy is finished with you, you'll be his next victim."

Sandra's eyes flashed in anger. Deana swore to herself. She had definitely taken the wrong approach.

"No, he won't!" Sandra said defiantly. "He loves me. He told me all about you." She held up a hand to display a flashy diamond. "As soon as we get rid of you, we're getting married."

Sandra took a step in Deana's direction and almost tripped. She took her anger out on Deana.

"No more talking, bitch. Now, drink that. It won't hurt. You'll fall asleep."

Deana looked at her quizzically and reached for the cup. "Sandra, what's in this?"

Sandra looked scared and nervous. "The pill is Andy's idea. I've never shot anyone before. You'll fall asleep, I'll turn the gas fireplace up as high as it will go, and I'll shut the room up tight." She paused. "It won't hurt."

Deana figured Sandra had somehow managed to rationalize that if it didn't hurt, killing Deana would be okay. She took another tack.

"I've got money. I'll give you whatever you want. Please, Sandra, don't do this."

"I'm through talking. Drink," she ordered. She grabbed a pillow and put it in front of the gun. Deana let the coffee mixture touch her lips and pretended to swallow.

"Good," Sandra said. "Now, I'll just sit here until you finish and fall asleep."

"Oh, I'm so tired," Deana moaned, feigning grogginess in the hope of getting rid of her.

Deana remembered Andy talking to the man when they installed the gas fireplace. Andy had wanted to put it in the bedroom, but they were not allowed to install an unvented fireplace in a bedroom. The man's words came back to her: *People close their bedroom doors. If the fire burns up the oxygen in the room, the occupants will asphyxiate.* Andy had obviously planned this scenario to make it easy for Sandra.

The word Andy used when he pushed Deana to close the open doorway to the living room with double doors was *cozy*. "Honey, the room will be so much cozier if we put double doors in that entry."

Deana shivered, remembering the rest of his sales pitch. He had put his arm around her and said, "Think about it. A nice fire burning and we'll keep all the heat in here. It will be a cozy spot on chilly nights."

Asphyxiation was obviously one of his possible scenarios for Deana's accidental death. She grimaced, wondering how many other contingencics Andy had planned for her.

"Sandra, I'll asphyx …" Deana started to say when out of the corner of her eye she saw her one-armed protector sneaking up behind Sandra. He hit Sandra over the head with his gun. Snooky caught Sandra's gun with his bad arm and knocked it across the room as she fell to the floor.

"You okay?" He asked Deana. "How much did you drink?"

"It just touched my lips. I think I'll be okay. Don't tell me, you were following me again?" Snooky was dressed in black from head to toe. He pulled off the black ski cap covering his head. He picked up Sandra's gun and handed it to Deana.

"Yes, ma'am. Lucky for you Kate called and warned me you were at your town house. I knew the policewoman was no longer in the house, so I drove up early this morning and have been sitting outside since 6:00 a.m. I watched you go for coffee and go back inside. A woman walked up to the front door. She seemed to be listening. She walked around to the back, as if she knew what she was doing. At first, I figured it was someone who knew you. Then I decided I better make sure. I saw the open door in the back, and the rest is history."

Deana watched Snooky pull out a pair of handcuffs. He rolled Sandra over and put the handcuffs on her. His ski cap was askew, and his all-black clothing made him look more like a criminal than Sandra. He had bags under his eyes. The man had been sitting in a cold car all day, keeping an eye on her. Snooky sat down in a chair but kept his gun on Sandra.

"Deana, could I have a cup of coffee?"

Deana laughed. "Snooky, you can have anything you want. Coffee coming right up. There's a bottle of champagne in the refrigerator. I was saving it for news they've caught up with Andy. You take it home to your wife. And tell her she's a very lucky woman to be married to you."

Deana stepped around Sandra's body to get to the kitchen. She was standing over a woman's inert body—albeit one who had just tried to kill her—and the only emotion she felt was frustration. Snooky's blow had done such a good job that Sandra might still be out cold when the police arrived. Deana wanted to ask Sandra a few questions of her own. She realized this was the third murder attempt she had survived. It hadn't quite become a ho-hum experience, but she felt oddly unemotional. It might have been the shock of looking down the barrel of a gun.

"Deana," Snooky said, "you've survived Andy's attempted murder and attempts by two amateurs. With his resources, he may enlist a professional next time. Ed wanted you to get out of town—maybe go back to Jasper—until the police catch Andy. I think Ed was right."

Deana didn't answer; she just nodded and went to get Snooky's coffee.

Randy arrived with the police just as Sandra sat up and started moaning about the pain in her head. Randy would work with the local police while Kate was holding tight in Pennsylvania, ready to move if they got a lead on Andy. They expected Sandra to cooperate and lead them to Andy.

Randy's interrogation approach was completely different from the one Detective Wheeler had used on Deana. Randy helped Sandra into a chair and gave her a glass of water before he began asking questions. Sandra started crying, but the tears did not touch Deana. Deana stood, arms folded, watching and listening in a corner of the room.

Randy spoke softly and encouraged Sandra to help them figure out where Andy was planning to go. Sandra demanded more than requested consideration for her help. Andy had met his match in Sandra. She admitted she had told him all about the sparsely populated coast line on the Canadian side of Lake Erie. They had talked about the empty cottages being a perfect hideout.

Sandra had shown Andy the tiny Canadian towns of Long Point and Port Rowan that were directly across from Erie. They were the same towns her sister had mentioned.

Randy asked, "Was Andy waiting for your call after you took care of Deana?"

She hesitated before answering, with a cunning smile, "Anything I did, I was forced to do to protect my family. He threatened to kill them if I didn't help him. I want a lawyer." After that, she refused to answer any questions.

Randy motioned for the police to take Sandra away. He called Kate, and they filled each other in on what was happening in short, quick sentences. After saying good-bye to Kate, Randy turned to Snooky and Deana.

"We're not 100 percent sure he's planning to cross into Canada. It's a little more complicated than we thought. The shoreline of Lake Erie on the Canadian side, especially the small bays, is still frozen. A boat could get out of the Erie harbor but wouldn't be able to get through to the Canadian side until Port Colborne, which is almost as far north as Buffalo. We can notify the harbors that are accessible, but the areas still frozen will be empty except for ice fishing shacks. The good news is that there isn't much small boat traffic out this time of year. The large freighters are still coming through the Welland Canal across Lake Erie to the large U.S. harbors, but the ice and changeable March weather make it too dangerous for small craft. The bad news is this has been their worst winter on record, and the ice is frozen three feet deep; it would not be impossible for Andy to drive the boat up against the ice and walk right across it to land."

Deana didn't say what she was thinking. With a bit of luck, Andy would hear the same frightening sound of cracking ice she had heard on the other side of Canada and would fall through the ice and become part of Davy Jones's locker. She wanted him to fall through the ice and die miserably, slowly freezing to death. Poetic justice indeed. She wondered if, in his last lucid moments, he would appreciate the irony of his meeting the fate he had planned for her. On the other hand, she wanted the body to be found. She didn't want to have to wonder if he was still out there, plotting and planning the deaths of more women.

Randy told her the RCMP and the border crossings at Detroit and Buffalo had all been alerted and had a photo of Andy. The harbor areas along the U.S. shore close to Erie had also been warned that Andy might try to rent or steal a boat.

Deana knew she couldn't keep following Andy's trail. She had to let go and try to get back to a normal life. *However,* she thought stubbornly, *we're so close. Maybe just a couple more days out of my life and the nightmare will be over.*

She looked at the maps and considered flying versus driving to Buffalo. Even if she drove, she didn't want to cross the border with a gun. If she couldn't take her gun, she might as well fly. She booked a flight to Buffalo and decided to stay in a hotel there until she heard from Kate. Andy might fool everyone again and head south or even up to Buffalo instead of crossing the lake.

Kate hadn't even bothered telling her to stay inside the Watergate.

Snooky had followed Deana back there and probably thought she was sitting inside, sipping a cup of tea, and trying to recover from the latest attempt on her life. She shook her head. No way she would let Snooky in on her plans and put him at risk again.

It was warm in Virginia—in the low fifties. Deana checked the Buffalo forecast, shivered, and grabbed her ski jacket. She called Jack from the airport.

After he heard she was headed to Buffalo, he said, "Change the ticket, and fly to Jasper. You'll be safer there. Let the police bring him in. You can stay at my place. I can leave D.C. tomorrow."

"Jack, I need to stay close to the action until they catch him. I know this sounds gruesome, but I need to see him either in jail or, even better, dead. I guarantee you if they need me to identify the body, you will not see the tears of a grieving widow!" She heard Jack laugh and continued. "Worst case, I'll see what Buffalo has to offer."

Jack joked, "That would be snow and buffalo wings."

A comfortable silence lasted a long minute. They understood each other. Jack knew Deana wanted an end to looking over her shoulder, and Deana knew Jack was worried about her.

Finally, Deana said, "It just so happens I like both."

"Look," Jack said, "I'm just worried about you. Your ex seems to have an incredible ability to talk people into doing his dirty work for him. He'll know Sandra didn't succeed and will be on the lookout for the police and you."

His voice dropped. Deana sensed his face clouding over and his eyes trying to look into hers through the phone.

"He could be anywhere," Jack said. "Deana, you think you're tracking him down, but he could be the one following you—even now."

Deana gulped and closed her eyes. In a horrible mental flash she saw Andy's face leering at her in the disguise of an airport security officer.

"Jack! Stop it. You're scaring me. Don't worry. I'll be careful."

She wasn't as confident as she wanted Jack to think she was. He was right. Andy had outsmarted everyone many times. It was stupid of her to assume she now had the upper hand.

"Okay, you win." Jack said with a sigh. "I'll get on a plane to Toronto as soon as I can. All this has got me thinking about the time I spent there as a kid. The marsh areas around Long Point are beautiful. This is probably not the best time of year to visit, but you know I like doing series sketches. If we like the area, we can return in the spring and catch the migrating birds."

Deana thought to herself, *I like the way he keeps saying* we.

"Jack," she said, "you could become even more famous for sketching ice shacks. I guess the title would be 'Ice Shacks on Long Point.'"

"Enough sarcasm. The correct term is *ice hut,* not *shack.* And it would be an interesting change from the mountain vistas. Call me when you find a hotel, and I'll let you know how soon I can get there. Just promise me you won't start detecting on your own. Wait for me!"

Jack's plea was a sobering reminder that Andy had a habit of escaping at just the right time. She could feel the excitement—they were close— but she needed to remember that she wasn't safe until they caught him.

CHAPTER 16

Buffalo lived up to its reputation. Walking through the airport in Buffalo, every fast food store advertised "Best Buffalo Wings." A poster-sized colored photo of a smiling man stopped Deana dead in her tracks. What appeared to be a gigantic chicken wing hat was perched on top of the man's head. The poster invited passersby to attend the spring Buffalo Wing Festival. Deana walked into the closest food kiosk advertising Buffalo wings. She was hungry and intrigued. A town that threw an annual Buffalo Wing Festival had to have good wings. She walked out of the airport with a carryout box holding a dozen Buffalo wings.

When Deana stepped outside the airport, she buttoned her coat. Jack had said to expect Buffalo wings and snow. He was correct. It was freezing, and the sky was gray. The piles of snow heaped by the side of the road were ample evidence the city was in a snow belt. The tops of the mountains of snow were no longer white. The dirt in the air had settled on the snowbanks and turned them from white to gray. The directions given to her by the rental car attendant took her on a route around the city of Buffalo. Century-old buildings that once housed booming factories now sported broken windows. The once-beautiful red brick was buried under years of soot. The city looked tired and shabby until Deana noticed the forms of people ice skating on the canal below the expressway. Colorful food trucks lined the canal. It appeared a little snow did not stop the locals.

Seeing the food trucks reminded her she was hungry. The box with the wings was sitting on the console between the seats. She reached for a Buffalo wing and groaned after the first bite. They were delicious. Jack would have to change his attitude. The wings alone were worth a trip to Buffalo.

Deana turned up the volume on the car radio when she heard the words *travel advisory*. The world stopped at the mention of snow in northern Virginia, but when Buffalo worried about heavy snow, she figured she should pay attention.

A lake-effect snowstorm was forecast for that afternoon. Listeners were warned to be prepared for possible blizzard conditions when the wind started to pick up. The phone started ringing, and a glance showed it was Kate. Deana took the next exit. Kate might have news that would make it feel like the sun was out in Buffalo.

Deana's mood brightened when she heard Kate's exciting news.

"A boat was reported missing from a small harbor outside of Erie. The owner is a commercial charter boat captain. He was on the Coast Guard boat that found his abandoned boat run up onto a frozen section of the lake between Long Point and Turkey Point. It looks like Jack's hunch about the area was a good one."

Kate usually stayed on an even keel, but this time her voice was uncharacteristically enthusiastic. She paused and said, "Now, for the really good news. A rental car found in the harbor parking lot was rented to a *Ron Morris,* the name Andy used when he rented the cabin. The car rental agent identified Andy as the renter from a photo. It isn't like him to make a mistake like this. He has to be getting tired."

Deana relaxed her grip on her phone. "Thanks, Kate. I'm afraid to ask. What's the bad news?"

"Well," Kate said, "the Coast Guard boat was equipped with ice rescue equipment, which included a special all-terrain vehicle(ATV). The bad news is the rescue crew decided it was too risky to use the ATVs to follow the tracks across the ice and opted for snowshoes. They had just started to follow the tracks when a warning came on the weather radio announcing a quick-moving snowstorm with high winds. The search had to be aborted, which means the blowing winds and snow will probably cover the boat thief's tracks before the search can be resumed. If—and

that's a big if at this point—Andy does make it to shore, it will be difficult to track him."

Deana's heart sank when she realized catching Andy might not be a
sure thing. He could slip away.

"Deana, your charming husband is one lucky guy. The local RCMP
in Port Rowan said they just didn't have the staff to patrol the whole
shoreline but would do what they could. It was already snowing so hard
there that visibility was reduced to zero. All the ice fishermen were off
the ice, but word was out to report any strangers. No one will be out on
the lake until the storm is over."

Kate sighed and spoke again with more energy. "Andy has managed
to stay a step ahead of us, but this time Mother Nature may be on our
side. I'm sure it has occurred to you he could freeze to death out there
on the ice."

"We can only hope," Deana responded laconically, without an iota
of guilt for wishing Andy would freeze to death on Lake Erie. "Talk
about poetic justice!"

Kate's voice didn't contain any of the discouragement Deana felt.
She said with energy, "The lake is frozen three feet thick several miles
from shore. The searchers think Andy had a forty-to-sixty-minute lead
on the search team. The storm is moving north to south, which means
he's heading into it as he tries to cross into Canada."

Deana remembered the start of their snowshoe trek in the Canadian
Rockies just a few weeks ago—sheer blazing white all around. For a
moment, she forgot the horrible ending and remembered the thrill of
making the first tracks in the snowy wilderness. Now, it was Andy trying to make an escape in the middle of a snowstorm. She thought about
him floundering in the drifting snow that covered the frozen lake. The
fleeting feeling of perverse satisfaction that he was now experiencing the
same trials and tribulations she had faced evaporated when she realized
Andy would be equipped with snowshoes. The jerk probably had the
foresight to include a tent and other necessary items for his survival—the
very items he had discouraged Deana from including in her backpack
on what was supposed to be a romantic snowshoe hike.

She pounded the dashboard of the car with her fist and spoke quickly, the words running into each other, "Kate, you can't let him get away! What if he backtracks to the U.S.? Maybe a boat rescued him, and he isn't heading toward the Canadian shore."

Kate said, "Deana, calm down. We've thought of that and have an alert out on both sides of Lake Erie. The Coast Guard said there were signs someone headed from the abandoned boat in the direction of Canada. RCMP will be ready to move out onto the ice as soon as the weather permits. The storm is a positive. It will hold Andy up until we can get into place."

Deana noticed Kate had stopped referring to the boat thief as "the man" or "the thief." Andy was on his own, making tracks across the ice. If his tracks were covered by the heavy snow, he was more likely to stumble around and lose his direction. There were no trees and no cover or shelter for him on the frozen lake. Deana started to feel more confident that Andy had been outsmarted by Mother Nature. Now, she started hoping for a record-breaking storm that would trap him.

Deana started searching the Web for a hotel close to Long Point or Turkey Point. She didn't think about the danger she would be in if she managed to find Andy. She just knew she had to keep moving in the direction he was going. She didn't have any luck with a hotel. The only two in the Long Point area were completely booked with ice fishermen. There was an ad for a B and B, but it was closed for the winter. On a hunch, Deana called the number anyway and pleaded her case for a room. The owner listened and finally said, "Oh, what the heck. You sound like a nice lady. And I wouldn't mind a bit of company. The only problem is there's a big storm brewing, and you might get into trouble on the road." Deana protested that she was driving an SUV. The woman laughed.

"You could be driving a snowplow and go off the road when the wind kicks up." In a stern voice, she warned, "If you can't see, you need to stop driving and get off the road. You might want to stay where you are tonight and head in our direction tomorrow. Why, just a week ago, a severe snowstorm moved in late one afternoon, and eight ice fishers had to be rescued."

Deana stubbornly ignored the woman's advice and started driving, figuring she could get there in two to three hours, around 4:00 p.m. She reached for another Buffalo wing. Even cold, they were seriously good. If anyone ventured out onto the lake to check for stranded fishermen, she wanted to be there. Andy might easily sneak through, disguised as a fisherman. As she continued west across Ontario, it started to snow. The snow got heavier until she had to admit it was too dangerous to drive. The radio warned drivers to get off the road. She crept into the next town—still about one hundred miles from Port Rowan—and pulled into the first Tim Horton's she saw. "Timmy's," as it was affectionately referred to by Canadians, was the Canadian version of Dunkin' Donuts and McDonald's—except that the food and the doughnuts were better. The only reason the Tim Horton's was open was that the weather was too bad for the employees to head home. Deana curled up in a booth with a sandwich, a donut, and a cup of Timmy's famous coffee.

She dutifully called Jack to let him know where she was. He couldn't fly into Buffalo or Toronto. The Buffalo airport was closed due to the weather. All the flights to Toronto were booked. He was stuck in D.C. and would get to Port Rowan as soon as the airports were open. Deana heard the relief in his voice after she told him she was stuck in a Tim Horton's for the night.

Jack said, "You're kidding! At least you won't starve to death."

Deana rolled her eyes but kept quiet about the dozen Buffalo wings she had polished off earlier that day. She gave him the name and phone number of the B and B and told him she would head out to find it as soon as the storm was over. There were concerned messages on her phone from Snooky, telling her to either stay put in a hotel in Buffalo or fly home right away. It was too late for that.

Deana slept in the booth at the restaurant and woke up early to a bright, take-your-breath-away cold morning. She looked out the window and was thankful to see a snowplow working in the restaurant parking lot. She stretched and worked the kinks out from sleeping scrunched up to keep from falling off the bench. The smell of fresh donuts baking brought a smile to her face. Thank goodness she had stopped at a donut joint and not a plumbing store. Her car was buried, but the windshield and windows had all been cleared. Deana asked the waitress who the good Samaritan was. She pointed to a group of men sitting at a table with a mountain of doughnuts in the middle.

"They pulled in behind the snowplow and cleared all our cars for us. They're regulars. Always stop on their way to ice fish at Port Rowan."

Deana thanked the men and ended up with the name and phone number of an ice fishing business in Port Rowan. She did have an honest curiosity about the appeal of ice fishing, but her real reason for asking about trying ice fishing was to learn more about the area between Long Point and Turkey Point.

She passed snow-covered fields and lonely barren fruit trees on the road to Port Rowan. The four-lane highway turned into a two-lane road. It was scraped clean, and Deana could see the snowplow ahead of her. The countryside reminded her of the winter landscape she had just driven through in the Midwest: white and flat as far as the eye could see. The signs to Port Rowan directed her to the center of a charming little town perched on a small bluff overlooking a frozen bay.

She pulled into a parking spot (no meters) and glanced around: small library, post office, small grocery store, pharmacy, a few shops, and some restaurants. It looked like everything was tidily arranged within a couple of blocks. A few merchants were out shoveling the walks in front of their stores. She sat in the car for a few minutes, surveying the street, on the lookout for Andy. There was a "Closed for the Season" sign on Judy's Ice Cream Parlor and just a couple of cars parked in front of the library. There was so little activity that anyone walking around would draw attention. She pulled out and continued out of town to the B and B.

Deana checked into the Bird & Swan B and B, left a message for Jack, and headed out in search of the bay closest to the point where the abandoned boat had been found. Drifting snow made the side road out of town treacherous. The road followed the shoreline above the bay. Deana knew the views would be spectacular in the summer. Now, the frozen water was an eerie, ghostly white. It felt like she was once again making first tracks into a remote, deserted winter wonderland.

At the end of the road, she followed the directions and turned right. Her eyes opened wide at the sight of a field full of trucks and SUVs with trailers on the back. There was a hand-painted sign that read "Parking $5.00 All Day + Trailer $8.00."

Driving slowly past the field, she marveled at the number of people who found their way to the remote area to ice fish. The main roads might not all be cleared, but the snowplow found its way to the ice fishing area without any problem. The road narrowed and continued straight down to the water. There was a ramshackle hut on one side of the shore advertising the rental of ice huts and one on the other side offering fish cleaning. SUVs and trailers were crammed in on both sides of the road. Men bundled up in snowmobile suits were coming and going, hauling sleds of gear to and from a veritable village of ice huts as far as the eye could see. The buzzing of ATVs and snowmobiles filled the air. Deana had always assumed ice fishing was a quiet, solitary sport, practiced on remote northern lakes. It looked like the heart of the town had been transported to the frozen lake for the winter season.

Deana felt a tingling sensation on her arms and sat up straight. She quickly scanned the men walking around her one more time. Heads were covered with thick knit hats; all bodies looked the same in the snowmobile suits. The only way to distinguish one blob from another was by the way the man moved. She carefully scanned the crowd moving to and from the frozen lake, watching for the twinge of recognition in a walk or mannerism. If Andy made it to shore, he could easily slip away unnoticed. Satisfied he wasn't right in front of her, she let out her breath and pulled out the paper with the name of the ice fishing business the men at Timmy Horton's had given her. She checked the name, *Hudson's Ice Huts*. That was the name on the shack at the edge of the frozen lake. She crammed the car into the only empty spot along the road and self-consciously walked into Hudson's.

She hadn't seen any women around and wasn't exactly dressed for ice fishing. Mr. Hudson would think she was trying to track down a husband or boyfriend, which was exactly what she *was* trying to do.

"Good morning!" Deana tried on the man behind the desk. "I've never been ice fishing before. Could I walk out on the ice and look around?" He nodded and reached for the phone.

She scooted out of the office and gingerly walked out on the frozen lake. In spite of seeing snowmobiles, ice huts, and burly men spread across the lake as proof it was safe, Deana was shaking with every step on the ice. The memory of the sound of cracking ice on the lake in Canada was still too powerful. She took a deep breath and turned back to shore as a snowmobile tore past her and screeched to a stop next to Hudson's.

The driver jumped off and ran inside. A group of men were gathered around the entrance. Deana moved up to the edge of the group and asked, "What's going on?"

"Stuart Ferris found a body outside his ice hut. His is the farthest out. There's no cell reception out there. They called the RCMP." He finished, pointing to Hudson's. "Stuart didn't recognize the guy, so he isn't from around here."

Time stood still for Deana. She took a deep breath and stared across the lake in the direction the snowmobile had come from. The image of Andy waving good-bye from the trail on the other side of Canada floated in her mind. It seemed so real she lifted an arm to push the image away. The body on the ice might be Andy. She stayed motionless yet conscious of the buzz of activity that surrounded her. The flashing light on an RCMP car that slid to a stop at the edge of the lake broke the spell. She pushed her way through the group surrounding the officer.

"Excuse me, excuse me. I may be able to help." Deana explained who she was.

The officer had received word about the search for Andy. He said, "So you're the wife?"

He gave her the choice of waiting on shore until they brought the body in or riding along on a snowmobile to retrieve it. The need to know if it was Andy overcame her fear of the ice. She climbed into the trailer behind the officer's snowmobile for the ride out to Ferris's ice hut.

Deana briefly considered what kind of person she had become when she had her fingers crossed hoping the frozen body was Andy. What was she supposed to do—hope it was him but that he was still alive? And if it wasn't him, it would mean some other poor, helpless, and potentially kind man lay frozen to death. If Andy was taken alive, it would mean a long and nasty trial. So she kept her fingers crossed. Guilt and her hard heart she would deal with later.

The sheriff pulled up close to the last ice hut. The wooden structure was the size of a telephone booth with a small window on one side. Delaying looking at the body, Deana squinted out across the ice and saw ragged clumps of ice in the distance. Just beyond that she knew was open water.

She followed the men to the lifeless form next to the ice hut. Deana held her breath as the officer rolled the body over. She felt like her knees would give way and reached for the officer's arm.

He said, "I'm sorry, ma'am."

Deana said, "No, no. You don't understand. It isn't him."

Her eyes rested on the face of the dead man. Strands of long gray hair had escaped from his pony tail. His face was contorted into a terrible grimace. Ice clung to his eyebrows and mouth. He didn't look anything like Andy.

She barely heard someone say, "Well, shit. Who is it?"

The officer guided her back to the snowmobile and helped her climb into the trailer. He pulled a blanket out from a pack on the back of his snowmobile and spread it over her. She couldn't talk. Somehow Andy had fooled everyone again. A feeling of exhaustion replaced the anticipation that had kept her alert.

The officer checked the dead man's pockets and pulled out a wallet. Deana heard him say, "This says he's from Erie, Pennsylvania." Deana watched him scratch his chin. In a quiet voice, he said to the ATV driver. "Stand back. I'm going to open the door."

Deana came out of her fog when it clicked in her brain what the officer was thinking. The man who froze to death might have come out on the ice with Andy. Might have been forced to guide Andy to a safe harbor in Canada. She sat up and watched the officer pull his gun out and turn the knob on the door of the ice hut with the other. He threw the door open and quickly looked inside.

"Man, oh man!" he said. "I'm afraid we've got another body. Carbon monoxide. The heat is still on."

Deana threw the blanket off and scrambled out of the trailer. She was outside the hut when the officer said, "It's too late. The dope left the CO2 heater on, and this hut didn't have any ventilation." He shook his head. "I don't know what happened. Maybe he pushed the other guy out, and he froze to death."

They turned to look at Deana staring at the man they pulled out of the ice hut. An olive-drab army pile cap covered the head of the man. The ear flaps were pulled down tight and tied under the chin. The forehead was hidden by the hat's brim. Only the eyes, nose, and cheeks were visible. That was enough for Deana to recognize the face of the man she had married.

"It's him. Greg Irwin, also known as Andy Harris," she said quietly and without any emotion.

She nudged his leg with her foot, as if making sure he was dead. Several minutes passed while she just stared down at the man who had been her husband and lover. Dying from carbon monoxide poisoning in an ice hut on a frozen lake would have to rank as one of the most ignominious ways to die for someone who considered himself the consummate outdoorsman. She could only shake her head when she noticed the snowshoes lying in the snow outside the hut. For her, it had all begun with the snowshoe trip. Andy's attempt to escape had ended with a snowshoe trek. He had planned so many accidental deaths for women in his life that it was fitting his own death would be considered an accident—an accident caused by his own bad decisions.

By the time they got back to the shore with the two bodies, there was a crowd of ice fishermen waiting next to the police car. A policeman approached Deana and told her to call Kate right away. She kept her eye on the activity and dialed Kate's number.

"Kate," Deana said. She realized just talking to someone she knew was enough to make her voice quiver. To stop it and prevent any tears flowing she made herself feel anger instead of pity.

"Damn it, Kate. Andy made it to a fishing hut, but he didn't freeze to death. He, he died of carbon monoxide poisoning."

Kate stopped her. "What are you talking about?"

Deana explained what they had found on the ice. Kate said, "Wow! Deana, I'm sorry we didn't find him first, so you didn't have to go through this."

"No, no," Deana interrupted, her voice stronger, "I needed to see it for myself. You were right, Kate. He started making mistakes. He should have known to leave a little ventilation in the ice hut."

Deana knew she sounded like a spoiled child, but she couldn't help saying. "I wanted him to freeze to death. His damn snowshoes were lying on the ground next to the ice hut."

Kate said, "Good. I'm glad you're angry and not crying, but you're going to have a big letdown in a few hours. Get back to your B and B, and I'll be in touch."

Kate was right. The shock of finding Andy dead hadn't quite sunk in. Deana kept telling herself the nightmare was over, but the adrenaline was so high she felt like she had downed ten cups of coffee. She didn't protest when the RCMP offered to accompany her back to the B and B. Stepping over the threshold into the quiet inn, the smell of fresh baking tickled her nose. She closed her eyes and felt the tension ease out of her as she inhaled the warm air tinged with cinnamon and sugar. The owner greeted her warmly and sat her down next to a pot of tea and a plate of date bars and butter tarts. It seemed so normal and civilized. One bite into the butter tart filled her mouth with a rich, sweet taste that brought a smile to her face.

There was a message from Jack saying he hoped to be flying out the next day. He still didn't know they had caught up with Andy. Deana called him and gave him the good news. She told him to save his ticket to Buffalo. She promised to fly out to Jasper as soon as everything settled down.

Kate had asked her to stay in the area for a couple of days. Deana would need to sign statements and get through a couple of police interviews. She was exhausted but didn't want to sit in her room by herself. She lingered over the tea. The innkeepers, Peggy and Keith, were a friendly, caring couple. They didn't pry. In all small towns news traveled fast. Deana assumed they knew most of the gory details by now. The local paper, which was published monthly, was sitting on the table. She flipped through it, marveling at the pace of life that only required a monthly report on the news. The front page was taken up with a photo of swans in flight.

Peggy said, "You're our only guest this week. We'll be full in a month or two. The birders will be here looking for the first migrating swans." She pointed to the front page of the paper, "The annual tundra swan migration. If you have a few minutes, walk over to the marsh lands and the beach. It's really quite lovely."

Deana knew Peggy was thinking, "And it might make you feel better."

According to the paper, the annual tundra swan migrations were an amazing sight. Deana wouldn't be there long enough to see them this time, but it was intriguing. Tens of thousands of the birds came through and covered the fields, marsh land, and the Inner Bay where Andy's body had been found. They used to be called "whistling swans"; their wings produced a unique sound in flight. She asked Peggy about the swans.

"Oh yes, they make quite a racket. As soon as the snow is gone, they'll start flying in." She gestured out the window overlooking marsh land. "I'm always glad to see them come because it means spring is here, but I'm also happy to see them go and a return to peaceful nights over the marsh. Don't get me wrong now. It is a once-in-a-lifetime sight to see thousands of swans flying and landing. Truly amazing! And we get to see it twice a year. It is part of the magic of the area."

Deana looked at the clock and decided to take Peggy's advice. She didn't have to meet Kate and the local police for a couple of hours. She walked to the beach and gazed out across Lake Erie. It was like looking at the ocean—you could not see land on the other side of the lake. She could just make out a lone freighter moving through the open water. Small cottages closed up for the winter dotted the lake shore. Sand had blown up onto porches, and the frozen waves and snow-covered sand made it impossible to walk along the beach. She walked along the beach road until it ended. The atmosphere was desolate, yet wild and beautiful. It was the first day in three weeks Deana didn't have to worry about being the target of Andy's grand plan. She took a deep breath and spread her arms out wide. It seemed impossible that so much had happened in such a short time. She turned, looked at her surroundings, and slowly exhaled. It was a new sensation to be able to look around and appreciate the view without worrying if someone was stalking her.

Her eyes narrowed as she thought about returning to Virginia. The town house she and Andy had shared would bring back ugly memories. Her hands made fists. He would not drive her from her home. Paint and a few pieces of new furniture would take care of some of the memories. New memories, good ones would, in time, replace the bad ones. *In the end,* she thought, *he didn't win; she did.*

She thrust her arms in the air and yelled, "I won. I won!" Her thoughts turned to Jasper, and she remembered the kindness of Jim, Linda, and Jack. It would be a good place to spend a few months while she decided what to do.

The top priority was finding the money Andy had stolen. He obligingly had an ATM card for a bank in the Caymans in his pocket. It was a good start on tracking down the money. Deana headed back to the B and B, thinking about the other victims of Andy's crimes who needed closure.

She called Michelle Grant first.

"Thank you, Deana," Michelle said. "Thank you. It doesn't bring my friend back, but it helps to know he didn't get away with it."

And then Sonny, the retired sheriff in Indiana. He told her the exhumation order for Meredith Givens had been approved. He was certain the results would confirm Andy's guilt in her death. He told Deana the FBI had also requested an exhumation order for Leslie Thompson.

She saved the call to Snooky for last. She knew it would be an emotional one. Snooky was very quiet after he heard the news. "Deana, you have been through a lot. Now, you need to take care of yourself." He made her promise to stay in touch.

Randy and Kate wanted to meet at the local RCMP office. Deana entered the room and saw what looked like paper money and a bingo card spread out on the table.

Randy explained, "Deana, these bills were found tucked under a flap in Andy's wallet. Take a look."

The bingo card and each of the bills had a woman's photo glued to the center. A date and a dollar amount were neatly written next to the photo.

"Is this what I think it is? His so-called trophies?" she asked sadly.

"They're in chronological order," Randy pointed out. "Do you recognize this woman?" he asked, pointing to a five-dollar bill between the trophies with photos of Meredith and Stephanie Randall. Deana shook her head.

No one pointed out her own photo. She touched it and shook her head. Anal and accurate, Andy had crossed out the date next to her photo, but the number *$2,500,000* was neatly printed under the date. The photos were face shots cut into an oval shape someone would put in a locket. The bingo card had a photo of a smiling sixteen-year-old girl, Leslie Thompson. The others were his mother, Meredith Givens, the unknown woman, Stephanie Randall, Deana, and finally, Sandra. Sandra's photo was glued to the bill, but there was no date. *Incredible,* Deana thought, *what goes on in the mind of a murderer. It was a competition—a game to him, and the photos were his trophies.*

Randy explained, "He moved around a lot and needed portable trophies. He could keep these with him at all times." He pointed to the photo of the unknown woman. "We'll find out who she is."

Deana left the meeting in a sober mood. Sandra was in jail where she belonged. It was over, but it wasn't over. She was no longer in danger, but she had to steel herself for reliving parts of the nightmare—at Sandra's trial and in the dark memories she knew would trouble her from time to time.

She checked her phone in Virginia for messages before driving back to Buffalo. The first message was from her attorney. The annulment was final. Deana thought about a quote she had read somewhere: "The arc of the moral universe is long, but it bends toward justice." She was lucky to have lived to see the arc bend to catch Andy.

On an impulse, she called Jack. She suggested he use his unused ticket to Buffalo to meet her in Long Point when the swans started their migration. She really wanted to see what Peggy had described as a once-in-a-lifetime sight. And she wanted to share it with Jack.

She could hear the smile in Jack's voice when he answered, "Nothing to match the flight of wild birds flying." He laughed and said, "Those are Edna St. Vincent Millay's words, not mine. Yes! I'll fly into D.C., and we'll go to Long Point together."

Deana couldn't resist reminding Jack about the attractions of Buffalo. "Jack, you were right about Buffalo; the town made snow famous, and they have really good wings. First stop when we got off the plane in Buffalo is the nearest Buffalo wing vendor."

She smiled at the sound of Jack's laugh on the other end of the phone. It would be the first of many good memories.

ACKNOWLEDGMENTS

Thank you to all the people who took the time to read and comment on early drafts: Mary Maher, Carolyn O'Hara, Benn Carr, and Mason Jewell. Barbara Stremikis and Annette Jareb, my writer friends, listened to rewrite after rewrite and provided unfailing encouragement. Many people were patient in answering questions. Thank you to Red Jenkins for sharing his experience and knowledge of police procedure, Ray Hansohn, of Hansohn Brothers, for his expert knowledge on guns and bullets, Chelsea Gottleib and Laura Kuhn for medical advice, Paul Schrecker for answering questions about the FBI, and the Virginia Department of Games and Inland Fisheries for their excellent Hunter Education programs. Michael Redhill poked and prodded me to improve the tension. Thank you to Bob Friedman for his advice and Devra Jacobs for her suggestions. I really appreciate the editing work done by Kendal Norris. I learned a lot from the detailed attention she gave to the book. Thank you to the folks at Archway Publishing for their professional and organized approach to publishing.

A special thank you to Kenny Marotta for all his patience, criticism, and editing work. Without his input, the book never would have been finished.

About the Author

Susie McKenna was born and raised in the Midwest. A successful career as a software entrepreneur led her to Virginia, where she now makes her home. A snowshoe trek in search of virgin snow was the inspiration for Last Tracks. The thrill of making first tracks in deep snow led Susie to the chilling realization that accidents can happen—turning first tracks into last.

CPSIA information can be obtained
at www.ICGtesting.com
Printed in the USA
BVHW032002130219
540221BV00001B/44/P